Terry & Christine —

Hope You Enjoy The Story!

            —Michael O. Bangberger

            May 12, 2021

D1733416

NAIMERA

THE **NAIMERA** SERIES: BOOK 1

ABSENCE OF GRACE

MICHAEL GANZBERGER

GANZBERGER.COM

Published by Michael Ganzberger.

ISBN: 979-8-5969057-3-1

Editors: Will Tyler, Elizabeth Ward, and Sara Kelly

Cover design, illustration and interior formatting:
Mark Thomas / Coverness.com

For Suzy
My love and inspiration.

PROLOGUE

Managua, Nicaragua

Over thirty thousand angry citizens flowed through the streets of Managua. The largest anti-government protest in recent memory halted traffic, bringing most of the city to a standstill. They had seen enough and were demanding change. Streams converged, filling the National University stadium parking lot, spilling over onto walkways and roads. Local news stations followed, capturing images of the noisy but peaceful crowd. Whistles blew and drums pounded. Nicaraguan flags waved in the breeze. Some attached to sticks, some draped over the backs of protesters. Shouts of anxious optimism filled the air. The young and naive believed there was safety in numbers, especially with TV cameras present. Their charismatic leader, the founder of the university opposition movement, hopped up on the bed of a pickup truck. He stood tall and held a bullhorn. The crowd immediately began to chant his name.

"Victor! Victor! Victor!"

He paused to admire the sea of brave compatriots draped in blue and white. Intensity grew with each chant, becoming louder and louder. His arms went up.

Cheers erupted.

"We are fearless and unstoppable."

The crowd responded with their rally cry: "Nobody surrenders, here!"

"Stop government-sanctioned violence!"

Thousands roared: "Nobody surrenders, here!"

"We demand free and honest elections!"

"Nobody surrenders, here!"

The protesters worked themselves up into a fever pitch of excitement. It felt like the start of a revolution, one that would finally free their country from oppression and corruption.

Victor shouted, "Release all political—"

Suddenly, rapid-fire explosions pierced through his words. Victor dropped, injured. Most continued cheering, assuming the loud pops were sounds of celebration from a continuous firecracker roll. Several protesters in front, holding up the poles of a large freedom banner, collapsed. Blood pooled around them. The cheers stopped, and a wave of panic swept across the crowd. Cries for help and screams of horror echoed through the campus. A few rushed to help the wounded, the rest scattered. Heads swiveled, searching for the source of the gunfire. From multiple directions, several canisters of tear gas shot up, landing near the speaker. Protesters nearby crawled, struggling to breathe; others ran while covering their faces.

Among the chaos, under the cloak of thick choking smoke, six men dressed in blue shirts and wearing gas masks rushed Victor. With military precision, they grabbed him and whisked him off into a waiting vehicle.

*

An hour later, a hundred miles to the north, Sergio Cruz, the leader of the notorious Nicaraguan paramilitary group and criminal cartel, PLVI, sat in his compound finishing his breakfast while watching the carnage replayed on TV.

A spokesman for the government appeared on screen "The president has issued a statement. The government of Nicaragua condemns this senseless act of violence. We will not rest until we bring the murderers of the eight protesters to justice."

Sergio reached for the remote and turned off the set. A wry smile crossed his face, followed by an involuntary snicker. He took a long pull of what remained of his cigar, then ground it out on his plate. His phone rang. Sergio had been waiting for this call. He raised his arm and waved for the servants to leave the room.

"General."

"Sergio, well done," said General Rafael Cortez, the chief director of the National Guard. "Have you interrogated their leader?"

"Not yet. They're still on their way back."

"I need to find out who's organizing these protests," said the general.

"We will make him talk."

"Sergio, the president is not happy with all the negative publicity lately. He wants the protests crushed but with less bloodshed. He's getting pressure from the church and the press to do something. He'll probably fire someone."

"I'll see to it my lieutenants get the message. So, General, any other news worth sharing?"

"Yes, I heard a rumor they're cutting your funding again next year. We need you, but voices are telling the president the PLVI has grown too big and you're going rogue."

"Rogue?" said Sergio in a dismissive tone. "Their money means nothing. General, I'll let you know what we find out."

Sergio hung up and called his lieutenant, Luis Ortiz.

"Boss, what is it?" asked Luis.

"I had an interesting talk with Cortez. No more waiting. We need to move forward with 'silver or lead.'"

"I told you we had enemies in Managua. Did he give any names?"

"I don't care who they are. I want them all here to see, that to our friends, we are generous."

"And to our enemies—just try to stop us," said Luis with a puff of confidence. "But boss, remember that quote from the arms dealer? We don't have that much."

"Work with Roberto; do whatever it takes, just get it."

CHAPTER 1

Austin, Texas

Grace Strauss stood silently with her arms crossed, looking down at her bulging luggage. "What have I forgotten?" she said to herself.

From another room, her fiancé Alan responded, "Nothing, Grace, we have everything. Don't worry."

Grace passed a hallway mirror and made one final check of her appearance. On her last trip back to see her father, he had commented that with her blue eyes and blonde hair, she resembled her late mother. For the first time she could see it, and she smiled. Like her father, she was a stickler for detail and obsessed with preparation. Their two-week trip to the Guatemalan Petén Basin and the Chiapas region of Mexico included visits to historic Mayan ruins, museums, and lots of hiking. She would combine her thesis research with a much-needed vacation. Then it was back to the University of Texas at Austin for the young twenty-three-year-old to continue her Ph.D. graduate work in Latin American Studies.

A doorbell buzz in two quick successions announced the taxi had arrived. The driver and Alan loaded the two heavy suitcases and carry-ons. Grace gave her cat Chisme a hug, placed the care and feeding instructions on the table for her friend Julie, turned on the family room light, and closed the door of their Austin apartment.

On the way to the airport, Alan looked up from his cell phone. "Your dad called when you were in the shower. He wished us a safe trip and asked if you'd call him when we arrive tonight."

"Oh, I'm sorry I missed his call. He's been super busy lately. I haven't talked to Daddy in over a week."

The taxi pulled up to the international departure terminal. Later that afternoon, they arrived in Flores, Guatemala and checked into their cottage. They chose it because of its central location to several of their destinations. It was also quiet and isolated. Grace called her father's office, but he was out. She tried his cell with no answer and left a message to let him know she and Alan had arrived safely and would call back.

Early the next morning, Alan and Grace headed out in their rented SUV. First stop, the ancient ruins of Tikal.

CHAPTER 2

San Benito, Guatemala

Policeman Javier Villalta and his partner Fernando Ramirez shuffled into their usual cantina to grab burritos and beer before heading home. Both were tired and bored after another monotonous eight-hour shift. They started on a pitcher and talked while waiting for their food. Tonight's topic of discussion was their low pay.

"I can't live on twenty-two quetzals an hour," said Fernando. "It's pathetic!"

The subject of one of their close childhood friends, Cesar, came up.

"Cesar joined a cartel and lives like a king! I drove by his hacienda last week," replied Javier. "Gigantic! The servant casita is bigger than my house!"

"How is this world fair to us?" asked Fernando.

As the conversation continued it grew more intense, along with their drinking. Among their fellow officers they were neither respected nor trusted. If money was missing from someone's locker or anything from the evidence closet, they were the first suspected.

Javier dribbled a glob of guacamole down his shirt as he tried to talk while slurring his words and waving one hand. Fernando watched with quiet amusement as it slowly slid down Javier's huge barrel stomach, curious when it would eventually stop. When it did, he looked up at Javier's face and noticed an unidentified remnant of food attached to his circular beard. Javier had an unpredictable temper. Fernando chuckled to himself; it took every bit of restraint for him not to burst out laughing. He didn't dare point out his friend's faux pas. Instead, he looked down at his own slender chest to make sure he hadn't dripped anything on himself. Then he nonchalantly patted his thin mustache, cheek, and chin. They both slowly stood up, finished their cigarettes, tossed them on the floor, and staggered out the door to their car.

*

Alan and Grace were both tired after a long day in the heat, examining ancient ruins. The sun slowly retreated behind gentle rolling hills. From the horizon, the sky transitioned in layered hues from bright soft red, pink, baby blue, and purple, overlaid with small wispy pewter clouds. It was a beautiful and peaceful night. Relaxed and content, both were becoming one with the tranquil beauty surrounding them.

The road back to their cottage was long and winding with no traffic. The paved asphalt, lacking middle divider lines, cut through lush dense jungle. It was as if an artist had painted a jet-black meandering path through a sea of green. Alan passed a sign warning of dangerous curves. He drove cautiously.

As they rounded a turn, a car suddenly appeared forty feet away, heading straight at them on their side of the road. Alan's eyes widened. With no time to think, he hit the brakes and swerved off the road to avoid crashing head-on. In an instant, their SUV skidded, spun, rolled over, and smashed sideways into a stone wall embankment. A plume of dust and smoke surrounded the scene. After a deep groan from the engine, it became eerily silent.

*

Javier slammed on his brakes. They glanced at each other.

Fernando shook his head and let out a long, deep breath. "Jesus. We're lucky they didn't hit us!"

The excitement jarred them both slightly from their drunken state. They opened their doors, got out, and approached the SUV. The driver appeared dead. They looked inside and saw an unconscious young woman in the passenger's seat with blood on her forehead, moaning. The airbags had deployed, but since the violent impact came from the sides, they offered no protection, especially to the driver. The rollover had caused every window to shatter into thousands of tiny pieces. Gasoline leaked from the fuel tank.

"We've got to get her out before this catches fire!" said Fernando as he tugged hard to open the passenger's door.

Broken glass poured onto the ground. He carefully reached in to free her from her seat belt. They dragged her away to safety near their car while she bled from small cuts and abrasions. Fernando stayed and knelt next to Grace, gently cradling her while wiping blood from her forehead and arms with his handkerchief, his shirt now stained with her blood. Javier returned to the SUV and took one more look inside to make sure the driver was really dead. He felt for a pulse and shook his head. Javier looked down and picked up a backpack lying on the floor. After shaking off pieces of glass, he froze, holding on to it without moving. It appeared he was thinking about something.

"We need to get her to the hospital," said Fernando. "Help me put her into the car."

They laid her across the back seat. Javier turned to Fernando. "We can't call this in. They'll know we've been drinking and caused this. That's manslaughter. I've got a plan. Trust me."

"What do you mean, a plan?"

Javier walked back, looked down the road in both directions, then tossed his cigarette near the SUV. It landed on a stream of gasoline. Fernando's eyes widened as he watched a low rush of blue flame race toward the vehicle. It burst into a huge ball of fire. Javier ran back to the car, slammed his door, and drove off.

"Are you crazy? Why'd you go and do that?"

"The guy's dead. I don't want to leave behind fingerprints."

"Fingerprints? What are you talking about?"

Javier's mind was apparently racing ahead, plotting his next move. Fernando's question went unanswered.

Fernando felt a sudden surge of uneasiness bordering on a mild panic attack. He'd known Javier all his life. He could be a factory of poor choices. Even in his now mildly drunken state, Fernando knew this was a bad idea. After several minutes, Fernando calmed down. He turned around to check on the woman lying in the rear seat who was still unconscious. The bleeding began to slow. He reached back and blotted her wound. While looking down at her bruised and bloodied face, he became curious. He opened her backpack to check for her identity.

"She's American, from Texas."

"Cell phone?" said Javier.

Fernando pawed through her belongings and unzipped a small pocket. "Yeah, why?"

"Shut that damn thing off! They can track us if it's on."

Fernando pressed every button and finally figured out how to shut it down. "It's off, relax, it's off!"

"That was nearly a disaster. Good thing we checked."

*

The next morning, Grace slowly opened her eyes. Her head throbbed; every part of her body ached. *Where am I?* Dim daylight filled the room through a dust-covered window on the door. She was in an old adobe structure with a dirt floor. She moved her arms and felt resistance. She lifted her hands and found a handcuff attached. Her breathing suddenly turned fast and shallow as her heart pounded. The single handcuff attached to her left wrist connected to an eight-foot cable, secured to the metal frame of her bed. She carefully sat up. *Where is Alan?* A plate of food and a water bottle were left on a nearby table. A rusty steel bucket with a half roll of toilet paper sat in a corner.

Grace's memory was drawing blanks. She lifted her hands against the weight of the handcuffs and cable then began to gently massage her aching neck and head. She recalled driving down a country road and seeing a car heading at them. That's all she could remember. *I've been kidnapped. What happened to Alan?* Her pulse continued to race out of control. The gravity of her situation turned her attention away from her injuries. Her thoughts scanned the terrible possibilities! *Rape, murder?* The handcuff hurt when she tried to pull. She wanted to call out for help but stopped herself. *Who would come? Help or my captors?*

CHAPTER 3

San Francisco, California

After eight years with the FBI, Agent Mike Murphy was moving on. It was his last week; he had accepted another job and was about to begin a new chapter in his life. He felt invigorated and distracted but needed to stay focused. There was still important work to do before leaving. A few ongoing cases within the International Violent Crimes Unit still needed his undivided attention. Then, at long last, a welcomed break and a well-deserved fourteen-day Hawaiian vacation. When he returned, he'd join Strauss Global Sciences Inc. (SGSI), thirty-five miles south in Palo Alto, as head of security.

During moments of downtime, Mike packed up his personal items. In a bottom drawer, he found a small box he had long forgotten was there. He opened it and smiled. It contained a group picture of him and several members of his former Navy SEAL team. There he was, Lieutenant Mike Murphy, along with Lieutenant Deandrea Williams, a helicopter pilot; Chief Petty Officer Santiago "Sandy" Lopez, a brilliant tactician; and standing on the end, Petty Officer First Class Kyle Miller, an expert sniper. That was nine years ago, a sunny and memorable day at Naval Amphibious Base, Coronado, California. They each received an award for their efforts during a dangerous but successful mission in Afghanistan.

When I'm in Maui, I'll have to look up Deandrea and Claire. He slid his finger within the box, moving aside dog tags and ribbons until he came across his Silver Star. He picked it up and pressed it between his fingers while reliving the events. Just the four of them attacked and destroyed an Al-Qaeda compound, killing twenty-seven terrorists and saving twelve captive coalition soldiers. *Damn, I am so proud of us. That was awesome. Not sure I could ever do that again. Not sure I'd want to. But we went after those bastards and we did it.*

A tap on his door brought Mike back; it was two coworkers. He left the box and picture on his desk, walked over to the door, and chatted with them.

"We heard you're leaving us," said Agent Cabral.

"Don't tell me it's because there wasn't a grand jury indictment in the yakuza case?" said Agent Tole while cracking a smile.

"No, no, but that would be a good reason. I poured my blood and sweat into that case. Those guys are guilty as hell," said Mike.

"So, where you going?" asked Cabral.

"Strauss Global Sciences. Heading up security," said Mike.

"SGSI—military drones?" asked Tole.

"That's right."

"It's been great working with you," said Tole. "You're leaving a huge hole."

"You can say that again. Bill told me I'm taking on most of your cases," said Cabral.

Mike patted Agent Cabral on the back, followed with a sympathetic smile. "Thanks for stopping by, guys. After I'm settled in, we'll get together for lunch," said Mike.

Since announcing he was leaving, the many friends he'd made over the years had come by to wish him well. He would miss them, but he craved new challenges, and this was exactly what he was looking for—SGSI made the most advanced military drones in the world, used exclusively to hunt down terrorists. A cause with deep personal significance to Mike.

CHAPTER 4

San Benito, Guatemala

Grace's attention shifted toward the side table. It had been almost twenty-four hours since her last meal. There was an apple and a bowl of stale-looking churros. *Yuck, but I'm starving.* The apple was gone in no time. When she reached for a churro, there was movement. "Oh, ants, disgusting!" she said out loud. She brushed them off and felt grease all over her fingers. She rubbed her oily fingers together, then under the handcuff that was chafing her skin. It felt better. It felt loose. She twisted a couple churros, extracting as much oil as she could, then rubbed her left hand. *I might be able to squirm out of this handcuff.* With a tight squeeze of her hand and a steady tug that took all of her strength, her left hand popped free. She paused momentarily to rub her sore wrist.

Grace slowly stood up. With weak and unsteady legs, she gradually made her way to the door. She held her breath and turned the handle. Surprisingly, it opened. Her body was still bruised and tender, but a surge of adrenaline negated the pain. She peeked outside. It looked safe to exit. The small structure holding her was a storage shed. A modest one-story adobe house stood nearby. It appeared quiet and empty with no cars in the driveway. Scanning the countryside; there were no other houses in sight across the expansive terrain. She hobbled from the shed. Moving as quickly as her aching body would allow, she headed down the gravel driveway toward a country road.

*

News of a dead American found in a burned-out SUV spread quickly. First to the police in San Benito, then to the local news stations. The police investigation determined the accident did not seem suspicious, perhaps a careless foreign tourist driving too fast on the unfamiliar hazardous road. Vehicle rental records revealed the driver, but there was a second name, a woman who couldn't be located. The police contacted the American embassy in Guatemala City and visited the cottage where the couple indicated they were staying. There were no signs of the woman, Grace Strauss.

Javier and Fernando stepped past a TV crew in the lobby and walked into San Benito Police Chief Torres's office together.

"Hi, fellas, what can I do for you?"

"Chief Torres, we want to join the team looking for the missing American woman," said Javier.

"That's great, we could use more help, but you both realize we're working this case around the clock. That means long hours and no days off," replied Chief Torres.

His phone rang.

He looked at the calling number. "Hold on, I need to take this. It's the FBI."

The FBI was working locally within the Transnational Anti-Gang Unit office.

"Hello, Chief Torres here."

"Hi, Chief. It's Agent Aguilar."

"I recognized your number. I assume you're calling about the fatal accident and the missing American woman?" said Chief Torres.

"Yes. What can you tell me?" asked Agent Aguilar.

"I have the report right here." The chief slid the document in front of him and opened it up. "The cause of the accident. The driver, Mr. Walter, lost control of his vehicle and hit a stone embankment. The passenger-side airbag deployed, and the door was found opened, indicating Ms. Strauss was present but had gotten out before the vehicle caught fire. She could be wandering in a daze. We have an APB out for her. We searched the cottage where they stayed and found the couple's itinerary. Their first day showed them visiting the ruins at the Tikal site museum. One of my officers drove out and collected security camera footage from the visitor's center. We reviewed it and saw the couple leaving in the late afternoon. Nothing suspicious. That's all we have, so far."

"Chief, we'll handle it from here," said Agent Aguilar. "I'll have someone stop by to pick up your report."

"The case is all yours. Hope your agents can find her." The call ended. The chief looked up at Javier and Fernando. "Thanks for your offer, fellas, but as you heard, the TAG office will be taking over."

The two officers walked away, now feeling nervous. Javier said he needed make a call and left. An hour later, they met outside the station next to a police car.

"Fernando, let's go for a ride." They got in and drove off.

Fernando was panicking. "Javier, I don't want any more to do with this kidnapping. Let's go get her and set her free now. It's not too late."

"Stop your worrying. I arranged to pass her on."

"Pass her on? To who?"

"Didn't you hear the news reporter at the station when they were filming this morning? Her father in America is a billionaire! I called Cesar and offered her to his cartel for a million quetzals. That's a bargain I'm sure they won't pass up. I bet they can get a hundred times that much."

"You made a deal with a cartel?" said Fernando, shocked.

"Yeah, we hand her over and collect our money. In an hour we'll both be rich with nothing to worry about."

The police car left the city. Within minutes, they were driving down a remote country road. Up ahead, a lone car came into view. Javier pulled over and parked behind it. Both officers got out and approached the driver's side window.

"Have you good news for us, Cesar?" asked Javier.

"I talked it over with my boss; he thinks TAG is going to be all over this."

"So, that's it? You could make two billion quetzals!"

"We know that. We'll make you an offer. It's too risky for us, but we have a contact in Nicaragua. The PLVI cartel wants her. You'll get two hundred thousand quetzals. Take it or leave it."

"Why the PLVI?" asked Fernando.

"Nicaragua has no extradition treaty with Guatemala or the US, and TAG can't operate there," said Cesar. "PLVI has the protection of the Nicaraguan government."

"I don't understand," said Fernando. "How come they get government protection?"

"Oh, you don't know? The PLVI first formed as a paramilitary group. Their members are former elite Army soldiers. When political leaders need them to break up anti-government protests, they do it."

"But they're super dangerous. I heard one gang in El Salvador crossed them, and they killed every member. Some they tied up and executed with antiaircraft guns just to be sadistic," said Fernando.

"That's probably bullshit," said Javier.

"No, really, I heard there's a video of it," said Fernando.

"Those stories are true. I saw it," said Cesar. "They sent copies out to all the gangs in the area. They kill like that to frighten their enemies. I can tell you this: it's working."

"Okay, okay, I don't care who they are. We'll take it," said Javier. "I want her off my hands as soon as possible. What's the plan?"

"Once I confirm we have a deal, they'll arrange to have a plane waiting at our airstrip north of San Andrés in two days," said Cesar.

"There's nothing there. That's in the Maya Biosphere Reserve?" said Fernando.

"Yeah, we built it for our business travel, and you better keep that to yourself," said Cesar. "Now go get her, and meet me back here in thirty minutes. We'll do the rest. I'll have your money after they pay us. Half an hour, no more, or the deal's off!"

CHAPTER 5

Palo Alto, California

D r. Peter Strauss was wrapping up a weekly status meeting at work when the door opened. His personal secretary walked over and quietly spoke to him.

"Excuse me, Dr. Strauss. There is an urgent call for you from the American embassy in Guatemala."

Peter's heart raced, and he got up quickly.

"We were about done. I need to take this call," said Peter. He hurried back to his office and closed the door. The consular agent told Peter there had been a fatal accident involving the vehicle rented by Alan Walters, who was found dead.

"No! Oh my god! What about my daughter, Grace?"

"We have no information on her whereabouts. We were hoping you may have heard from her?"

Peter's heart rate skyrocketed. "No, nothing. I'll check my cell phone for messages. If she were in trouble, I'd be the first she'd call." Peter picked up his cell phone and checked. "No messages from her. I want to help. Can I do anything?"

The consular agent replied, "Please try to stay calm, Dr. Strauss. We made a call to the TAG office; the Transnational Anti-Gang Unit will be handling this. They're notified when a missing person might have been abducted. Their team includes FBI agents, so you should expect a call or visit from an agent soon." The consular agent gave Peter her contact information and asked him to call back immediately if he heard from Grace.

After the call ended Peter sat motionless, staring down at his desk. He could almost hear his heart pounding; he needed fresh air. He stood up and walked down the hall, by the door to the conference room. A few people were still inside talking when they noticed Peter walk past. Someone called out. "Peter?"

He paused with a vacant look. "Grace... Grace is missing."

Two employees jumped up to go check on him but Peter left the building. He found a bench and sat quietly as he tried to calm himself. After fifteen minutes he pulled out his phone and made a call.

CHAPTER 6

San Benito, Guatemala

Still aching from the accident, Grace walked gingerly along the edge of the road, struggling to conserve energy and not further injure herself. After less than a mile in sweltering heat, she was exhausted and thirsty. The asphalt was too hot even with shoes, and the shoulder littered with large rocks. She walked twenty minutes and only saw two cars. Both sped by, refusing to stop. Heatstroke was now her biggest concern.

Up the road, she spotted a small house. She approached cautiously, fearing the owner might have a vicious dog running loose. She reached the front door and knocked. A young child could be heard crying through a half-open window. No one answered. Desperate, she knocked again, harder. She waited a minute; still no answer. She sat down on the porch. Overwhelmed, she began to cry; confused, in pain, thirsty, and exhausted.

*

Hearing Grace weeping, Maria opened the door slowly and stepped out, holding her baby in one arm. Judging by the stranger's condition, she was not a threat and needed help. Maria invited her in and offered her water. She first sipped, then guzzled a large glass. Maria knew the water was warm and tasted like iron. *The poor girl is thirsty.* Maria refilled her glass. Grace emptied it in seconds. She told Maria that she had been kidnapped. She escaped from the first house down the road.

"It must have been Javier. He drives too fast and late at night shoots his gun. He scares us," said the woman.

"Javier, I'll remember that. My name is Grace Strauss. I'm an American. What is your name?"

"Maria … Maria Hernández."

Grace looked around the room. "Maria, do you have a phone I can use?"

Maria shook her head. "No, my husband Miguel needs it in case his truck breaks down."

"When will he get home?"

"Between seven and eight o'clock tonight."

Grace looked frustrated as she checked the time. "I don't want to wait six or seven hours."

Maria realized Grace had been through a traumatic ordeal and needed to relax. She was probably hungry. "Can I make you something to eat?"

"Yes, please. I'm starving."

Grace had dried blood and dust still on her face and arms.

"I'll start lunch, but first, you could use a bath."

Grace looked down at herself. "Thank you, you're right."

Their water came from a well. Maria led Grace outside to a small enclosure with a standing tub. She handed her a bucket, a towel, and a bar of soap, then glanced over to the hand pump.

Grace smiled and got to work. Pumping each bucket of water was slow, but it appeared to help take her mind off her ordeal and restore a sense of calm. After a refreshing sponge bath and a simple lunch, Grace said she was heading out to find a ride back to the nearest town. Maria tried to talk Grace into staying. She looked too frail to walk, especially in tropical heat. But a determined Grace wanted to try, hopeful someone would stop and give her a ride. Maria told her if she continued down the same road, it would lead to San Benito, about two miles away. Maria filled a plastic bottle with water, wrapped a small snack, and handed them to Grace.

"Here, take these with you. Not everyone is good, not even the police. Please be careful," she said. "Goodbye and good luck."

"I don't know how I can ever repay you for your kindness." As Grace walked toward the road, she paused and turned around for one last look at Maria, wearing a slightly puzzled look. It appeared as if she was wondering about Maria's parting comments.

*

The two policemen had only thirty minutes to drive to Javier's house and return with Grace to rendezvous with Cesar. There was no time to waste. They used their police siren to move traffic out of their way as they raced down the road. They sped up Javier's driveway and jumped out.

"Fernando, in my front closet is her backpack. Go grab it. We'll give it to Cesar. I'll get her."

Javier walked back toward the shed and noticed the door was not closed. Immediately, his nostrils flared and teeth clenched. He kicked the door open and looked around the empty room.

"Damn! How'd she get out?" He picked up the cable with the handcuffs still attached; it was not cut or unlocked, so she must have slipped out.

Javier stormed outside and called Fernando. "She's gone!"

"She escaped?"

"Yeah, she's on foot and can't have gone far in this heat unless somebody picked her up."

Fernando tossed her backpack into the back of the car and jumped in. The sudden acceleration of the rear tires caused rocks and dirt to erupt, leaving behind a lingering cloud of dust that followed them as they frantically sped away toward the road.

"We're in luck! There she is," said Javier. "Be calm. Don't scare her. Let's get her in the car and off this road before anyone drives by and sees us."

Grace was only fifty yards from Maria's driveway when the police car pulled up next to her. Both officers rushed out and approached.

"Are you Grace Strauss, the American?" asked Fernando.

"Yes," replied a grateful Grace.

"Are you okay?"

"Oh, I am now. Thank you."

"You know, we've been looking for you. Come with us; we'll take you back to town."

Javier reached for a pair of handcuffs, then remembered she could slip out. *Need to make them tighter.*

"What are you doing?" asked Grace as Javier applied a pair of handcuffs on her wrists.

"Standard procedure when anyone's put in our police car."

"Ouch! They're hurting me."

"I'll take them off when we get to the station. Don't you worry."

Grace dropped the water bottle and snack on the ground, which caught Javier's attention. He knew it wasn't the one they left for her, and they definitely hadn't made her a sandwich. He paused and stared back at Maria's house. She was standing by her front door but quickly went back inside when he looked her way.

CHAPTER 7

San Francisco, California

Agent Mike Murphy was at his desk within the FBI's San Francisco field office when his phone rang. "Agent Murphy, FBI."

"Hello, Agent Murphy, this is Peter … Peter Strauss. I need to talk to you. It's urgent."

"Dr. Strauss, what is it? You haven't changed you mind about hiring me?"

"No, no. I can use your FBI help."

Mike was first worried, but now puzzled.

"I got a call from the consular agent at the American embassy in Guatemala. My daughter's fiancé died in a car accident, and she's missing."

"That's terrible. What did they say?"

"A unit called TAG will be handling the investigation. Apparently, that includes FBI agents."

"That's right, the Transnational Anti-Gang Task Force. If TAG's been called in, they must assume a gang or cartel's involved and she's likely been abducted. Since we're the nearest office to you, I'm sure we'll be working with them from our end."

"Agent Murphy, I am losing my mind. Can you please do me a favor and find out what's going on?"

"Absolutely. Dr. Strauss. I realize this is very difficult for you. I've worked with TAG in the past. I can assure you they are very good at what they do, probably the best in the world dealing with gang-related kidnappings. So, you haven't been contacted by anyone from our office yet?"

"No. Not yet."

"All right, it sounds like we haven't assigned an agent to the case. I'll look into it and let you know what I find out."

"Thank you. That makes me feel a little better. Call me once you learn anything. Anytime, I don't care. Please."

They hung up. Mike walked down the hall and tapped on the door to his boss's office, Special Agent Bill Andrews.

"Bill, got a minute?"

"Sure, what's up?"

"Have you received a call from TAG in Guatemala?"

"Yes, in fact, I just got off the phone. How'd you know about that?"

"The missing person they're looking for is the daughter of the CEO of the company I'm being hired into. What's the status?"

"They're just beginning the investigation. No leads yet. They asked us to collect some info from her family."

"I've got some spare cycles this week before I leave. Mind if I take this one on?"

"Sure, it's yours. Here's what they sent me."

Bill reached over to the printer and handed Mike a copy of the Grace Strauss case file.

"Call and let them know you're the lead agent up here."

"Thanks. Not exactly the way I imagined I'd begin working with

Dr. Strauss," said Mike, slowly shaking his head.

Bill shrugged his shoulders and gave Mike a pat. "Let's hope she's safe and they find her soon."

CHAPTER 8

San Benito, Guatemala

FBI Agents Antonio Garcia and Roxane Allen, assigned to the Guatemalan TAG office, were working on the case. They arrived at the crash site. Although San Benito police initially inspected the accident scene, they needed to investigate it themselves. It was the day after, and the SUV had been towed away. They found small pieces of the vehicle, broken glass, and an area of scorched earth. They checked the road for skid marks and discovered a pair in both directions, indicating another car had applied its brakes directly in front of the SUV. Next, they examined where the SUV left the road and, based on the length of each skid mark, determined the speed of each vehicle. Tire prints remained from the approaching vehicle and were clearly visible. Everything was carefully measured, recorded, and photographed.

As they approached the area of charred earth, Agent Garcia noticed something suspicious. A single half-burned cigarette lay on the ground where gasoline channeled away from the SUV. This could offer a key piece of evidence. While he knelt and began taking more pictures, Agent Allen discovered something else: a line of dried passive blood drops. They started where the SUV had come to a rest and led back to the road, where they abruptly stopped.

"Antonio, when you're done, come take a look at this."

Agent Garcia stood up and walked over, the camera hanging to his side in one hand. "Well, if that's what I think it is, we either have Ms. Strauss's blood or one of the kidnappers. This could be a huge break."

They photographed and collected the cigarette along with the blood samples. After an hour, they completed the accident site-investigation and left.

The two agents returned to the TAG office. The complex was originally an old Guatemalan military base. There were no signs out front, and the complex was a fortress; surrounded by an eighteen-foot barbed wire electrified fence topped with security cameras, floodlights, and motion sensors. A guard checked everyone coming and going. The TAG building contained dozens of offices, a front lobby with a receptionist, a large conference room, an interrogation room, and several holding cells.

The agents stopped to submit three samples for lab DNA analysis. Next, they wrote their report and created a summary presentation. They walked into Director Rick Aguilar's office.

"Agent Aguilar, we completed the site-investigation and are ready to present our findings," said Agent Allen.

On the way to the conference room, Rick poked his head into Deputy Director, Major Hugo Rojas's office and asked if he would join them.

"This accident was the result of an oncoming car approaching from the wrong side of the road," said Agent Garcia. From his laptop, he brought up a slideshow on a central screen.

"We found evidence both vehicles attempted to stop, each traveling an estimated forty to forty-five miles per hour. The tire prints of the approaching vehicle were evident enough we should be able to tell the tire type and derive a list of all possible vehicle makes and models. We are treating this as a crime based on a key piece of evidence. We discovered a burned cigarette, seen here, indicating the fire was intentionally set. We also found a trail of blood drops leading away from the SUV back to the road. It was likely from Ms. Strauss but possibly one of the kidnappers."

Agent Allen stepped forward. "We've requested rapid DNA analysis on the cigarette and blood samples. San Benito police turned over the couple's luggage they found at the cottage. We collected hair samples with follicles attached from a woman's hairbrush and sent that to the lab as well.

"With Major Rojas's help, we issued a subpoena to obtain records from the regional cell phone providers in order to track all phone activity in that area during the afternoon and early evening of the accident. We hope to collect locations, times, names, and phone numbers of anyone present. If Ms. Strauss had her cell phone and it remained connected, it might provide insight into her disappearance."

"How soon can they pull those records together?" asked Rick.

"I spoke with the managers from the two cell providers," said Agent Allen. "All their clerical staff left for the day, but both agreed to have managers work late to retrieve the logs. They promised to have them later tonight or early tomorrow morning."

"Early morning?" asked Rick.

"By 0400," answered Agent Allen with a slight frown.

"Agent Allen and I will stay here processing records as they arrive," said Agent Garcia.

"You'll both be exhausted. I'll present what we find at a 0600 meeting," said Rick. He stood up and thanked the two agents for their extraordinary effort and sacrifice. "I'll continue to manage this case, but I'd like you both to take on the lead roles. If this is a kidnapping, we should be hearing from her captors soon. The less information that gets out the better. Let's keep our findings strictly confidential. You two focus on the case; I'll handle any inquiries. See you all tomorrow morning," he said as he walked out.

*

Javier, Fernando, and Grace sped along in the police car down the road leading toward San Benito. After a mile, the car slowed briefly and turned abruptly on another road while still maintaining a high speed. Grace became confused. Maria told her the way back to town was to continue straight on that first road for two miles. Now they were heading in the opposite direction. She worried the police car was going too fast. Grace checked that her seat belt was secure, then looked down and saw her backpack on the floorboard.

"How did you get my backpack?" Grace asked, confused.

"Keep quiet!" said Javier. His harsh tone was alarming.

She was beginning to feel scared. *We can't be heading into town; this place is desolate.* She saw a vehicle up ahead.

"There's Cesar," said Fernando.

Who's Cesar? Who are these guys? Are they really policemen? Grace began to panic.

The police car pulled behind a van parked off the road. Both officers got out and greeted Cesar as he emerged from the van. Cesar walked to the rear and opened the back doors. Grace watched with increasing horror as all three turned and approached. They opened the door and dragged her out, forcing her into the back of the van while she kicked and screamed for help.

"Tie her legs!" ordered Cesar. "I may need to gag her if she doesn't shut up!"

Javier grabbed hard and pinned Grace's ankles, using excessive force.

"Come on, Javier. Don't be rough with her," said Fernando.

Javier paused and glanced at Fernando with a look of contempt, then applied zip-tie handcuffs. "Good, that should hold you," he said.

Grace watched Fernando toss her backpack next to her in the back of the van. He turned around and walked back toward the police car. Cesar and Javier remained, looked down at Grace momentarily, then slammed the doors. The van was dark and the steel floor uncomfortable, especially on her already aching body. She could hear their voices.

"Wait a second. She can identify us. All of us."

Grace recognized the voice; it was Javier's.

"The PLVI will make sure she doesn't live that long. That's part of our deal. Better not tell your partner. He might start crying."

They both chuckled.

Javier, looking back at Fernando sitting in the car, slowly shook his head in disgust.

"Yeah, the guy's become a wimp."

Tied up and in pain, lying on the floor in the dark, Grace heard every word.

CHAPTER 9

San Francisco, California

Agent Mike Murphy returned to his office and reviewed the Grace Strauss missing persons' file. He called the Guatemalan TAG contact listed.

"Guatemalan TAG, Special Agent Rick Aguilar."

"Good afternoon, Agent Aguilar, I'm Agent Mike Murphy out of the San Francisco office. Special Agent Bill Andrews assigned me to the Grace Strauss case."

"Great. Welcome aboard. I'm the director of the TAG office here in San Benito. And I'll personally be overseeing the case."

"Thanks, I read over the file. There's not much."

"Not yet, but we're making progress. We need you to contact her family as soon as possible and gather some information for us."

"No sense wasting time. If I can reach her father, can you join us on a three-way call?"

"Yes, good idea," said Rick.

Mike put Rick on hold and called Dr. Strauss.

"Peter Strauss here."

"Dr. Strauss, Mike Murphy. I have the TAG agent leading the case on the phone. Can you join us?"

"Yes, definitely!"

Mike set up the call.

"Hi, Dr. Strauss, I'm Special Agent Rick Aguilar from the TAG office here in Guatemala."

"Thanks for everything you're doing. Any news on the whereabouts of my daughter, Grace?" asked Peter.

"Dr. Strauss, this is an ongoing investigation. Everything we discuss is confidential," said Rick.

"Understood."

"As you may know by now, the vehicle Grace and Alan were driving was in an accident on a remote stretch of highway outside San Benito in Guatemala. It appears Alan swerved off the road to avoid hitting an oncoming car. We're certain Grace was a passenger and was not killed. But since she vanished, we believe she was abducted."

Peter made a clenched fist and popped the edge of his desk, which could be heard over the phone. "Damn it! That's what the consular agent told me might have happened. But you think she's okay, right?"

"There's no reason to believe otherwise, at this point. We haven't heard from anyone and assume you haven't either?"

"Nothing."

"Can you confirm this is Grace's cell phone number?" Rick recited the numbers out loud.

"Yes, that's it."

"Aside from your wealth, can you think of a reason why anyone would have kidnapped her? Do you have any adversaries?"

"No. None. Although, I am the owner and chief executive officer of SGSI, a high-tech military defence contractor. That possibly could be their motivation."

"If you receive a call from the kidnappers, record the conversation. Do you know how to do that?"

"Yes. No problem."

Mike spoke up. "Dr. Strauss, right after this call I'll send you a list of questions you should ask the kidnappers. Hopefully, they'll cooperate and not hang up. Take a look at them and try to commit them to memory. I'll stop by sometime tomorrow and walk you through the protocol. Let me know if they call you before then."

"All right, gentlemen," said Peter, "since I have you both on the phone, there's something I've been thinking about since I spoke with the consular agent. If Grace was kidnapped, I can help."

Mike listened while trying to imagine what Dr. Strauss was offering.

"Will the FBI or the Guatemalan police be the ones who rescue my daughter?" asked Peter.

"FBI agents assigned to the TAG office here in Guatemala, most likely, will be on the case," answered Rick.

"How many agents are we talking about?"

"Well, initially, two. Our resources are limited. Especially with regard to the number of available FBI agents who are currently working on other ongoing cases. For short-term highly critical situations, I can temporarily reassign all available agents, but that's usually only for a day or two," said Rick.

"If the goal is to rescue her unharmed, I think two agents wouldn't be enough, especially if there's a gang involved," said Peter.

"Dr. Strauss, the FBI's mission in any kidnapping case is to recover the victim. There are no assurances Grace will be found unharmed or alive. I know that sounds harsh, but that is the reality."

"I was afraid that might be the case. I have an offer. I am in a unique position to provide support," said Peter.

"Support?" said Rick and Mike simultaneously.

Mike immediately flashed back several weeks. When he interviewed at SGSI, everyone was deliberately vague discussing the work they did. He knew about drones, but little more. Upon his selection as the head of security, he learned he would get immersed in the details. His military and FBI backgrounds were a definite plus because of the high level of secrecy required. He felt he was about to get an early introduction.

"My company is at the absolute cutting edge pioneering smart drones. They have many versatile capabilities. This may seem a little vague, but for this purpose, imagine a flying bloodhound. I'll need to inform my contacts in Washington to let them know, but I'm sure it won't be an issue. It's more a courtesy than a request."

"A flying bloodhound, huh?" said Rick. "If it might help to get your daughter back, I'm interested. Mike, since you're up there, take a look, and if you think it's something we can use, we'd like to have one. We're still working on leads, so we couldn't use anything like that yet. But hopefully soon. I'll let Mike know about the timing."

"Great. Mike, when you show up tomorrow, I'll give you a tour of our R&D lab. I promise, you'll be impressed. You were going to get this introduction in a few weeks anyway, after you start."

"What's that?" asked Rick. "Are you joining SGSI, Mike?"

"Yes, this is my last week with the FBI."

"This is some transition from one job to another. One more thing before you hang up—Dr. Strauss, would you be willing to publicly offer a reward for information leading to Grace's safe return? It might help get your daughter back sooner, heading off a prolonged ransom demand."

"Definitely! Whatever amount you think will get her free. Is one million dollars enough?"

"Yes, very good. That should generate some interest. I'll send a memo out immediately. Okay, that was productive. I'll be in touch as things develop down here. Mike, let me know what you think of those smart drones. Dr. Strauss, I want you to know we will do our best to bring your daughter home safely."

CHAPTER 10

San Benito, Guatemala

Fernando watched Javier remove a small bag of cocaine from the evidence locker. When he asked what he was doing, Javier disclosed he planned to plant it in Maria's house to make the murder appear drug related. Javier told Fernando he had a .22 caliber pistol he confiscated from a burglary suspect but never turned in. No one could tie its ballistics back to him.

Fernando followed Javier into the bathroom within the police station. After they closed the door, Fernando ducked low to check if anyone was sitting in the stalls.

"Damn it, Javier! You're crazy. First the kidnapping; now you're talking about murder. Kill Maria and her whole family? I absolutely won't be part of it. It's insane."

"Shut up before someone hears us. I know what I'm doing. I'm saving your ass too. If my neighbor reports us, it's over. Prison. You want that, coward?"

Fernando was frustrated and angry. No matter how this played out, he'd had it with Javier. His eyes squinted and were on fire after hearing

Javier's last insult. He stared at Javier like he wasn't sure he knew who he was looking at anymore. They used to be friends, but now Fernando wasn't so sure. He turned and stormed out to try to cool down.

After work, they got into Fernando's car without saying a word. They'd spent the better part of the afternoon going back and forth, debating how to deal with Maria. Javier was adamant he had to kill her. If her husband was home, he'd kill the entire family. Fernando was afraid this was spiraling out of control. He felt strongly they should handle it without violence. Maybe just threatening Maria would keep her silent. Whether he could change the events that were about to unfold or not, Fernando still felt he had to keep an eye on Javier.

As Fernando drove to Maria's house, his mind raced, trying to find a way out of this mess. He turned off and headed up her driveway. There were no cars. It meant her husband wasn't home. A small relief. He and Javier got out. They approached the door and knocked. It was quiet, and no one answered.

"Senora Hernandez, where are you? Are you okay? We know you're here," called Javier.

After less than a minute, Javier grew impatient and kicked the door open. The small house was empty.

"Nobody's here. Okay. Let's go, Javier."

"I know she's hiding. She saw me looking at her from the street. In this heat, she won't have gone far."

Javier stepped outside and looked around. Fernando followed. In the back there was a chicken coop and small square bales of hay. They walked toward the coop. Fernando caught a glimpse of the edge of a pink baby blanket protruding from behind one of the bales and hoped Javier wouldn't notice it. He tried to think of something to say that might get him to leave, but Javier saw it and started his approach. He found Maria, cradling her baby tightly, staring up, petrified.

"There you are."

Fernando was right behind. Both stood looking down at Maria.

"Why are you hiding? Come with us, we want to talk to you," said Javier. "You're not in trouble. Don't worry."

Maria slowly got up, her arms quivering. "I'm not hiding. Can't I sit in my own back yard with my baby? Why are you officers here? Has something happened?"

The conversation stopped. A vehicle could be heard approaching. Maria's husband's old pickup truck drove up the driveway, making loud rumbling noises and spewing black diesel smoke from the tailpipe. Miguel Hernández stepped out of his truck, appearing surprised to see a strange car in his driveway.

"Maria! Maria!" he shouted.

"Over here, Miguel," she called back.

Miguel rushed over to Maria's side. He looked at Javier. "You're our neighbor. What's going on?"

Javier and Fernando knew this was the worst-case scenario. Javier's hand began to move for the gun sticking out of his back pocket. Fernando had to think of something quick. He reached over and touched Javier's arm to stop him. Both Maria and Miguel noticed. Fernando spoke up quickly.

"We are San Benito policemen. Today an escaped criminal, a young American woman, was in the area. We arrested her but wondered if she stopped here and tried to rob you?"

Maria answered, "Yes, she came up to our house. I gave her food and water. She didn't rob us. We have nothing to steal."

"She tells people she was kidnapped to gain their sympathies, then asks them for money or takes anything she can grab. Don't believe a word she told you."

"Oh no, I didn't."

"A criminal came here today?" asked Miguel.

"Yes. But you're safe now," said Fernando. "She was arrested and deported."

"Thank you for warning us," said Maria. "You are good policemen."

Fernando turned to Javier. "We're done here."

*

The couple stood and waved as the two officers drove off. When they were out of sight, Miguel turned to Maria. "What really happened today? That policeman, Javier, our neighbor, he looked like he wanted to shoot us. Did you see?"

"Yes. Javier kidnapped an American woman named Grace. She told me the whole story. She escaped and came here for help. I gave her food and water. She was bloody and bruised. And needed a bath. Just as she left, they showed up and put her in their car and drove off. The baby and I spent the day hiding behind the chicken coop. I was so scared. Thank God you arrived when you did."

"Oh, Maria, an angel is watching out for you. They sent me home early; otherwise, I'd still be at work."

"Yes, we are blessed. But I hope that poor girl is all right. She was so nice. What should we do?"

"Nothing," said Miguel. "They'll come back and kill us if we say anything."

Maria handed the baby to Miguel and walked into the house, her pulse still racing. She sat quietly at the kitchen table, made the sign of the cross, put her hands together, tilted her head down, and prayed. Seeing Grace bruised and frightened reawakened memories of abuse she endured growing up. "God, I want to help her," Maria whispered to herself. "Please, dear God, show me how."

CHAPTER 11

San Benito, Guatemala

The investigation started moving rapidly in the Guatemalan TAG office. In order to expedite matters, Rick pulled in several more agents from other cases. He also included his deputy director, Major Hugo Rojas, an attorney in the Guatemalan Army assigned to TAG. His insights on legal matters were invaluable.

Agents Allen and Garcia worked through the night collecting records of interest from the major cell phone providers. They knew every minute counted in the first few days of a kidnapping.

Rick arrived to work at 0500, and started examining files as they became available. He began the tedious task of selecting and sorting relevant information and combined them into a presentation, along with the initial local police report, the TAG internal investigation findings, and preliminary DNA results. A team of twelve tired-looking agents entered the conference room for an early morning status meeting to discuss their findings. They sat around the long rectangular table, their attention focused on a large screen. Rick finished typing on his laptop and stood up. He leaned forward, placing both hands on the table with outstretched arms as he looked around the room.

"Here's what we know. We've mapped the locations of Ms. Strauss's cell phone on the day of her disappearance, November twenty-first."

A map of northern Guatemala appeared with red dots and time stamps representing her locations.

"This is the site of the accident. Based on the phone location data collected, we believe it occurred at 1843. That's when it abruptly stopped its movement."

Rick pointed at the map. "After seventeen minutes, her phone began moving along this road, but soon after, transmission terminates. The phone was either shut off or low on battery power. We tried calling, but it's dead."

"Did we pick up any other phone activity in the area?" asked Agent Allen.

"Good question." The next slide displayed a map cluttered with time-stamped multicolored dots. "There is one cell phone of particular interest right here"—Rick circled a spot on the map— "identified in blue dots. It approached from the opposite direction and stopped at the crash scene exactly at the same time as Ms. Strauss's; the car that we suspect caused the accident. The name associated with that phone number is a police officer from San Benito, Fernando Ramirez."

"Was he one of the first responders?" asked Agent Garcia.

"No, the call to both the police and fire departments didn't come in until twenty-two minutes after phone activity showed Ms. Strauss's and Mr. Ramirez's phones left the area at exactly the same time. Small blood samples taken from the scene match DNA from hair samples found in her luggage. That confirms she was definitely in that SUV. Unfortunately, DNA results taken from the half-burned cigarette recovered at the scene of the accident were inconclusive."

The room began to fill with low-volume chatter between agents.

Someone could be heard above the others. "Great, another crooked cop."

Rick turned his head in the direction of the voices, showing a slightly displeased look.

The agents went silent.

"Who made the call to the police?" asked one of the agents.

"A passing truck driver called it in," said Rick. "Agent Garcia, get Officer Ramirez's home address. Agent Allen, pull together all cell records of Officer Ramirez's phone since November twenty-first. We need to find out where he's been. Major Rojas, arrange an arrest warrant. With that in hand, a team will pick him up this morning. Don't alert the San Benito Police Department yet. I need to pay a visit to their chief first. We don't know how deep into their department this goes. Thanks, everyone, for showing up so early. Be back here in two hours for your assignments."

Rick called police Chief Torres and requested an urgent meeting. On the way to the San Benito police station, he had some thoughts run through his mind. *The chief is definitely a good cop. I can't imagine he would stand still knowing he had anyone on the force who would do this. Who is this Officer Ramirez? Some new guy? Never heard his name mentioned.* Rick arrived and made his way to the police chief's office. He closed the door behind him.

"Chief Torres, thanks for meeting with me," said Rick.

"What's going on? Is there a problem with the case?"

"There's no easy way to say this. We have evidence linking one of your policemen, Officer Fernando Ramirez to the abduction of the American woman."

"One of my men!" replied Chief Torres. "Christ. Are you sure?"

"Positive," said Rick with a slight nod.

Chief Torres shook his head slowly while showing his disgust.

"There's nothing good about this. A woman is missing, a family that's probably worried sick. It tarnishes the image of our entire department and erodes trust among the community."

"You're right. One senseless act can do a lot of damage," said Rick. "What can you tell me about him?"

"You know, he pretty much stays to himself, a real quiet guy."

"Does he have any friends you know of, especially within the station?"

"One for sure, Officer Javier Villalta. They're partners and close friends. Hold on. Those two came to me and asked that I put them on the case right before we turned it over to you. Those sneaky bastards!"

"Yeah, probably wanted to make sure evidence never pointed back at them. Do they have any friends within the station?"

"No, not that I'm aware. In the past, I've heard other officers make disparaging comments in passing about them both. I don't think either is well-liked."

"Interesting. I have an arrest warrant for Officer Fernando Ramirez. Would you ask him to come here, now? Then we'll step out back. I'd like to take him in quietly so as not to alert anyone else in case others within the station are part of the kidnapping."

"Unfortunately, both officers aren't scheduled to work today—a rotational day off."

"We need to pick him up immediately. We'll have to go to his house and get him." Rick paused for a moment, imagining how the arrest might play out. "If he's home, we'll need a reason to get him to come out. If he's holding Ms. Strauss inside, I don't want to risk creating a standoff. Would you call Officer Ramirez later this morning and ask him to come into work?"

"Sure, I know what to say."

Chief Torres walked Rick through his plan.

"Good, that should work. I'll call when we're in place."

Rick thanked him for his help, they shook hands, and he left.

*

Rick returned to the TAG office and immediately called Agents Allen, Garcia, and Major Rojas into his office.

"Unfortunately, Ramirez has the day off; we'll need to arrest him at home. Agent Allen, take a team and head out after this to pick him up. I'll come along and observe. Agent Garcia and Major Rojas, I want you two here working on something. The chief mentioned Ramirez has a close friend, another officer, Javier Villalta. Scan the records and see if there's any connection. If so, we need to move quickly to bring him in as well."

Later that morning, ten agents mustered at the rear of the TAG building. Rick and Agent Allen approached each agent one by one and handed out their assignments. It included a diagram of Officer Ramirez's house and their exact position and role. Although they assumed this would be a routine arrest, they had to prepare for every contingency in case all hell broke loose. Rick unlocked the armory storage shed. Inside, they had laid out equipment for each team member. There were helmets, handguns, and bulletproof vests for everyone. Three members formed the entry-breaching team. They were given tools that included explosives and short-barreled shotguns with special ballistics to blast open doors or walls, if necessary. The four members that made up the arresting team would carry handcuffs and nightsticks. Rifles were given to three members assigned as snipers. Rick carried the arrest warrant and binoculars; he would observe. They gathered everyone around, and Rick walked them through his plans. Agent Allen would lead the operation. Rick handed her the bullhorn.

"The best-case scenario would be if we get Officer Ramirez to leave his house and arrest him outside without incident. If that doesn't happen and we're spotted, he could get desperate and threaten to kill Ms. Strauss if she's inside. It goes without saying: be careful."

After answering a few questions, they loaded up in three large SUVs and drove off. When the TAG agents arrived, they parked a quarter-mile away and discreetly moved in toward Fernando's house. The first task was to cordon off the area to make sure his neighbors would not be harmed nor interfere with the arrest. Next, they took up their positions. Agents observed Officer Ramirez moving around inside, apparently oblivious to the fate that awaited him. Rick called Chief Torres.

"We're all set. Call Officer Ramirez."

The chief used a station phone so as not to raise suspicion. Fernando's phone rang. Rick watched through binoculars as Fernando answered his phone.

Rick had the script memorized. *Right now, Chief Torres is asking Ramirez to come into work to help out with an emergency. Then he'll offer him double-time pay. That should get him motivated. Hope this works; otherwise, it could get ugly.*

After the call ended, Chief Torres called Rick to let him know Officer Ramirez took the bait.

"Excellent!" Rick said softly. "Thanks for your help. I'll call later with an update."

Rick waved and showed a thumbs-up to Agent Allen, indicating it was proceeding as planned.

*

Fernando hurriedly changed into his police uniform, slipped his shoulder holster around his arms, then grabbed his wallet, cell phone, and keys. He jammed his feet into his police shoes without bothering to tie them, stepped out, and turned to lock his door. Suddenly, he felt as if something wasn't right. He paused momentarily to listen. *That's odd, nothing. It's dead quiet.* The morning sounds of the neighborhood were missing, especially kids shouting and playing noises conspicuous by their absence. He resumed locking his side door.

"Freeze! TAG agents! You're under arrest. Put your hands up slowly," said Agent Allen through her bullhorn.

A stunned Fernando complied. He was familiar with the routine. His hands moved slowly away from his sides and up over his head. No sudden movements.

Within seconds, the agents pounced. They applied handcuffs, patted Fernando down, and confiscated his gun and personal belongings.

"Mr. Ramirez, would you like me to recite to you your rights?" asked Agent Allen.

"I know what they are. Why am I being arrested?"

"Kidnapping," replied Agent Allen.

Agents led him over to a large black TAG SUV as it drove up. They put him in the back seat, pushing his head down to avoid hitting the top as he slid in. Five agents, led by Agent Allen, stayed to search Fernando's property. The rest drove back to the TAG office with Fernando.

Handcuffed, sitting quietly alone, Fernando thought about his options. He had rights under Guatemalan law, he knew what to say, and, more importantly, what not to say. Fernando felt anxious wondering how much they knew. *How did they know to arrest me? Did they find the American woman? Have they arrested Javier? Did they get Cesar too? Did Maria or her husband turn us in?* He could only hope the evidence against him wasn't strong enough for a conviction. The best path forward was not to disclose anything and let them show their cards first.

CHAPTER 12

Palo Alto, California

Mike arrived at SGSI, looking forward to a tour of the R&D facility and learning about the smart drones Peter mentioned. The guard checked the guest list and examined his identification. His name looked familiar.

"Agent Mike Murphy," said the guard. "I read a memo that you're our new head of security."

"That's right."

"Welcome. Please pull over to the parking lot to your right."

As he did, Peter stepped out of the administration building to greet him.

"Agent Murphy," Peter said while reaching out for a handshake, "thanks for jumping on this so quickly! Let's head to my office." Peter handed Mike his access badge. "Here, you'll need this; fortunately, you've been here before, so we can dispense with the security formalities."

Mike had been to SGSI twice, but both times, his interviews had taken place in the administration building.

They headed toward a more secure part of the complex. Peter swiped his badge and entered through an access-controlled turnstile. Mike followed, and he noticed security cameras monitoring their movements. They walked into a four-story office building. During Mike's interviews, he always sat across the table from everyone. He hadn't noticed much about Dr. Strauss's appearance. Mike assumed he was in his early fifties. His brown hair was thinning on top and transitioning to gray. As they walked together, he could tell he was about five-foot-eleven with a medium build.

"This will be your office, next to mine. By the way, may I call you Mike?"

"Yes."

"Good. Please call me Peter. I realize it's early, but is there any news?"

"I talked to Rick briefly before heading out. They're working on some promising leads," said Mike.

"Sounds encouraging."

"Let's hope. Now, if you get a call from the kidnappers, here's a list of questions to ask. Try to keep them talking. Maybe they'll reveal something we don't yet know. Convince them you intend to fully cooperate. But given that kidnappers often communicate with encrypted text, I think it's unlikely they'll call."

They spent the next twenty minutes rehearsing discussion techniques.

"If we're ready to move on, I'm curious what you meant by 'smart drone' support," said Mike.

"The company you're about to start working for is at the absolute cutting edge, pioneering what I call NAIMERAs along with attack drones. When deployed together, they form a 'smart drone.'"

"NAIMERAs?"

"It's a word I conjured up to describe what they are—a Naturally and Artificially Intelligent Chimera. NAIMERA for short. Think of one as a living, high-tech, independent reconnaissance 'brain,' using both natural and artificial intelligence, capable of directing one or more attack drones. You look a little puzzled. Bear with me. It will become clear after you get a glimpse of our R&D facility."

What is a NAIMERA, a living creature? A mystified Mike was about to start working at a place and suddenly realized his understanding of what they did was way off base. *What on earth are they doing here?* "I'm dying with curiosity to learn what my new employer really does. While serving in Afghanistan, I remember SGSI mentioned as the vendor providing us with AI-directed high-tech drones. I assumed that was the core of your company. Is that right?"

Peter slowly shook his head with a polite smile. "You have many fine qualities we were looking for in someone to head our security team. But having both a top-secret and sensitive compartmented information clearance definitely helped make you stand out. As you know, it can take many months or years for those to go through, if they're granted at all. What we do here must be kept secret. The fact you know so little is actually good news. Let's move this to the sensitive compartmented information facility. I can give you a better overview there."

Mike's curiosity grew exponentially. Peter led him from his office toward a three-story building surrounded by a ten-foot fence topped with barbed wire. They entered a small booth, the door closed, and Mike heard a bolt lock from behind. A woman's voice spoke.

"Good afternoon, Dr. Strauss. It's been exactly twenty-three hours and four minutes since you last visited," said the voice.

Mike looked around, intrigued.

"Hi, Maggie. I'm taking my visitor into the SCIF."

Several cameras in the booth emitted red focus beams at Mike's face and body.

"Yes, Agent Mike Murphy, FBI. Age: thirty-five years, weight: one-hundred and ninety-one pounds, height: six-feet-three inches. TS/SCI clearance verified and valid. By the way, Agent Murphy, your clearance is up for renewal in four months and twelve days. Your paperwork has yet to be submitted. Do you prefer Mike or Michael?" said Maggie.

Mike's eyebrows raised, not knowing to whom or what he was talking.

"Ah, Mike would be fine. Thank you for the reminder about my clearance … Maggie?"

"Yes. You are welcome. Mike, before you exit, a cell phone in your left pocket is active." A small cabinet stood off to his right with several one-foot-by-one-foot lockers. One of them slid haltingly open. "Please leave your cell phone and smartwatch before exiting."

Mike complied while shaking his head. The locker drawer quietly slid closed. "Why my watch?"

"GPS tracking could reveal who visited our SCIF as well as other locations," replied Maggie. "They can also serve as listening devices. A prudent precaution."

"Of course. Thanks for catching that."

"You are welcome. Access granted."

The sound of a bolt clicking was heard, and the door leading out slowly opened. As they left the booth Mike looked back over his shoulder.

"Okay, who or what is a Maggie? How did she know I had a cell phone … and a smartwatch?"

Peter smiled. "She is our AI security goddess. Runs everything. You will be working with her."

"No one mentioned Maggie during my interviews."

"We interviewed over two dozen candidates for the head of security. We never disclose our security details or what we do until we hire someone. And even then, we restrict what they learn of our operation to a need-to-know basis."

"Okay, I get it. So, you built her or it?"

"Yes. As you're about to find out, we are pretty diverse here at SGSI."

Along the way, they passed several small groups of workers, all of whom appeared engaged in conversations as they walked. Many wore white lab coats and carried notebooks.

"This place has the atmosphere of a college campus," said Mike. "Vibrant and intellectual."

"That's not by accident," said Peter. "It was one of my goals. Those five over there are physicists. The three entering that building now are biochemists. I'll take you by and introduce you to all the teams when things settle down."

Mike was becoming keenly aware of his surroundings. He noticed several security cameras on their way up to the entrance. The door opened.

Mike turned to Peter. "Did Maggie just perform facial recognition on us?"

"Yes."

They walked into a large room with a thirty-foot-high ceiling. It looked pristine, still retaining a slight smell of fresh paint and new carpet. Peter led Mike down a long hallway, where they encountered another security entrance with a door that resembled a bank vault. They stepped up and walked across a slightly raised platform consisting of several large octagonal-shaped rubber pads pieced together with sensors beneath.

Mike looked down, curious. "What is it we're walking on?"

"Earlier, Maggie recorded your unique gait as part of your personal profile. A number of different pressure sensors help confirm it's you. She's also scanning our faces and verifying weight and height are within known tolerances. She performs multiple security checks at every entrance."

Maggie's voice spoke up. "Gentlemen, please place your right hand on the glass plate." Mike and Peter complied. "Would you like to open the vault manually or shall I do it for you, Peter?"

"Open it, Maggie. Thank you."

A dark plexiglass cover dropped down to conceal the combination lock. The dial on the lock began to turn. Mike could hear the soft irregular clicking of the rotations, and then it stopped. The sound of a massive bolt could be heard and felt with a slight vibration. The dial spun one last time, and the plexiglass cover lifted. The vault door slowly opened.

"This is new to me. Is the gait security analysis a necessary tool for the extra effort and expense?" said Mike.

"Absolutely. It not only helps confirm who you are, but we found another surprising benefit. A year ago, we had some visitors. Maggie alerted one of the gentlemen he was displaying early stages of Parkinson's disease. Of course, he remained skeptical until he had it checked out. He called back and thanked me, grateful, since catching it early helped slow its progression. Maggie's been programmed to check for a number of neurodegenerative diseases. Not making use of the full benefits of any technology would be a disservice, don't you think?"

CHAPTER 13

Palo Alto, California

Peter led Mike into a small auditorium. "Have a seat. You mentioned in your interview you were familiar with our drones. Tell me about your experience and what you know about SGSI."

"What I know about SGSI? Not as much as I thought. We used one of your drones in Afghanistan. They said it was a prototype, so nobody had any high expectations. The thing that fascinated all of us was how it differed from the others. An operator only needed to provide general coordinates of suspected Al-Qaeda activity, the nature of the mission—reconnaissance or kill—and send it off. Once launched, not long after it left, the drone would vanish from radar, sometimes for hours, then suddenly reappear. No one was sure what it was doing. Heck, on its first mission, we assumed it was shot down. But it returned safely. Every one of our mission debriefing reports showed the kills were clean and complete, never a friendly fire or civilian casualty. The thing seemed to have 'brains,' possessing the intelligence of an expert sniper. We were all pretty impressed with the results."

"That was our first attempt at 'wetware,' the HBC-100. A pioneer," said Peter. "The first drone, or any device for that matter, to use human brain-celled microprocessors for sensing and decision-making. Cells separated and grown in cultures derived from stem cells."

"Excuse me ... what on earth does that mean?"

"Maggie, start up the animated slideshow 'Introduction to SGSI,'" instructed Peter.

Lights dimmed, and the title came up across the top in bold letters. One after another, images appeared. First, a picture of the SGSI complex in the center, and surrounding it, smaller graphic pictures gradually materialized along the edges. There was a double-helix DNA strand, a military attack drone, a row of beakers filled with organs immersed in fluid, a room packed with computers, scientists in white lab suits working around research equipment, and a couple of bats flying through the sky firing lasers.

Mike looked at the images, baffled. *What in the hell is that all about?*

"My background is bioengineering," said Peter. "Building on my Ph.D. dissertation, I cofounded a spectacularly successful biotech company, PureBioX. After I sold it in ninety-eight, I took some time off to reassess my life. Meditation retreats, reading, traveling, and pondering my place in the world. I realized being wealthy and talented is a blessing but also carries great responsibility to myself and humanity. I set my sights on pursuing a long-held dream of mine, to uncover every mystery surrounding the deoxyribonucleic acid molecule, especially the evolutionary process. Simply put, to understand every minute detail of DNA—how and why it works, then how all the various pieces fit into making the process of creating and evolving life possible. That was my original goal by founding this company."

"How did the drone business enter the picture?"

"I make it my business to learn as much as I can about the people

I meet, especially the ones I hire. It turns out we share a common thread," said Peter.

"A common thread?" said Mike with an inquisitive look.

"Unfortunately, yes. Not long after I started this journey, the infamous 9/11 attacks occurred. Of course, I was upset and angry, not only for the nation but for the friends I lost. I wanted to do something. Something significant. That's when I took what seemed, at the time, to be a short-term detour. It started with a casual conversation with a friend from the DoD. He mentioned there was a desperate need for intelligent reconnaissance and killer drones in the hunt for Al-Qaeda."

"So, you know about my father?" said Mike.

Peter nodded. "I'm sorry. It must have been terrible for you and your family."

"It was, for us and all the other families of FDNY firemen along with everyone else who lost love ones on that day. That was a big reason I wanted to become a Navy SEAL. For a chance to go after those guys," said Mike.

"Oh, I understand, and thank you for your service. Maggie, next slide."

A picture of a soldier in full military combat gear came up, alongside him an attack drone with a satellite station, an operations trailer, and finally, support personal appeared. All slowly converged, transforming into a single drone. Mike tried to make sense of these images. *What's the story with this?*

"As I said, I was determined to contribute to the cause. At that point, we were making huge strides in creating a computer program capable of inputting a list of desired physical features of a living organism and outputting the necessary DNA sequences, or genomes, to create it. A team of us got together and identified the requirements necessary to build AI drones. We felt confident by using our research, we could do something spectacular. Of course, there were major obstacles: the drone must function independently, and time was of the essence. If we wanted the AI drone to possess human-like cognitive capabilities, and soon, we had to think outside the box."

A slide came up with a graphic showing a human brain across from an array of computers. The title read "Comparable Processing Power."

"Is that suggesting it takes a room of computers to match a human brain?"

"That's right. Your observation distinguishing our drones in Afghanistan from all others was right on the mark. Up until then, military drones were exclusively managed by human operators using remote cameras. We set out to make autonomously operated smart drones, incorporating actual human brain cells for cognitive processing. Our first drone, the HBC-100, combined both ordnance and intelligent AI reconnaissance together into one flying structure. Although it was successful, it had limitations. In order to locate and identify terrorists inside vehicles, homes, caves, or other hidden enclosures, we needed another smaller reconnaissance unit to accompany the lethal drone. It called for a small, independent, intelligent, agile, stealthy, and mobile system—hence the NAIMERA was born."

The next slide showed a military drone with a small door opened on one side. Inside the door was something that resembled a bat.

"Is that bat-looking thing a NAIMERA?"

"Yes, but let me explain. Here's how it works. A NAIMERA rides inside a much larger attack drone until they approach a suspected target. The drone hovers and lands in a safe staging area, awaiting instructions. The small NAIMERA exits the drone and flies off to perform reconnaissance. After identifying precise targets, the NAIMERA calls in and directs one or more lethal drone strikes to finish the job using the appropriate ordnance."

Mike leaned forward in his seat. He couldn't believe what he was hearing. "Okay, what you're talking about is, excuse me, freaking insane. You need to step back a bit. How are you able to use human brain cells?"

Peter grinned. "When we started this journey, the common belief was that AI was only available on silicon-based chip computers. As our team discussed the limitations of previous drones and examined the requirements of what we'd like our drone to do, we encountered a potentially show-stopping hurdle. The processing power needed would require a computer larger than the size of this room.

"The true genius of any invention is distilling the solution down to its most optimal form. I pondered the problem from every angle. A human brain is made up of roughly one hundred billion neurons. When you factor in the interconnectivity, we're looking at a staggering quadrillion synapses. In fact, memory cells can have over ten thousand connections where a silicon logic gate has a max of four fan-outs. The solution jumped out and seemed so obvious: merge the two."

An image of a computer chip with brain cells inside showing ports all around the sides appeared. The animation showed the cells growing and attaching to the surrounding encasement.

"The HBC-100 only needed a human brain-enabled chip integrated within existing silicon circuitry to work. But to incorporate that chip into a living organism with an existing brain, a NAIMERA, we needed to make a small modification. Every chip socket pin, as well as the pins within the chip itself, contains specially coated connections offering locations where synapses attach naturally. We begin by placing brain cells within the body of the chip. As they develop, they seek out and connect to the coated pins along the inside perimeter. The same way your brain cells connect to each other. Next, we memory map that brain-celled chip with any number of cognitive skills we want it to perform—for example, languages. Finally, we surgically insert one or more chip sockets within the host brain. Within a few hours, the host's brain cells connect to the coated pins of the socket. Once that's in place, a memory-encoded human brain-celled chip is inserted into the socket. Later, it can easily be removed and replaced with another."

A picture appeared showing the head of a pin next to the chip.

The material, Peter's fast pace and enthusiasm made the entire presentation exciting. *Man, this is amazing stuff!*

"Nearly a million neurons can exist on that pin head. When we built our first successful chip, we knew we were on to something ground-breaking. Our imaginations went wild."

"Wait a minute," said Mike. "Cells are the basic structure of living organisms. They need things like glucose and oxygen, not to mention a proper temperature range to survive."

"True. We addressed those issues by circulating nutrient- and oxygen-rich absorbable chemicals around the environment within thin membranes. The body of the NAIMERA offers some degree of temperature stability, but like anything, extreme heat or cold will cause malfunction. So far, we haven't seen that happen."

An oversized image of a battery appeared on the screen next to a small drop of nutrient-rich liquid.

"One more compelling benefit, computer chips with neurons are over a million times more energy-efficient than silicon-based devices. As a result, our NAIMERAs are small, lightweight, and much more efficient. The smartest silicon-based AI computers in the world really only excel at a limited array of tasks. We recognized that and, frankly, had little choice but to look beyond silicon-based chips."

Mike shook his head. "A tiny drop of that is equal to that battery?"

"That's right." Peter smiled.

A slide entitled "Disciplines" displayed.

Mike scanned down the list, pausing to try to understand what role each discipline would play. He saw molecular, evolutionary, and synthetic biologists, neuroscientists, physicists, chemists, engineers, geneticists, mathematicians, computer scientists, and lawyers.

"Armed with this new low-powered, miniature but powerful computing potential, as I said, our imaginations went wild contemplating the possibilities. The handful of scientists we had wasn't adequate. But I didn't want to grow too big or too fast and paralyze our efforts. So, I assembled the small teams of professionals you see here. I always hire either three or five highly motivated world-class scientists per group. I pay them very well but expect great results."

"Three or five. Why is that?"

"It's my policy based on years of experience. Our research guidelines are such that each group must agree on one single best path forward unless there's a compelling reason to follow multiple research options. But normally, I prefer we focus our energies and resources on one. The odd number guarantees no ties. This might seem counterintuitive, but I also try to hire scientists who may not agree—devil's advocates, if you will. However, they must do so respectfully. They should logically and methodically assess both the positive and negative sides of each approach. If you populate groups with yes men or naysayers, you could miss critical flaws or important opportunities. Of course, we conduct periodic reviews, and if a research path is not working out, we learn from our efforts and choose another. Failure is beneficial as long as you recognize it early, analyze why it failed, and move on."

"Have you ever had a stalemate between the three?" asked Mike.

"Not yet, but if that happens, I would be the tiebreaker. There's no delay in deciding since I attend every proposal review."

"I noticed you listed lawyers," said Mike.

"Yes, it's crucial we do not violate laws with respect to our DNA research, as well as international law with our drone development. Plus, I need to legally protect our R&D as much as possible. Our patent attorneys are the most overworked group on-site."

Mike paused and rubbed his eyes. He saw Peter watching him.

"Don't worry if you don't understand much of this," said Peter. "It's a lot to absorb. Just try to get the big picture."

"Thanks," said Mike smiling. "I am a bit overwhelmed."

A slide with the title "Memory and Cognitive Milestones" appeared. Underneath were pictures of rectangular computer chips with open tops and brain cells occupying the center, connecting to the output pins.

"Our researchers tackled many complex issues. They made significant progress in our understanding of memory mapping and cognitive models. You see, the brain is essentially a predicting machine, an idea that's been around for years. Making sense of the world around us, developing language skills, interpreting behavior, performing tasks are all built primarily from the memory of our experiences. We've learned how that works, how to assemble and map hierarchies of experiences that perform predictions, and finally how to transfer those memories and skills within living brain cell computer chips. Once a NAIMERA matures physically, we implant the human-celled chips. They come preprogrammed with advanced functionality to get them kick-started with any special skills we want them to do. Plus, NAIMERAs are continually in information-gathering mode. In order to fast-track their ability to process what they learn, we encoded several AI machine learning techniques into their brain cells. In essence, the minute they're born, they can immediately begin to organize and assimilate information as if they were graduate students.

"Our scientific research requires massive computational power, especially for AI and DNA R&D. So, we brought in a 500-petaflop supercomputer. That's five hundred quadrillion calculations per second. That massive horsepower made quick work of the language-development effort. Once in place, the language infrastructure was memory encoded and ready to stage on one of our homegrown human brain-cell chips. We currently have all 6,500 spoken languages that fit nicely onto one tiny living chip. Within minutes, we can insert that chip into one of our NAIMERAs' preinstalled chip sockets, and suddenly, it speaks every language. *Voilá!*"

"Let me get this straight. They can speak and understand every language on the planet?"

"That's true."

"And the mind you created for a NAIMERA has infinite learning capacity?"

"Potentially. However, we realized early on as soon as we enabled their 'brain' to form questions and acquire knowledge on its own, it began to experience overload. Organic neurons started dying from overload, basically too much stress. Also, the unrestricted accumulation of information began saturating its memory storage capacity. The solution was obvious. Sleep. Their brains have two hemispheres. We evolve them to include the gene to perform unihemispheric sleep. Periodically, each side of the brain of a NAIMERA moves from active into either a no-stress sleep state or maintenance cleanup mode. Duplicate or extraneous information gets discarded in maintenance mode. All done while they never lose consciousness."

Mike's head was spinning. Without noticing, he began rubbing his temple until he realized Peter was looking at him.

"What do you say we take a short break. Coffee, water?" asked Peter.

"You read my mind."

CHAPTER 14

San Benito, Guatemala

TAG agents filled the conference room to review the latest information and discuss interrogation strategies.

Rick stood up. "Now that we have an arrest, we need to move quickly if we have any hope of saving Ms. Strauss. Whoever has her might feel keeping her alive is a liability. I'd like an update before deciding how to approach this interrogation. Agent Garcia?"

"I heard from Agent Allen. They searched Fernando Ramirez's house, car, and property. No signs of Ms. Strauss, but they did discover a bloody handkerchief and shirt in a laundry basket. It seemed fresh."

"Excellent! Let's have that analyzed, immediately."

"The chief pointed us in the right direction. After the accident, Fernando's phone showed him traveling to his partner Officer Javier Villalta's house. They must have been together."

"Great, we're getting closer. Maybe that's where they're keeping Ms. Strauss?" said Rick.

"We already got the warrant for his arrest," said Major Rojas.

Rick nodded with approval.

"Agent Allen and her team are on their way at this moment to pick up Officer Villalta and search his property," said Agent Garcia.

"Excellent! Anything else?" asked Rick.

"Yes, one more. Phone records revealed one day after Ms. Strauss disappeared, Officer Ramirez visited a neighbor of Officer Villalta's. The home of Mr. Hernández. Agents will stop and have a chat with him after they leave Officer Villalta's house. Otherwise, his phone locations and activity seem to follow his typical workday."

"Agent Garcia, let me know when the team returns. I'll want an update immediately. Perhaps with a little more information, we can persuade Officer Ramirez to cooperate. Major Rojas, Agent Garcia, I'd like you both to join me in the interrogation room," said Rick.

Major Rojas spoke up. "Agent Aguilar, if you don't mind, I'll lead the interrogation. I'm the most familiar with our legal system."

Rick nodded his head in agreement; he was curious what new interrogation techniques Major Rojas could show him. "Sure, can you give us a hint of what you have in mind?" asked Rick.

"I expect Officer Ramirez to demand a public defender. Here in Guatemala, that is a common stalling tactic. We only have four public defenders per one hundred thousand people in the entire country. Requesting one usually pushes a case off months or years, sometimes resulting in charges being dropped altogether. As a police officer, he would be aware of it. But I have many high-level connections that, from time to time, come in handy. If he tries it, watch what happens."

The door opened to the interrogation room. Major Rojas and the two agents walked in. Fernando looked dejected; hunched over and handcuffed to a steel ring bolted into the large wooden table. He stared up. There appeared a hint of anger in his eyes. They calmly introduced themselves and displayed their FBI credentials and Guatemalan Military IDs.

Fernando spoke first. "I won't answer any questions without an attorney."

"Certainly, Officer Ramirez; do you have one in mind whom we should contact?" asked Major Rojas in a stern, confident voice.

"No, I want a public defender."

Major Rojas smirked and shook his head. "Of course," he said nonchalantly, in a calm tone. "Agent Garcia, call the Court for High Risk Crimes and tell the assistant attorney general Major Hugo Rojas requests him to assign Officer Ramirez a public defender. Send one here immediately."

Fernando's eyes opened a little wider in surprise.

Agent Garcia got up and left to make the call.

"Officer Ramirez, we can hold you in jail for a very long time while we investigate this crime. You could be sitting in a cell with many, many others through this process. Of course, if you care to answer a few quick questions, we might be able to clear this up now and send you home."

Fernando thought for a minute, apparently weighing his options.

"All right, but if I feel the questions make me uncomfortable, I'll stop."

"Fair enough," said Major Rojas.

Major Rojas and Rick looked at each other with tight smiles. Rick reached down and discreetly activated the video recording system.

Then Major Rojas began: "Officer Ramirez, are you aware of the car accident just outside San Benito that claimed the life of an American tourist, Mr. Alan Walters?"

"Of course, that's a big story here in town."

"Were you on duty at the time?"

"I don't think so. I don't remember. What time did it happen?"

"It was reported at 1843 on November twenty-first."

"I get off work at 1700, so I definitely was not on duty."

"Have you visited the crash site?"

"I drove by to check it out. Everybody's curious to see what happened."

"How do explain that your cell phone was at the scene of the accident exactly when it occurred?"

Caught off guard, Fernando squirmed in his seat. It was obvious to everyone in the room he was beginning to panic. There was a long pause.

"Officer Ramirez?"

Fernando tried to compose himself. "I want to wait to talk with my public defender."

The door opened.

"Excuse me, Agent Aguilar," said Agent Garcia.

Rick knew this meant there was an update from the team sent out to arrest Officer Villalta. He stood up and turned toward Fernando. "We're not done talking, Officer Ramirez. We'll pick this up when your attorney gets here."

Agent Aguilar, Agent Garcia, and Major Rojas walked down the hall into the conference room.

"We have some encouraging news," said Agent Garcia. "I received two calls from Agent Allen and her team. They found Officer Javier Villalta at home and placed him under arrest. They're still on-site conducting a thorough search of his property. So far, they found an unregistered handgun and a bag of cocaine in his car. His home has a small adjacent storage shed that showed evidence it recently held someone captive. There was a bed with a pair of handcuffs attached, water, and some food. They collected human hair samples for DNA analysis. Unfortunately, Ms. Strauss was not found."

"Interesting. Did Officer Villalta say anything?" asked Rick.

"No. Clammed up. We'll try to pry something out when we have him in here, but I don't think he'll cooperate," said Agent Garcia. "While that was happening, two agents left and paid a visit to his neighbors, Mr. Miguel Hernández and his wife, Maria. Both were home. They appeared frightened at first. The agents explained they were not in trouble and only wanted to know why Officer Ramirez came to their house. It wasn't until they learned their neighbor Officer Villalta and Officer Ramirez had been arrested that the wife began to open up. She said Ms. Strauss had come by asking for help and the policemen took her away. Ms. Strauss had told Mrs. Hernández she had been kidnapped by their neighbor, Officer Villalta. Later that day, the officers stopped by her house and told them not to believe anything Ms. Strauss said. Officer Villalta had a gun, and they felt he would return to harm them if they said anything. She added Officer Ramirez may have stopped Officer Villalta from killing them. I don't have to tell you how incredibly brave it was for Mrs. Hernández to disclose what she experienced. Having an eyewitness who can tie both policemen to Ms. Strauss's abduction is just the break we needed."

"Yes, it is, and you're right," said Rick. "Mrs. Hernández deserves tremendous credit. When this is over, I'll stop by and thank them personally. Now I want to know what they did with Ms. Strauss! Damn, we're really close. We need to get one of those officers to start talking."

Rick turned his head and scratched his chin while trying to think of his next move.

"All right, let's get that hard evidence. Run DNA analysis on the hair samples they collected. A positive match will be another nail in the coffin of our two policemen. Thank you. Good work. Let's head back to the interrogation room and check on Officer Ramirez."

During the break, the public defender arrived and requested a private session with Fernando. In that meeting, Fernando told him what happened leading up to the accident and what questions were asked in the brief interrogation session.

The attorney opened the door and told the agents his client was ready to resume questioning. The agents, Major Rojas, Fernando, and his attorney sat across from each other around the table in the interrogation room.

"Let me repeat my last question, Officer Ramirez," said Major Rojas. "Kindly explain how your cell phone was at the scene of the accident, exactly when it happened?"

"I —Yes, I actually was there when the accident happened. We—I mean Officer Javier Villalta and me—were driving home and saw it. We both had a couple drinks. We stopped, but the vehicle exploded on fire. There was nothing we could do, and we didn't want to get in trouble for being drunk, so we left."

Major Rojas stood up, walked over to Fernando, crossed his arms, and looked down sternly, ignoring his attorney. "Officer Ramirez, our mission is to find Ms. Strauss alive and return her home safely. We think you know where she is. Now I don't want to play any more games with you. I'll be straight. We have a mountain of evidence pointing directly at you. We can place you at the scene of the accident. We have a burnt cigarette that proves the vehicle fire was deliberately set. A man died. That is enough to charge you with manslaughter and fleeing the scene of an accident. Blood samples collected match hers. We know for certain Ms. Strauss was in that vehicle at the time of the accident. We can charge you with kidnapping. Our agents found a bloody handkerchief and a blood-stained shirt when they searched your house. We'll know soon if it's her blood. There was someone handcuffed to a bed on Officer Villalta's property. We have their DNA. And finally, we have an eye-witness who will testify you and Officer Villalta were partners in the kidnapping."

Fernando's posture slumped as if his insides had deflated.

Rick watched this unfold. Major Rojas was brilliant. They had Officer Ramirez exactly where they wanted him: cornered with no options.

"Now I want the truth. What happened to Ms. Strauss?" said Major Rojas.

The public defender turned to Fernando and put his hand up to stop him from saying any more. But it didn't register quickly enough.

"Why should I tell you anything? There's nothing in it for me."

His attorney interrupted and asked for a quick recess to have a chat with his client. The meeting lasted about a half hour.

During that time, Rick and his agents had time to talk among themselves.

"From what I've heard, our best chance at getting one of these officers to talk would be with Officer Ramirez," said Rick. "He may have saved the lives of Maria Hernandez and her family. I get the impression he's not a bad guy. Perhaps he got caught up in a situation that got out of control."

Major Rojas slowly bobbed his head. "If that's right, and I think it is, he's in there right now disclosing everything to his attorney. I'm sure they're trying to figure out the best plea deal. If that attorney is good, he'll have thought of more than one option. We'll soon find out."

The door to the interrogation room opened, and the attorney called the agents back to resume.

"My client needs to hear your answer, why he should cooperate with you," said the attorney.

Major Rojas stood up and addressed Fernando. "You and your partner are both in serious trouble. If you help us, I will recommend some leniency to the judge. That could be in the number of years you serve or where you serve. I'm sure you're familiar with Pavón Prison?"

Fernando squirmed in his chair. From his reaction, Rick could tell Fernando was well aware of its reputation. No one has ever escaped, and it was dangerous, especially for an ex-cop.

"So, you are offering me a minimum sentence at a safe VIP prison, like Mariscal Zavala?" said Fernando.

"I'll see what I can do, but you are facing some serious charges," said Major Rojas.

"But I didn't burn that SUV; that was Javier! I didn't want to kidnap her; he did. It was all his idea. I just happened to be there. Believe me!" said Fernando.

"Actually, I do. So, tell us what happened to Ms. Strauss," said Major Rojas.

Fernando turned his head and looked at his attorney.

"If Officer Ramirez helps you, we have some demands. First, he must have guaranteed protection. For the rest of his life."

This request dropped like a bombshell. Major Rojas glanced over to Rick, showing a puzzled look.

"Protection! From whom?" asked Rick.

Up until this point, the agents had thought the investigation was leading down a predictable path. Two low-level bumbling policemen tried to pull off a kidnapping. Convince one or both to disclose Ms. Strauss's location—case closed.

"Before my client answers any more questions, we'll need a guarantee for his safety. He'll have a target on his back for the rest of his life."

"Over the years, we've provided witnesses and some defendants protection and, in extreme cases, a complete change of identity," said Major Rojas.

"Yeah, that's what I want. New identity and relocation. In writing! Then I will tell you who has her," said Fernando. "But you need to do it now. She's about to be taken out of the country by some extremely dangerous people."

Rick looked at Major Rojas and nodded his head with approval.

"I know the assistant attorney general. If I can reach him, I think I can get approval," said Major Rojas. He left the room and headed back to his office.

"If anyone needs a quick break, go ahead," said Rick.

Major Rojas called the assistant attorney general's office and used all of his influence and pleading to have them send someone immediately to hopefully agree to the terms of the plea deal. A woman's life was at stake and time was running out. Within minutes, the major received confirmation a representative was on his way. Major Rojas returned to the interrogation room.

"Okay, a representative from the assistant attorney general's office will be here shortly to review your request. You want a new identity and protection. Any other demands?" said Major Rojas.

"No prison," said the attorney. Major Rojas turned to Rick, who agreed. That type of arrangement usually accompanied a defendant on a witness protection program.

"We can accept that, but it's up to the representative. If he approves it, you must testify for the prosecution when this goes to trial, and Ms. Strauss must be returned, unharmed. We want to hear everything," said Major Rojas.

Fernando turned to his attorney, who responded with a quick head nod.

"Agent Garcia, could you get Officer Ramirez a bottle of water while he waits?" asked Rick.

Rick tapped Major Rojas's arm and gave a hitchhiker's thumb for them to leave the room. Rick led back to his office. On Rick's desk, he had everything laid out: photos, phone records, the defendant's own statements, and eye-witness accounts.

"I think we have enough time to put together a polished presentation for our rep."

"Good thinking, Rick. And the final page needs to explain the time urgency of securing Fernando's cooperation. We've got to make sure we have solid answers for every likely question. Although, if they send a clerk, it might just be rubber stamped."

Rick and Major Rojas were both too experienced to leave anything to chance.

CHAPTER 15

Palo Alto, California

Mike and Peter ambled to the break room, pausing occasionally. The bright white walls of the hallway were periodically interrupted with framed posters containing photos of historic figures. Under each were quotations.

"Here's a name I'm familiar with: Admiral Hyman G. Rickover. The father of the nuclear navy—love that guy," said Mike, admiring his picture. "Which quote did you pick? Ah yes, 'Success teaches us nothing; only failure teaches.' True, but you need to have a few failures under your belt and the right mindset to appreciate that one."

They continued a slow-paced walk down the hallway.

"It's exciting to learn of the work you're doing here," said Mike. "I can't wait to see a NAIMERA. If they're as good as I think, we need to send a few to the TAG agents as soon as we can."

"Yes, I'm anxious to make that happen too," said Peter. "Once Agent Aguilar gives the word, I can have them on my private jet heading down. But doing that before you at least have a basic understanding of a NAIMERA's potential would be counterproductive. You'll definitely need to advise your agents in Guatemala how best to use them. Bear with me. We only have a few minutes more before heading over to the lab."

"Right. By the way, I'm impressed with how much of the infrastructure you've pioneered and built yourself."

They paused in front of an early photo of Richard Feynman giving a lecture.

"I had my first college physics classes from Professor Feynman at Cal Tech," said Peter.

Under the photo was a quotation, "What I cannot create, I do not understand."

"Unfortunately, he passed away far too young. A few of us stopped by his office after learning of his death to pay our respects and saw that quote up on his blackboard. It was a defining moment for me, igniting something deep inside. I wrote it down and ever since applied it to all my projects. I feel I'm keeping his legacy alive." Peter paused and stared at the picture longer than Mike considered a passing glance.

"It's good to have role models," said Mike to wake Peter from his thoughts.

"Definitely." Peter glanced up at a wall clock. "Oh, it's getting late. Maggie, ask Kim not to go home yet. I'll be giving Mike a tour of the lab. We'll be there in fifteen minutes."

"She said she'll be there waiting," said Maggie.

They stepped into the break room and could smell freshly brewed coffee.

"Why thank you, Maggie. Organic Sulawesi. My favorite."

"You're welcome, Dr. Strauss."

Mike didn't know why Peter thanked her at first. "Did Maggie make this for us?"

"Yes, she's very perceptive," said Peter.

Mike shook his head. *This place is wild. Is there anything Maggie can't do?*

They sat down at a table with their coffee and talked.

"I'm sure you're familiar with DNA and understand its enormous complexity. The human DNA molecule uncoiled is about six feet long comprised of various combinations of nucleotides. As I mentioned earlier, I started this company with the goal to understand every nuance of DNA and cell development: what every gene does, how it does it, and why it works. Of course, it includes following an organism's complete life cycle through the gene expression processes, such as DNA replication and transcription. Our efforts cover not only DNA from all living organisms but synthetic as well, exploring combinations not found in nature. You'll see some examples in the lab.

"Applying our ever-increasing knowledge, we're creating both well-known and new never-dreamed-of gene combinations. It doesn't stop there. We can amalgamate living tissue with inanimate high-tech components to assemble the most optimal devices possible to address virtually any task. In cases where we need to fabricate something unconventional, we use 3D bioprinting. We started with brain-celled memory chips but continue to add more as requirements grew. For example, short-range lethal lasers are added to all of our NAIMERAs.

"We needed tools to help us turn this information into something interesting. Making use of our knowledge of DNA and cell development, our computer scientists engineered software that mimic the combinations and relationships. The result is a very reliable and powerful DNA simulator. We try billions of combinations before ever empirically experimenting with it in the lab. For example, starting with a base organism and evolving its DNA into anything we want."

"Let me get this straight," said Mike. "You can start with any organism's DNA as input into your simulator, then run it to produce a new, evolved DNA genome with targeted characteristics?"

"Yes, you got it."

"But how do you specify the targeted characteristics?" asked Mike.

"As I mentioned earlier," said Peter, "I created groups with a minimum of three world-class experts. They work together to pioneer one aspect of a project. Every group contributes to or is involved in some way with the DNA computer simulation effort. Have you ever watched a computer animator work?"

"No, never," replied Mike, while wondering where this was leading.

"Well, they build the look, features, and movements of their characters, starting with 'bones' for movement and structure. Then they move on to defining shape, behavior, and so on. We have something similar but much more sophisticated. We design our NAIMERAs in augmented reality using a software tool: MARS. You can specify the look, functionality, and other characteristics, with the output being all the DNA sequences and instructions to create it."

"MARS, as in the Roman god of war?" asked Mike.

"Actually, Magical Augmented Reality Software. But the god of war connection did cross my mind when thinking up a name for it. To MARS, military power was a way to assure peace. A concept our NAIMERAs embrace."

"A computer software program can do all that?" asked Mike.

"Absolutely. In fact, we have another software tool, a simulator, used to train them for military missions, which is just as impressive."

"Train them for military missions? So, it's a combat simulator?"

"Yes, but more powerful than anything you can imagine. We can create a realistic holographic battle ground, wherever it might be, cities, villages, mountain caves, compounds and so on. Next, we populate it with adversaries and their weapons—all their decisions guided by complex AI algorithms. Then in augmented reality, which the NAIMERAs fully participate in, they run through tens of thousands of combat scenarios. When finished, our NAIMERAs can confidently tackle any hostile situation," said Peter.

"This I've got to see," said Mike.

"It's how our NAIMERAs are prepared to deploy into combat so readily. I'll have Kim show you how that works in the lab. But I'd like to get back to their design. A NAIMERA might have skin color characteristics of a baby flamboyant cuttlefish, the hearing of an owl, the sense of smell of a bloodhound, the vision of an eagle, or the sonar of a bat. They can flatten like a pancake, form wings to fly, basically take any shape they need. For self-defence purposes, we've added some powerful capabilities. For example, the high-voltage jolts of an electric eel, which can also power a lethal laser, or the venom of a golden poison frog. Each capable of killing, if necessary."

Peter looked at his watch. "It's getting late. Better head over to the lab."

CHAPTER 16

San Benito, Guatemala

Suspense was growing. TAG agents learned that unless they could stop it from happening, Grace would soon be turned over to a dangerous cartel and taken out of the country. But they needed a legal agreement signed off before they could learn where she was. Agents anxiously awaited the arrival of the representative from the assistant attorney general's office with the plea deal paperwork. They paced impatiently in the lobby. Heads turned almost continuously, checking the clock, then out to the front window. Over and over. Fernando remained tight-lipped, advised not to discuss anything about Grace's whereabouts until after the paperwork was legally signed off. In the meantime, Agent Allen and her team returned with Officer Villalta, placing him in a holding cell. Rick and Major Rojas wrapped up their preparation just in time.

At last, a dusty black sedan drove up and parked in front. The large man struggled to push his portly frame sideways to exit his seat, then slowly strolled up to the TAG building with a pouch tucked under his left arm. The agents stood near the door as if called to attention. Major

Rojas and Rick walked to the entrance to greet the representative.

"Assistant Attorney General Zapatero, how are you?" said Major Rojas. "Thank you for showing up on such short notice."

Mr. Zapatero casually nodded with a sullen face.

They expected a low-level attorney or clerk from the assistant attorney general's office, but instead, they got its leader.

"Have you met the director of our TAG office, Special Agent Rick Aguilar? Agent Aguilar, please meet the Honorable Mr. Zapatero," said Major Rojas.

Mr. Zapatero glanced momentarily over to Rick. "Director," said Mr. Zapatero, acknowledging his presence.

"Your Honor, pleasure to meet you. Thank you for coming," said Rick.

Rick led Mr. Zapatero toward the interrogation room. He turned around and told the team to wait in the lobby. Rick hoped this would be quick, just a couple of signatures. Fernando, his attorney, Agents Garcia and Allen, Major Rojas, Rick, and Mr. Zapatero sat at the table.

Rick stood up and gave a brief overview of the case to Mr. Zapatero. He asked the paperwork granting immunity and a new identity to Fernando be signed so they could learn of Ms. Strauss's whereabouts.

Mr. Zapatero listened, and when Rick stopped, he partially raised his right hand. "I want to hear everything about this case from the beginning. Show me the evidence you have against this officer and explain why we should offer him immunity with a new identity," said Mr. Zapatero.

Everyone in the room seemed to release a collective sigh. Rick and Major Rojas exchanged eye contact, knowing they were ready. Rick slid the twelve-page document he and Major Rojas had prepared over to Mr. Zapatero. He picked it up, removed a pair of reading glasses from his jacket, and slipped them on. His head tilted down, and he began to read, pausing periodically to fire a stare toward Fernando.

Mr. Zapatero removed his glasses. He first glanced over at Rick and Major Rojas, then fixed his eyes on Fernando. "I agree the plea deal is necessary to help find Ms. Strauss," said the Mr. Zapatero, "except I read nothing that compels me to grant a new identity. Officer Ramirez, who are you afraid of, your partner Officer Villalta?"

"No. I mean yes, Your Honor, him a little. But the El Zapote cartel and the PLVI, they will all be hunting to kill me as long as I live."

The agents in the room looked at one another in stunned disbelief. Rick suspected this case might have a few bumps along the way, but this was huge. Mr. Zapatero's eyes widened as he stared at Fernando, slowly shaking his head. "I agree. You will need a new identity and lots of prayers. Officer Ramirez, and this is the last time you'll be addressed with that title, you are a disgrace to your uniform. The people of Guatemala trusted you, and you let us down. I will sign this plea deal, but you understand it comes with revocable conditions. You must disclose everything truthfully. If we discover you lied or provided incomplete information, the deal is null and void. You will then be given a trial, and after you're convicted, of which I have no doubt, you'll be sent away to prison for the maximum sentence. Do you understand?"

"Yes, Your Honor," said an obviously contrite Fernando.

"Good." Mr. Zapatero took out the plea deal and signed it. He slid the documents over to Fernando's lawyer.

The attorney scanned over the papers and nodded to Fernando to sign them.

Mr. Zapatero gathered the paperwork and put it back into his pouch. He stood up slowly and looked at Rick. "Agent Aguilar, after you take his statement, send him to the witness protection program facility in Guatemala City. Mr. Ramirez, I understand you have no wife or children, which will make this easier. If you have family in the country, call them now and let them know they will not be hearing from you again, for their safety and yours. Agent Aguilar, have a unit go to Mr. Ramirez's house. Empty it out. Collect all his possessions and put them in storage. His house and car will be confiscated by the state and sold. Those funds, along with his belongings are to be returned to him after he gets his new identity and settled somewhere safe."

Rick nodded his head in agreement.

"Mr. Ramirez," said Mr. Zapatero, "as part of this arrangement, you're required to testify in court as a prosecution witness at some point in the future. When that time comes, you will do so over video from a safe, secluded location so you will never have to return here again." Mr. Zapatero turned and left.

Every eye in the room was now fixed on Fernando. Rick pressed the video recorder button to start. "Mr. Ramirez, now tell us what happened to Ms. Strauss. Where is she and who has her?"

CHAPTER 17

San Benito, Guatemala

Fernando took a sip of water, followed by a deep breath. "After we found out TAG was involved in her case, we panicked. It was more than we could handle, so Javier—I mean Officer Javier Villalta—arranged to sell her to a childhood friend of ours, Cesar Ruiz. He's in the El Zapote cartel. We met with him. He told us the American was too high-profile for his cartel to take. They didn't want to have TAG after them, either. But Cesar offered to pass her on to PLVI in Nicaragua. We would get a cut. Nicaragua has no extradition treaty with Guatemala or the US, and the TAG can't operate there were his reasons. Cesar has the American woman in a hiding place until PLVI can send a plane to get her."

"Cesar Ruiz, huh," said Rick, slowly recalling a familiar name while turning his head to Major Rojas.

"Do we know him?" asked Agent Garcia.

Rick slightly lifted his right forearm and raised his index finger in the direction of the agent and mouthed the words *I'll explain later.*

"So, the plane hasn't picked her up yet?" asked Rick.

"I think that's right. We gave her to him yesterday. He said a plane would be waiting at a secret airstrip north of San Andrés in two days."

"We know of that airstrip," said Rick. "It's one of a few dozen around the country. So that's tomorrow. We still have time. Is that everything?"

"Yes," said Fernando. "I want to add I'm sorry. I wish I'd stopped Javier at the beginning."

Rick showed a hint of a frown while accepting his apology. "Thank you for your cooperation, Mr. Ramirez. Hopefully, we'll find Ms. Strauss before she's removed from the country."

Rick stood up and opened the door. He called in two agents who were waiting outside. "Would you both take Mr. Ramirez to a holding cell and arrange for his transportation to Guatemala City. We need to get him out of here as soon as possible."

Rick motioned to the rest of the agents. "Everyone else, follow me to the conference room. Let's do some brainstorming."

The room filled with over a dozen agents.

"So, who is Cesar Ruiz?" asked Agent Garcia.

Major Rojas spoke up. "A lieutenant for one of the cartels, El Zapote, we believe. Cesar arranges transportation of everything from drugs to human trafficking through northern Guatemala. In addition to a handful of hitmen, he oversees several dozen falcons, who serve as his eyes and ears."

"We suspect he also does some freelance smuggling for other cartels on the side," said Rick, "which is why we could never pinpoint his exact affiliation. What we do know is he's a slippery character."

Major Rojas interrupted. "We've tried to bring him down for years. We traced several dozen murders and disappearances back to him. But either our evidence wasn't strong enough, or when it was, he managed to bribe or intimidate the judge. This might finally be our chance to nail him."

"Rick," said Agent Allen. "Why aren't we immediately going after Cesar? We know where he lives, right?"

Major Rojas and Rick both looked at each other.

"If we arrested Cesar now and searched his house, we wouldn't find Ms. Strauss, and he definitely would not tell us where she is," said Rick.

"That's true. His hitmen would likely kill her. If we want to get her back alive, our only option is to try to intercept her during the rendezvous," said Major Rojas.

"Regardless, if we do or don't find Ms. Strauss by tomorrow, we're going after Cesar," said Rick. "Fernando will testify to his involvement, so this time we'll have a great chance at a conviction. Okay, if there are no further questions, everyone, break up into three groups."

The agents looked at each other and slowly moved into evenly divided groups.

"What I'd like is Team PLVI over here," he said as he pointed to one group. "You are the pilot and his contacts within PLVI. And Team Cesar, you'll represent Cesar, his falcons, and hitmen. I'll lead the last one, Team TAG. Major Rojas, lead Team Cesar. Agent Garcia, lead Team PLVI. Given what we now know from Fernando's testimony, take a few minutes to discuss from your team's perspective what strategy you'll likely follow using all the resources you have at your disposal. You can assume by now they know we arrested the two policemen. Our goal is to devise a plan to arrest Cesar and rescue Ms. Strauss."

The discussions started quietly and slowly but soon grew louder, with multiple agents speaking at once. After twenty minutes, the chatter died down.

Rick interrupted. "All right, everyone, take a seat but stay in your groups." He fired up his laptop and brought up a satellite map of Guatemala and the surrounding area, projected on a large screen.

"If Fernando is right, a plane will land at this airstrip off Highway

PET-14 sometime tomorrow," said Rick, pointing at the map. "Now, teams, I'll begin by explaining our strategy. I'd like to know what you think they'll do. This exercise should help us put together a plan with the greatest chance of success.

"From Team TAG's perspective, here's our game plan," said Rick. "Twelve agents head to the airstrip; Major Rojas and I will stay here and direct activity. We'll load up two armored vehicles. Each AV holds six agents. They'll drive up PET-14 and turn off on this forest access road that leads all the way to the airstrip. Riding along in the helicopter will be one agent with a high-powered assault rifle. See this clearing next to the airstrip just past the access road? I want one AV to park here. It's also large enough for the helicopter to land. The other AV will drive to the airstrip and park under trees out of view. Once in place, they'll both wait. I'll request radar reports of any small plane movement in or near the departments of Petén, Izabal, Escuintla, Quiché, and Alta Verapaz. About the time their plane lands, Cesar should show up with Ms. Strauss. Once he drives in, the first AV will pull out and follow right behind. The other AV races over in front of the plane, blocking it from leaving. As that's happening, the helicopter will lift off, offering extra fire power from above. We'll have Cesar cornered with no option but to surrender. Okay, that's our plan. Tell me why it will fail from your perspective."

The groups huddled back together, first talking among themselves and then between Team PLVI and Team Cesar.

About fifteen minutes later, Major Rojas from Team Cesar spoke up. "Assuming Cesar learned of the policemen's arrest, he'll be cautious. His falcons will watch for and report any unusual police vehicle movement. You might replace your AVs with two public works trucks. We've borrowed them in the past, and they don't mind getting a paid day off from road repair when we do."

"Anything else?" asked Rick.

"Yes. If the goal is to rescue Ms. Strauss unharmed, they may kill her if you corner them in their vehicle. So, on the access road, lay out some tire spikes just short of the entrance to the airstrip. With Cesar's vehicle disabled, they'll be forced to walk fifty feet or so to the airstrip. Placing three or four snipers in the jungle on the north side of the entrance will allow you to easily eliminate them, if necessary. One last suggestion. Position a few snipers around the airstrip to prevent their plane from taking off. That way, there is no way they can remove Ms. Strauss from the country, regardless of what happens on the ground."

One other member of Team Cesar spoke up. "Until the arrest of the policemen, Cesar had no reason to move her from where she's being held. Let's assume Ms. Strauss is still in the area. However, Cesar may fear one or both policemen broke down and confessed. A cautious Cesar will assume we know about the airstrip, so he might use another nearby."

"Excellent suggestions, Team Cesar!" said Rick. "Team PLVI, anything to add?"

Agent Garcia spoke up. "PLVI will use a pilot skilled at getting in and out unseen. He'll certainly try nap-of-the-earth, but it won't be easy since the north is void of mountains. Of course, they may not need to do anything evasive. Radar systems in Guatemala, as we all know, are unreliable. If they're not offline, the military that operates them has a history of complicity with drug cartel plane movements. Sorry to say that, Major Rojas."

The major pressed his lips together and nodded his head in disheartened agreement.

"There's a good chance you may not know when or where the plane lands," said Agent Garcia. "Oh, and another issue. If the pilot detects any suspicious activity on the ground or in the air, he'll alert Cesar, and I'm sure they'll call it off or do something else. So, try not to be detected."

"Interesting, thank you; those are all good suggestions," said Rick. "We know of three airstrips, all within ten minutes by helicopter from the police station helipad, so we'll keep it on standby where it is. The other airstrips in the country are too far or remote to easily drive to from here. Plus, they're outside Cesar's territory, all built by other cartels who won't allow access without a huge price. Of the three possible airstrips, only two are currently capable of landing a plane. One was recently bulldozed into large mounds and ruts by the military's antidrug force a couple of weeks ago. That leaves him with only two. Major, contact the Guatemalan Air Force and ask if they would track planes in and out of the area for us."

Rick pointed them out on the map. "One's off PET-3; the other is the original off of PET-14. We'll split up into two groups—P3 and P14," said Rick. "Agent Allen, you'll lead P14. Agent Garcia, take P3. The plan is the same for both groups. Each will get one truck. As you head down your access road, find a secluded spot to park short of the airstrip. Three agents are to head to the airstrip with rifles and wait for the plane. The other three will deploy tire spike strips and wait off to the side of the access road with their rifles. Once we know which airstrip they're using, the helicopter will leave to intercept the plane on the ground. Snipers around the airstrip and the one on board the copter will stop the plane if it attempts to leave. We'll just have to hope Ms. Strauss survives."

Rick turned to Team Cesar. "We'll take your suggestion and not use police vehicles to avoid suspicion. I want six agents in each. Agents Allen and Garcia, I'll give you each a satellite internet system along with a hat fitted with two-way audio and an HD camera on the crown. I'd like you to wear that so we can tell what's going on. Major Rojas and I will stay here to monitor the situation and relay commands back to the field as events unfold. Agent Garcia, come with me. Let's go get a couple public works vehicles. This stakeout could take a while, so everyone pack food and water to bring along tomorrow morning at 0600. Sharp. I'll have the combat gear locker open when you arrive so you can begin loading up."

CHAPTER 18

San Benito, Guatemala

M ajor Rojas called the commander of the Air Defence Wing of the Guatemalan Air Force to request their help.

"Commander, this is Major Rojas. I'm an attorney in the army assigned as the deputy director of the Transnational Anti-Gang Unit here in San Benito."

"I've heard of you, Major, and of the fine work TAG is doing. What can I do for you?"

"We need your help. We've learned a kidnapping victim will be picked up sometime tomorrow from one of two jungle airstrips in the Maya Biosphere Reserve. We'd like you to track any suspicious planes for us. Probably originating from Nicaragua. Can you do that for us?"

"As of now, all three radar stations comprising our air defence monitoring system are operational. I want to assure you our staff has been thoroughly vetted."

"That's good to know," said Major Rojas.

"Of course, Major, I need to caution, there are known deficiencies in the system. As I'm sure you have read, our stations are prone to go offline periodically, and some geographic areas aren't adequately covered. We suspect some drug traffickers know where they are. But we will do our best."

"I understand, Commander, but thank you for the warning."

"Major Rojas, would you like us to intercept the plane when it enters Guatemalan airspace?"

"We've been debating that possibility. Any intervention before the plane lands will likely result in the death of the hostage. So that definitely should not happen. But if the plane were able to take off with the hostage on board, a midair interception might be necessary. Let's not rule it out."

"All right. Is that all, Major?"

"One more thing, Commander, if you don't mind. I'd like to request a spotter plane be launched to follow the kidnappers' plane when it appears on radar. Their plane will definitely be a type that's small and slow-moving to land on dirt runways."

"Not a problem, Major. All communication will go through the duty officer."

Major Rojas was given a direct line to the duty officer, who would provide real-time flight movement updates.

After the call, Major Rojas walked down the hall to Rick's office, tapped on his door, and walked in. He shared the conversation he'd had with the commander.

"Excellent. That is a relief," said Rick. "If they send a plane, we'll have a pretty good idea when and where it's heading."

"We discussed intervention—definitely not coming in—but if by chance they manage to elude our net, we'd still have the option to intercept it before it can leave the country."

"Good work. Thank you, Major. Please close the door on the way out."

Rick sat quietly at his desk, still feeling apprehensive. He removed his glasses and pressed the heels of his hands over his eyes while slowly shaking his head. *A young lady's life depends on us getting this right. Our plan seems solid, but I can't shake the feeling I'm missing something.*

*

At home, just outside San Benito, Cesar's phone rang. It was one of his falcons, Alvarez.

"Cesar, I heard two San Benito cops got fired this morning, Javier Villalta and Fernando Ramirez. The rumor is they've been arrested, but they're not at the station and nobody's talking."

"Idiots! TAG must have them. If you learn any more, call me." Cesar hung up and immediately called his contact within the PLVI, Sergio Cruz. It was a call Cesar did not want to make.

"Yes?" said Sergio.

"We have a little problem," said Cesar.

"Go on."

Cesar cleared his throat. "The two jackasses who gave us the girl got arrested by TAG."

"What do they know?"

Cesar cleared his throat again. "Our arrangement; the pickup day and place ... and that she's being handed over to PLVI who will kill her."

"My friend, if you want to keep doing business with me, you must learn to keep your *damn mouth shut!*"

"You're right, you're right. I'm sorry."

"I need a little time to give this some thought. I'll call you tonight with new instructions. TAG has become a pain in my ass. I want to give them something they'll remember for years."

CHAPTER 19

Palo Alto, California

Mike and Peter talked as they made the short walk from the SCIF to the NAIMERA Lab.

"You remember Kim from your interview panel? She'll introduce you to the NAIMERAs, explain how they were created, and what they're capable of doing."

"Oh, yes, she left an indelible impression. It was like being cross-examined on a witness stand. I got the impression she only asked the first question just to set up the follow-up questions."

Both men laughed.

Kim was the most demanding member of the interviewing panel. She never asked a simple question. Each one required careful thought, before answering.

"Although, I have to say, her intellect is impressive," said Mike.

"No argument here. I brought her on as an intern when she was a grad student. Hired her as soon as she graduated," said Peter. "She has a reputation of expressing her opinions without much of a filter, but to her credit, they're always honest and sincere. And amazingly perceptive. I admire that. To people who don't know her, they can be misinterpreted as mildly rude."

"I've known a few like that. It has the effect of chasing off new friendships," said Mike.

"Outside of work, I get the impression she doesn't have much of a social life," said Peter. "Which might explain it. But, for anyone who takes the time to look past that, they'll find her bright, curious, adventurous, and witty with a great sense of humor and, of course, a captivating smile. She makes working here more enjoyable."

"Thanks, I'll keep that in mind."

"Good, I hope you'll never be too put off. Periodically, you both will be working together when you come on board."

As they got closer, Mike could read the sign out front: "NAIMERA Lab." Suddenly, the door opened, and several young men and women came out, walking briskly.

Mike and Peter stepped aside, allowing the group to pass.

"Hi, Dr. Strauss," said one cheerful male voice.

"Good evening, gang. Where you all rushing off to?" asked Peter.

"Heading over to the Goose to shoot some pool. Care to join us?"

"Not tonight, thanks," said Peter with a smile.

Peter and Mike resumed walking up to the entrance.

Mike looked back over his shoulder and watched them vanish behind a building. "Friendly bunch. What do they do?"

"Computer scientists. They work for Kim."

They both stepped up on a raised platform in front of dark tinted glass double doors. Their faces scanned and access was granted. The tinted glass door slid open. Like the SCIF, this building was new, with large white tiled floors, white walls, and blue-tinted windows. To their right was a row of computer workstations.

A young woman, of petite size with dark hair sat working in front of one. She turned her head. "Dr. Strauss."

"When will you start calling me Peter?"

Kim stood up to greet them.

"Sorry to keep you, Kim. Hope you didn't miss out on a little R&R with your team?" said Peter.

"Thanks, but that's not for me," said Kim.

"You two, of course, have met. I brought Agent Murphy by to see the NAIMERAs," said Peter. "Kim Harrod's full title is chief scientist and cocreator of the NAIMERAs."

"Nice to see you again, Ms. Harrod."

"Interview's over, Mike. Kim will do. You're still with the FBI, right? Who's out looking for Grace?"

"We're working on it," said Mike, slightly taken aback but not offended, remembering what Peter told him about her.

"Just finished the daily DNA database updates. So, what did you have in mind for our soon-to-be security chief?"

"Mike needs to assess whether NAIMERAs can be of use hunting for Grace. I've been thinking about what he needs to know," said Peter. "We could go straight to the NAIMERAs, but since we have a little time and Mike will be joining us soon, he really needs to understand the science behind the scenes. At least an overview. How about a brief explanation of MARS: design, development, and assembly? A tour of the lab, then introduce him to the gang. We'll finish with a walk-through of the attack drone facility."

"You need to know if NAIMERAs can be useful hunting for Grace? I can save you the time, Mike. The answer is *yes!*"

Kim turned and took a sip of chai tea latte, moved over in front of a large screen terminal, and set her drink to the side. Sliding the mouse until it hovered over an icon, she toggled a button and brought up the software program called MARS. The program came up on the large monitor in 2D.

After a momentary pause, she swung her chair around and looked up at Mike. "Let's get started. Have a seat," she said, pulling one over next to the workstation. "I'm sure Peter gave you the intro, so you're probably pretty confused by now. But for you to understand what I'm about to show you, we need to cover some fundamentals.

"What is a NAIMERA? It's a living creature not found in nature, since we design and grow it here in the lab. To make it the smartest living thing on the planet, we integrate preprogrammed, memory-mapped living brain cells into their existing brains. In order to operate in a combat environment alongside attack drones, we develop and train them to perform many functions, like a skilled soldier and military working dog."

Mike listened but couldn't imagine how any of the science worked. It was intriguing but frustrating at the same time. He opened a fresh water bottle and took a sip, anticipating another marathon lecture session. Kim reached over and handed Mike and Peter augmented reality goggles. Kim put hers down on the table. She reached over and unplugged a pair of space-age-looking red gloves hanging from a charging rack. The fingers had black plastic cone-shaped tips on the ends, wires embossed along the surface leading down to the base, and two rows of white buttons dotting the back hand portions.

"This program displays objects in either 2D or 3D," said Kim. "These gloves are stylus tools I use to explore and sometimes alter specific portions of our NAIMERA in 3D augmented reality space."

As he listened, he slipped his goggles on to see how they fit. Then he tried to place his water bottle on the table but knocked Kim's latte over.

"Sorry, sorry."

Kim had it wiped up almost instantly. "It's all right, no harm done, everything's fine," she said. "Fortunately, I only had a little left."

"I'll buy you another," insisted Mike.

Kim shook her head, showing a soft smile. "Thanks, but it really is okay. Goggles come off for now. So, how do we begin to create a NAIMERA? We evolve it. We're basically a DNA shop. Our teams uncover, identify, sequence, and store DNA information to classify traits or gene-determined characteristics. As you may know, genes are segments of DNA. Chromosomes are structures that contain those genes found in cell nuclei. Chromosomes can contain thousands of genes. For one or more types of biological cells, genes hold the code for a specific protein functioning within those cells. DNA is often called the blueprint of life. It holds all the instructions an organism needs to determine its appearance as it develops, its physiology, and even influences how it behaves. Evolution occurs when there are changes in a DNA molecule. We call those mutations."

"Kim," said Mike. "Excuse me, but I'm already familiar with this topic. At the Naval Academy, I took a couple biology classes. We covered genetic engineering, human genomes, and DNA fingerprinting."

"Oh, great, thanks for telling me. Well then, let's jump ahead. So, what do we do with the DNA information we collect?" Kim nonchalantly slid one hand after the other into the stylus gloves and placed her AR goggles over her head. "We have several high-value applications in mind, but for now, we're using it to create NAIMERAs. In a nutshell, we design NAIMERAs on a computer with our software application, MARS. A newborn rat's sequenced genome becomes the base input into our program. It's computationally evolved to create the NAIMERA's DNA. Let me explain.

"Here are the steps. I'll begin by defining the NAIMERA's desired body characteristics, like skin type, physical size, olfactory sensitivity, number of eyes, vision parameters, exterior colors, physical structure such as bones or hydrostatic scaffolding, behavior, and so on. Next, I specify the functions we want our NAIMERA to perform. For example, generate electric shocks, fire a laser, detect scents, fly, slither, walk, interact with analog or digital messaging, and so on. These steps are a bit tedious but critical if you want a NAIMERA to match your specs. Menus provide numerous characteristics and functional options to choose from to help make the selection process manageable. At any step, I can request a unique feature not found in any known DNA. I don't worry about how the body organs are interconnected or arranged. The program decides that for me based on input criteria. Finally, the last step: I'll supply the sequenced genome of a base life-form, a rat. Now put on your AR goggles."

Wearing her stylus gloves, Kim pointed a finger at the screen, selected "3D Mode," then selected a predesigned NAIMERA object set from the gallery of saved 3D models, one entitled "Marty." It contained a "Before" and "After" avatar. She dragged both out and positioned them together. Like a wand, wherever she pointed, the objects repositioned. They appeared to float in the air right in front of them but in augmented space. The "Before" avatar was a rat. The "After" looked similar to a rounded cone. Through Mike's AR goggles, the objects appeared a foot in front his face. He reached out, trying to touch them. His hand moved right through the image.

Kim continued to talk. "DNA mutations can go on indefinitely. Which means under the right circumstances or environmental stresses, any organism will evolve, if carried on long enough, into something else."

Mike crossed his arms while slightly pushing out his lower lip and dipping his head in agreement. "Sure. All life originated on this planet as stromatolites, right? What, four billion years ago?"

"Three point seven to be more precise. But that's correct. Mutagenesis is a driving force of evolution. It's a process that happens naturally when genetic information of an organism is changed, resulting in mutations. Up until now, that could only occur spontaneously or when exposed to mutagens. We added one more method, 'deliberately targeted mutations' or 'hyper-evolution,' as we like to call it. It's all designed on our computers, starting with an organism's current genome. For reference, the human genome has over three billion DNA base pairs. A copy is present in all cells that contain a nucleus. Not trivial.

"Beginning with a NAIMERA's desired characteristics and a rat's genome, as I mentioned, the computer program performs a simulated evolution as defined by the targeted requirements. As output, we get the DNA blueprints for a NAIMERA. We follow those final instructions for creating a new, completely evolved, synthetic DNA sequence."

Mike was following. It started to make sense.

"We start with a recently impregnated rat. The new synthetic DNA replaces the original DNA in a rat's one-day-old embryo using genome editing techniques. By doing so, the embryo develops and grows organs with minimum risk of rejection. Another reason to perform this as early as possible in the fertilized embryonic stage is that we avoid unintended mutations, which might cause cancer after the original DNA is altered.

"The NAIMERA avatar floating in front of you is named Marty. I built him a few months ago. You'll get a chance to meet the living version after we're done here."

"Is that what he looks like, a cone?" asked Mike.

"At rest, yes, he can, but virtually any form is possible," said Kim. She slid her finger through the air. After making a few selections, suddenly Marty transformed into a bat. "I can transform and visualize the avatar Marty into any shape his body will permit," said Kim.

Her finger slid through the air. Within the AR screen, she selected an editing feature from one of the side panels. Cupping her hands and moving them together, the model compressed in size. She moved them apart, causing the avatar to expand. She selected another editing feature and used it to cut away the exterior, revealing Marty's internal organs.

"With these tools, I can explore minute aspects of his body. It helps me confirm the NAIMERA's evolution succeeded in creating what I specified."

"I think I understand a little of what's happening. Beginning with a rat's genome, you computationally evolve its DNA sequence into a NAIMERA," said Mike.

"That's right."

"But explain how it is you grow a Marty?"

"We're getting there. As I said, once we define all the NAIMERA characteristics, we move on to the next phase." She pointed to a door labeled "Lab Rats." "The day before we submit our creation request in MARS, we combine two rats for mating. Timing is critical. Exactly one day after fertilization the embryo is in the single-cell stage. That's our window to replace its DNA. We extract and sequence the DNA from the embryo. Then we supply the sequenced DNA as input data to MARS as a starting point for the computational evolution of the rat to begin."

"Why did you choose rats instead of worms, let's say?" asked Mike.

"Several reasons. The evolution to our eventual target requires less computation. They're easier to breed and work with. A rat has many of the basics we want, especially the brain, which includes the cerebral cortex, amygdala, hippocampus, and so on. Also, the female rats' bodies are just large enough to accommodate and give birth to an infant NAIMERA. Although, we're currently working on creating an artificial womb in the lab to one day grow a NAIMERA from embryo all the way through birth.

"Now we're ready to initiate the evolution process. MARS's first task is to evaluate the input. For each desired characteristic, one after another, it explores every possible known gene sequence. If nothing matches that can satisfy it, the program conducts a controlled 'mutation' on the closest gene to achieve the target characteristics. We're performing 'hyper-evolution' on the rat's DNA. It may require hundreds or possibly millions of mutations, one generation at a time. The complete evolution is performed on our 500-petaflop supercomputer. It simulates a full life cycle one generation at a time. Between each generation, it takes a snapshot and stores it. Sometimes the results of a particular series of mutations don't yield the desired or anticipated outcome. MARS iteratively evaluates what it did, then alters the input, and starts over from a previous snapshot. If results continue off-target, we've likely uncovered a deficiency in MARS; an area for improvement. When the program finally derives results that satisfy the original design objectives, it's done with the evolution process.

"As the program is chugging away, you'll observe the evolutionary progression in the simulator. Displayed first as the 'Before' avatar of the original organism, a rat, you'll witness it morphing gradually into the targeted organism, eventually evolving into the 'After' avatar, a NAIMERA. It's my favorite feature. Finally, as output, not only will you see how your NAIMERA will appear, but MARS assembles a detailed recipe. We take that and follow the instructions carefully, step-by-step, to create the NAIMERA here in the lab. As I mentioned earlier, the recipe includes the complete final synthetic DNA, detailed instructions for embryonic electroporation of DNA into the pregnant rat, care and nurturing guidelines after birth through maturity, and so on.

"Once born, we nurture the NAIMERA as it develops, all in the lab, until it matures. As it develops, we surgically add a variety of miniature circuitry, like the brain-celled memory chips. Every chip socket has specially coated connections offering locations where synapses or nerves grow and attach naturally."

They stood up and removed their AR goggles. Kim slid off the stylus gloves and set them on the table. "That pretty much covers the general introduction to the NAIMERAs design. Let me show you the next step."

Mike stood up slowly. What he heard was bewildering. The process seemed plausible, but he still couldn't comprehend the science involved. There was more to come.

CHAPTER 20

Palo Alto, California

Peter reached and patted Mike's shoulder as both followed Kim into the NAIMERA Lab. "You're about to discover why we couldn't disclose everything we do here during your interview."

Two large automatic sliding glass doors opened. They entered and continued down the hall until they encountered a transition room. Once inside, Kim handed them white sterile full-body suits complete with gloves, head covers, and face masks.

"Slip these on." Kim picked up a small device and inserted it into her right ear. She reached down and grabbed two more and offered one each to Peter and Mike. "Here, you'll need one of these."

"What is it?" asked Mike.

"Secure multiparty electronic transmission to better communicate with the NAIMERAs. Especially when they're in the air."

After everyone was adequately suited up, they stepped forward. Another glass door slid open. Inside were several rows of tables lined up with space to walk between. On each table, separated a foot or so apart, were dozens of beakers of various sizes. In addition, there were flat three-foot-by-two-foot rectangular containers several inches high. Liquid circulated in every container, propelled by small pumps through clear plastic tubes. Primarily a pale red, but colors ranged from clear to dark blue.

"This liquid. What is it, plasma?" asked Mike.

"It varies, mostly oxygen and nutrient-rich fluid media," said Kim.

Organs and organisms filled the room. Several beakers held brains of various sizes and shapes. There were lungs breathing, hearts pumping, skins of many types. One was transparent like jellyfish. Another flat and thin but pulsating, appearing silky smooth with irregular texture and stretching flat, similar to octopus skin. Several trays held flat, dark, shiny membranes laced with thin veins, like a bat wing.

"Why are there so many organ experiments?" asked Mike.

"We're in a hypothesis testing phase," said Kim. "Most of these organs began as embryonic stem cells. We recently discovered the trigger to direct a stem cell to differentiate into a specific tissue or cell type. Some developed as instructed by turning certain genes on or off; others activated by introducing chemicals. So far, the research shows great promise. One of our goals is to publish our organ-generation techniques, making them available to help augment existing organ donations."

"Outstanding!" Moving at a slow pace, Mike walked from one container to another, examining their contents. Some had devices attached. He stopped in front of three long snakelike organs connected together, leading to a laser target apparatus.

"What's all this?"

"A proof of concept," said Kim. "We often need some extraordinary capabilities, which we try to perform through biology. For example, a laser. To power it, we combined three electric eel organs, the main, Sach's, and Hunter's. They're found naturally in Amazonian freshwater electric eels. Our team performed a transcriptome analysis on a half-dozen or so electric fish. We found all electric organs' DNA used the same protein components. In this experiment, we evolved and grew the equivalent of forty-eight electric eels. Enough to power a laser and provide a pretty serious wallop. We typically like to include these organs in our NAIMERAs to power delicate electronic devices. The organs can discharge both low and high voltage. In either case, we include tiny organic inverters and voltage regulators to manage the appropriate power requirements.

"The pioneering breakthrough to enable this was an electrically pumped organic laser diode with a two-nanometer spectral width. In general, not too different from organic LEDs or OLED displays you'll find in smartphones or larger displays. It's the eye-shaped organ you see attached. The high electrical power, laser diode, lenses, and even the focusing apparatus are all organic. As I said, included in every NAIMERA."

"That's fascinating! I know we're tight on time, but I'd love to see a NAIMERA demonstrate a laser strike. The bad guys who kidnapped Grace may need a little persuasion."

"Sure, I think that can be arranged," said Peter.

"This looks interesting," said Mike, looking down at a flat container holding an unusual patch of weaved fabric-looking skin.

"Another unique creation," said Kim. "It's a natural silk-like thread fiber skin not found anywhere in nature. Similar to collagen fibrils. As the skin layer grows, fibers weave into tight, dense patterns about one-quarter of an inch thick. The result is a pliable exterior stronger than Kevlar. It's the ultimate natural body armor. It's the exterior of one of our NAIMERAs named Baron. You'll have a chance to meet him too."

"That's damn freaking amazing! Pardon me. I need to see this Baron. A Kevlar-coated laser flying around sounds awesome."

It was as if he'd wandered into a scientific toy store. Mike walked slowly from one beaker or tray to the next, pausing to try to grasp what was in front of him. Peter and Kim followed, answering his questions. He moved past, then stepped back to observe a curious-looking undulating blob. First a pale white, it slowly transitioned into pulsating waves of various colors. It looked like a large rainbow-colored wavy pita bread. The surface suddenly began to change from smooth to jagged. Two eyes, which blended into the skin without detection, suddenly popped wide open, looking straight up at him.

"What the *hell*!" shouted Mike, jumping back.

The eyes began pinning. The pupils quickly and rhythmically dilated in and out, focusing on Mike. The skin color transitioned to flashing bright red, while the body began to reshape fluidly like wax in a hot lava lamp. Transforming gradually, it elevated two feet into the shape of a tall rounded-top cone. It now had a better view to examine the stranger.

"Careful," said Kim, holding back her laughter. "Mike, meet Marty. Our latest NAIMERA creation. He's almost complete. I need to add one or two things, and he's ready to go."

"Kim?" asked Marty. "Please explain the meaning of 'What the hell?'"

"Marty, that is an idiom *some people*," she said, looking over to Mike, smiling, "use when they are suddenly surprised by something."

Marty's skin texture was contorted with little bumps and tall spikes but slowly receded back to a smooth surface interrupted by small, periodic surface veins. At the same time, his color transitioned from flashing red to red to light pink and finally back to a calm pale white.

"Marty's surface DNA is similar to a cephalopod, giving him wild texture and color variations that match his mood changes," said Kim, smiling. "Don't worry. There's not a mean bone in his body."

"Funny," said Mike, his heart still racing. "No bones, period, I get it." As Mike's pulse started to return to normal, he slowly stepped closer to Marty's container. "It talks! Oh my god. It can talk. How can it do that?"

"What is your name?" asked Marty.

Mike turned his head and saw Kim and Peter standing behind him with smiles on their faces. Mike moved a little closer. He was a little late answering Marty's question while busy trying to locate from where on its body the voice originated. But he heard him clearly through the earpiece he was wearing.

"My name? My name is Mike. Mike Murphy. Pleasure to meet you, Marty," said Mike as he continued to process what he was talking to.

Marty's eyes continued to follow Mike, still slowly pinning while adjusting to the light.

"You are the first stranger Marty's met since achieving consciousness," said Peter.

"How old are you?" asked Marty.

"Oh my god, he wants to know my age. Okay, I am thirty-five years old," said Mike in a careful, clear voice, slightly pausing between each word. Mike turned to Kim and Peter. "Is this the same Marty I saw in 3D?"

"Yes," replied Kim.

"Then he can turn into a bat to get around, right?"

"Marty can reshape himself however he likes," said Kim. "He's perfectly capable of flying like a bat, slithering like a snake, or even walking. Whatever is most appropriate at the time. He uses muscular hydrostats to reshape his body, similar to the arms or tentacles of a squid. Your tongue is another example. His muscles provide movement and, when necessary, some skeletal structural support."

"Amazing," said Mike, "and he has a laser?"

"Yes, they all do. Marty, would you fly around the room once for Mike?" asked Kim.

On her command, Marty began to shrink, stretching flat and wide. As he gradually reshaped into a bat, a bone-like hydrostatic skeleton formed into a pair of wings. Two small legs emerged from beneath his trunk. He stepped up on the edge of his tray and in a smooth, effortless motion flapped and lifted off, gracefully flying around the room in an oval pattern. He paused and hovered over his tray, then delicately landed. His body transitioned into a snakelike shape with a broad base for stability as he settled down.

"Thank you, Marty," said Kim.

"Don't let his size fool you," said Peter. "Our little Marty is a formidable hunter. Around the surface of his exterior are thousands of small tube-shaped capillaries that take in, sample, and expel the surrounding environment. Both in air and water. From the air, his scent membranes—roughly three hundred million olfactory cells—can distinguish odors at least two thousand times better than humans. Underwater, they can detect odors at one part per ten billion. Obviously, he can fly or move about, swim, contort into any shape, camouflage, communicate in any language, send and receive electronic messages, and defend himself with high-voltage shocks or a powerful laser. As you can imagine, he would be a tremendous asset when tracking down Grace. A virtual scent hound anywhere."

Mike turned to Kim. "Peter mentioned a combat simulator you use to train NAIMERAs. Could I get a glimpse of it?"

"Sure." Kim walked over to a workstation and fired up the software.

"I'll show you one scenario around a cave complex in eastern Afghanistan." Kim picked up a set of AR goggles paused to turn sound selection to 'On', and handed them to Mike.

He slipped them on. A mountain range appeared with several small caves dotting the hillside. The terrain, sky, and terrorists all looked and behaved realistically. Clouds inched across the sky and trees, and grass swayed in the breeze. Mike scanned up and down but couldn't find anything that didn't look like the real thing. Suddenly, he felt as if he were back in Afghanistan.

"I can't believe my eyes! It's absolutely authentic. Even the sounds."

"In this exercise, the bad guys are heavily armed," said Kim. "Marty has been using it to practice getting in and out of caves discreetly to perform reconnaissance. Each terrorist's actions are guided by realistic AI decision algorithms to mimic their likely thought process. Marty can run through these in less than a second, but in real-time, it takes hours. I'll fast forward and replay a minute of his last session so you can watch how he operates."

Marty flew toward one of the cave entrances, his colors constantly changing to match the background of the sky and trees. When he landed, his skin transformed to blend perfectly with the rocks—in color and texture. He appeared almost invisible unless you knew exactly where to look. And look hard. He inched along the rocks and vanished inside. Seconds later, he reappeared and flew off. Terrorists stood close by without noticing.

"Very impressive. Would it be possible to send this simulator to the TAG agents along with NAIMERAs? They might use it to plan a rescue."

"No need. NAIMERAs have it already installed in their memory. They can create realistic holographic environments of anything they observe and run tens of thousands of simulations in moments," said Kim.

"I'll definitely make sure they know this tool exists," said Mike.

"Marty is our latest addition," said Kim. "Let's go meet the other NAIMERAs."

Peter and Kim led Mike back inside the transition room, where they removed their sterile suits, head covers, masks, and gloves. They exited and turned down the hall toward another room with a sign above the door: "NAIMERA Development."

Immediately after stepping inside, three different voices rang out almost in unison. "Hello, Kim. Hello, Peter."

Mike looked around, not sure where the sounds originated.

"Who is this?" asked one soft squeaky voice.

"Buttons, Trinity, Baron," said Peter, "come over and meet our guest."

Within seconds, the NAIMERAs removed their camouflage, flew over, and landed on a stainless-steel bar in front of Peter at chest level. Each one was different in texture, size, shape, and appearance.

"I'd like you to meet our three adult NAIMERAs," said Peter. "This is little Buttons here on the left, Baron in the center, and the largest, Trinity, on the right."

Mike's mind was gradually accepting these fantastic, strange creatures as real and not puppets or robots of his imagination.

"Dear God, I cannot believe my eyes. They're incredible."

"Everyone, this is Agent Mike Murphy from the FBI," said Peter.

"Why are you here, Agent Mike?" asked Baron.

"We usually refer to him as Mike or Agent Murphy, Baron," said Peter.

Mike smiled.

"So, Agent Mike, why are you here?" asked Baron.

Now Mike started to chuckle.

Peter shook his head.

"Okay, they're funny as well as amazing," said Mike.

"As you will come to find out, each NAIMERA has their own distinct personality," said Peter.

"Our Mr. Baron has become slightly more stubborn and independent than the others," said Kim.

"He's quite the entertainer," said Mike.

"Everyone, Mike is here because he needs our help," said Peter. "You remember my daughter, Grace. She's been kidnapped in Guatemala. Mike is trying to find her. He's here to assess your skills to determine if they would be useful in locating her."

Buttons spoke up. "Peter, I am very sorry to hear that. I would like to volunteer if there's anything I can do to help."

Her minuscule size and soft high-pitched voice made Mike smile.

"Buttons is unlike the other NAIMERAs," said Kim. "Intuitive and highly observant, she's also the smallest. Buttons has many of the same attributes as her larger companions but in a tiny package. She can obviously squeeze into small places."

Mike crouched down to take a closer look, still wearing a grin. "You can't be more than an inch tall. Buttons?"

"She's cute as a button," said Kim. "That's what popped into my head when thinking of a name for her."

"It's perfect," said Mike.

Mike's mind began imagining a long list of possibilities of how she could enter places undetected and provide clandestine reconnaissance. *We could definitely use her on a number of cases the FBI is working on right now.*

"If your rescue plan requires aerial surveillance, I can be quite effective," said Trinity.

"Trinity is the largest of the NAIMERAs," said Kim, "standing four feet tall in her flying form; designed for high-altitude aerial reconnaissance. Compared to the other NAIMERAs, her personality is more serious and methodical."

"I'll volunteer too," said Baron.

"Baron is half the size of Trinity," said Kim. "As we mentioned, his exterior is a uniquely developed skin, tough as Kevlar but extremely pliable. Baron, would you fly by the target bay and fire on the five-millimeter steel plate? Mike would like to see a quick demonstration of your laser."

"A full burn-through?" asked Baron.

"Sure, why not," said Kim.

Baron, in the form of a bat, leapt up and flew across the room, paused, and hovered twenty feet above the floor directly in front of a target practice area consisting of several rectangle metal plates aligned side by side. Located within his upper chest, a lens covering resembling an eyelid opened. Baron fired his laser. It produced a bright flash only lasting a few seconds as he directed the beam across the plate. It was enough to slice the nearly quarter-inch steel target in half. A metal piece could be heard hitting the ground as Baron flew back to his perch.

"Wow!" said Mike. "I'm speechless. That was impressive. I'm curious about Baron's exterior. What's the ballistic rating?"

"His armor level is at type III," answered Peter. "The only thing that can penetrate it with a single strike is an armor-piercing rifle. Of course, multiple direct hits from lesser weapons could also breach it."

"Hard to believe. That's pretty damn good," said Mike while shaking his head.

"Thank you, Baron," said Kim.

"And thank you all for volunteering," said Mike. "I'll meet later with Peter and Kim to review each of your special capabilities. The decision is in the hands of the lead agent searching for Grace in Guatemala. Once he learns what a great contribution you all can make, I'm sure he'll accept your help."

"Yes, thank you," said Peter, addressing the NAIMERAs. "It's getting late. Let's head over to the drone facility." Mike turned back as they walked away. The eyes of the NAIMERAs followed him out of the room.

"They're absolutely incredible!" said Mike. "I'm at a loss for words." Peter, Kim, and Mike left the NAIMERA lab and walked down a path cutting through a lush flower garden. On the way, Mike asked what NAIMERAs ate and drank. After all, they were living creatures.

"They all have a single gastrovascular cavity," said Kim. "We feed them one condensed slow-release energy pellet every day. Each should cover all their nutritional needs, in addition to fresh water. That shouldn't be a concern, though. Either Peter or I or maybe both of us will certainly want to accompany the NAIMERAs to Guatemala and will manage their care and feeding."

"What did you mean by 'should cover their nutritional needs?'" asked Mike.

"Typically, one pellet is adequate. But if they become overly excited or spend an extended period flying around as bats, their metabolic rate elevates, requiring more food."

The three approached an industrial-looking building. The procedure to enter was the same: Maggie verified their identity and access privileges. A tinted glass double door automatically slid open. They entered and walked down a hallway to another door labeled "Drones." After one final security check, the door opened.

Mike stopped and looked up. The room was enormous, two-hundred by three-hundred feet with a sixty-foot ceiling. It was like walking into an airplane hangar with dozens of drones of various sizes, assembled in partially completed states. Four technicians were working on one of the larger drones. They paused and looked in the direction of Peter. One nodded, and then they quietly went on with their work.

"Don't tell me you designed and built all this from the ground up?" asked Mike.

"No. I bought the entire drone subdivision from another defence contractor. I kept most of the personnel and moved the operations here," said Peter.

"Who's in charge?" asked Mike.

"I am at the moment. The manager left a few months ago," said Peter.

"But when a request comes in for a NAIMERA to accompany a mission, who goes along?" asked Mike.

Kim and Peter looked at each other.

"That would have been the manager," said Kim.

"My plans to hire another unfortunately will have to wait until things settle down."

Mike walked over to one corner where there were dozens of light-gray "coffins" for transportation. The largest, twelve feet long and three feet wide. Each contained military drones awaiting shipment. One large drone appeared fully assembled on the far end of the room. It had a wingspan of one hundred feet. Two large rotors on the wings supplied lift vertically. When airborne, the wings were designed to rotate ninety degrees for forward motion.

"Now this reminds me of the ones we used in Afghanistan."

They continued to stroll, pausing while Peter described each type.

"Every drone is completely autonomous. No need for a nearby manned satellite uplink vehicle or ground control station. It makes rapid deployment to remote locations much safer and faster. Each contains its own AI unit capable of making quick decisions without a remote pilot or operations crew. As I mentioned in the introduction, if a clandestine operation calls for up-close intelligence and guidance, a NAIMERA can fit inside the fuselage. When the drone approaches a suspected target, the NAIMERA is deployed."

Stopping in front of the largest drone, Mike spoke up. "The wings are huge!"

"Can be," said Peter. "They dynamically extend and retract between twenty and one-hundred feet across. They can hover just above ground or soar up to fifty thousand feet. See these?" Peter pointed to tiny, microscopic holes in the wings. "They weep out de-icer during cold, wet flights."

"What armaments do these things deploy?"

"Whatever the customer requests. We don't make them. But we do integrate some critical components for our unique communication. A variety of ordnance is kept on hand at our test range. For example, this drone was specced to deliver two HellFire I-n missiles."

"We used HellFire Ones," said Mike. "What's the difference?"

"The missiles you used were directed to their target by laser or a remote operator," said Peter. "The 'n' version includes the option to receive precise guidance to a target from our smart AI drones or one of our NAIMERAs. For example, to destroy a camouflaged tunnel, it might guide the missile at the target, providing a specific approach trajectory, then for the last fifty yards, instruct it to drop down to six feet, level off, and enter the tunnel entrance. Surprise! It's proven highly effective. All our drones, including the NAIMERAs, can capture-single frame full-motion video. They carry both variable aperture and infrared cameras."

"Day or night?"

"That's right," said Peter. "Also, synthetic aperture radar when there's smoke, haze, or clouds."

"How about communication?"

"Encrypted Ku-band satellite for the high bandwidth stuff and LEO sat-phone technology for basic communication," said Peter. "They also can use short-range radio within several hundred yards."

They strolled over to an odd-shaped, relatively small drone. It had two propellers in the hollow center, one above the other, enclosed in a circular saucer-like body about three feet in diameter. All around the body were compartments that could open and close like angled doors.

"We call this one the 'carrier drone.' It's used for two missions. One, to deploy NAIMERAs, land and wait in a secure area, then retrieve them when the recon mission is complete. In addition, they can carry small glider-type bombs when a single discrete target needs to be neutralized as directed by a NAIMERA."

"What ordnance do they carry?"

"High-Explosive Anti-Tank. Basically, a slow-moving RPG. Again, very effective."

"I don't think the TAG office in Guatemala will need HEAT, but if they asked for small ordnance, could you get several?'"

"The Guatemalan government would need to approve it, but yes, getting a dozen would be no problem." Peter looked over his shoulder at the crew working on the large drone, then turned toward Mike. "Well, that's it. Unless you have any more questions, let's call it a day."

"Thank you for the awesome tour," said Mike. "I'm thrilled to be a part of this company. Honored, really. And from what I've seen, with help from the NAIMERAs, I'm confident they'll track Grace down."

"That's my hope," said Peter. "I'll leave you two now. I need to go check on the progress of that drone."

Kim and Mike walked back.

"You must love it here," said Mike.

"I do. Sometimes I pause in the middle of the day and chuckle to myself. I actually get paid for doing this. It's a total blast."

*

The traffic from Palo Alto up Highway 280 to San Francisco was unusually slow. Mike seemed not to notice. His brain was still reeling from everything he'd seen. He couldn't wait to call the TAG office in Guatemala and tell Rick. But it was so extraordinary, he didn't know how to describe it without sounding like a lunatic. It was something you had to see for yourself.

As traffic crawled to a standstill, Mike's phone rang. It was Rick.

"Agent Aguilar, I was about to call you."

"Hi, Agent Murphy. I wanted to give you a quick update. We've arrested two San Benito police officers who kidnapped Grace Strauss."

"Police officers! You're kidding?"

"I wish."

"But that's good news, right? Did you find her?"

"Not yet. She's been turned over to a local cartel. One of the officers is fully cooperating. We know where they're taking her, and if everything goes well, we should have her on a plane heading home tomorrow."

"That sounds encouraging. I take it you won't need the help Dr. Strauss offered after all?"

"Never say never, but let's hold off and see how things go. We're fairly confident we have a handle on the situation," said Agent Aguilar.

"I'll take it as good news. Thank you for the update. Call me as soon as you find her. We're all anxious to have this ordeal over with."

CHAPTER 21

San Benito, Guatemala

The next morning, Rick pressed ahead with his plan. If Fernando's information was correct, the rendezvous should occur sometime today. Rick, Major Rojas, and Agents Allen and Garcia walked out to inspect the vehicles; two large yellow-and-orange trucks with eleven-foot utility bodies. The tires looked in good shape, both gas tanks were full, and when started, the engines sounded fine. Both trucks had garage-style roll-up rear doors, which they pulled up to inspect inside. Air circulated nicely inside the cap, and two dome lights above offered illumination. Installed against the sides were metal benches with seat cushions allowing enough room for four agents and their equipment in the back.

"These are perfect," said Agent Garcia.

Agent Allen nodded with approval. Major Rojas handed each agent a laptop-sized satellite internet device and a hat with an HD camera on the crown of the cap.

"Here you go, remember to keep them on," said the major. "Both audio and video are enabled."

"Keys are in the truck," said Rick. "Good luck."

"All right, everyone. Let's go!" shouted Agent Allen.

One by one, agents made their way over and loaded their equipment into the trucks. The two most senior agents from each team sat up front. They wore road worker uniforms to avoid suspicion. Agents carried satellite phones since cell coverage was not assured. Every truck and agent had GPS tracking devices, all monitored from TAG headquarters. It was 0600 local time. Agent Allen started up Team P14's truck and left heading up the PET-14 highway from San Benito toward the airstrip Cesar originally mentioned. The second truck, driven by Agent Garcia, followed carrying Team P3. It turned south toward PET-3, a slightly longer trip.

Team P14 took under a half hour to reach the turnoff. The next ten minutes would be the most uncomfortable. Everyone knew what to expect. Potholes and rocks littered every small access road cutting into the Maya Biosphere Reserve. As scripted, the truck stopped fifty feet short of the airstrip and parked in a secluded spot.

Rick and Major Rojas sat in Rick's office, monitoring the movements on his computer screen. Team P14 exited the trucks but remained clustered around in a circle, moving around each other. The video feed became blurred and cloudy. Rick called the Team P14 lead.

Agent Allen answered, but she was coughing.

"Team P14, are you all right?"

"We are now." She coughed after almost every other word. Rick could barely hear her.

"Agent Allen?"

"We stepped out and realized we forgot to put on mosquito repellent. They're everywhere! It's hard to breathe right now. There's a cloud around me, but we're covered."

"Since I have you. Want to give me a status update?" asked Rick.

"Give me a second." Agent Allen stepped away and took a few deep breaths. "Okay, I'm better. There were no problems getting here. Didn't see anyone yet. Tire spikes are now laid across the access road. Three agents with sniper rifles are on one side or the road near the airstrip. The other three agents are lugging their stuff, headed to the airstrip. Should be in place soon. That's all."

"Okay, thanks. I'll let you get back."

A short time later, Rick observed that Team P3 arrived at their designated airstrip. They moved into position.

*

Minutes turned into hours as the day dragged on. Each team called every hour to check in with Rick. They both reported a few brief rain showers had passed through the area, making this typical hot and humid day even more uncomfortable. Neither reported any sighting of a plane or vehicle. Rick wondered if Cesar had canceled the rendezvous.

It was almost 1500 when Major Rojas received a phone call from the air defence duty officer. They'd spotted a suspicious plane. Tracked originally leaving from Nicaragua, it had just entered Guatemalan airspace. Flying low, trying to evade radar detection, it shut off its transponder and kept radio contact silent. A spotter plane scrambled. It followed discreetly a thousand feet above and a mile behind. Major Rojas remained on the phone with the duty officer, relaying information to Rick, who passed it on to the lead agents at each airstrip. With growing anticipation, Teams P3 and P14 remained in their positions. Snipers were down, rifles resting on bipods, all ready to fire.

The duty officer gave an updated location of the plane. It was heading directly for the original airstrip; the one Fernando had mentioned. Closing fast, it was now fifteen miles away. Major Rojas reported its position to Rick, who relayed it to the agents at the airstrip. Rick ordered the helicopter to immediately head to the P14 airstrip. Excitement intensified by the second for everyone except Rick, who remained puzzled. *Surely by now, Cesar must know they arrested the officers. He told them his plans. Why wouldn't he have changed locations? It doesn't make sense.* But there was no time to ponder that now.

Major Rojas turned to Rick. "Five miles from the airstrip and closing."

Rick relayed the news to the agents.

Suddenly Agent Allen spoke up. "I see a large van driving up the access road … it just ran over the tire spikes."

"Thanks, Team 14. We're picking it up on video, but tell me everything you're seeing," said Rick.

"The van hobbled to a standstill, with four flat tires," said Agent Allen.

"Two guys got out … walking around the van, inspecting. They look pretty upset … sounds like they're shouting profanities. Oh yeah. Definitely."

One flung the spike strips into the jungle.

There was a long pause.

"Team 14, what are they doing?"

"They're talking to each other. Wait. They walked to the rear of the van and opened the back doors. They're pulling out a ramp. Now they're sliding out a long … a six-foot wooden crate … placing it on a dolly. It looks heavy; they can barely handle it. They shut the doors. Now they're both behind the dolly. Pushing it toward the airstrip. Still hear them shouting profanities."

Rick could see Agent Allen draw her gun and heard her chamber a round.

"Arrest them, now!" ordered Agent Allen.

Rick heard the agents in the background yelling out, "Freeze! Put your hands up where we can see them."

Agent Allen approached the truck.

Rick listened but couldn't hear anything. The video focused on the two drivers. "What's going on? Do you see Ms. Strauss?"

"Sorry, Rick, this is a little confusing. The two guys look scared. They don't look like cartel members to me. We got them surrounded. They're not going anywhere. But so far no sign of Ms. Strauss."

"The crate, check the crate," Rick insisted in a frantic tone.

"What the hell is in that crate?" demanded Agent Allen.

The two men looked at each other, puzzled, but appeared too terrified to speak.

Two agents rushed back. One opened up the van doors and looked inside. "There's nothing in the van," shouted one of the agents. Another opened the large crate. The agents stared down. Baffled.

"Rick, the van is empty and the crate filled with bananas."

Rick turned to Major Rojas. "They brought a crate of bananas to the airstrip?"

"Rick, we're about to interrogate these guys. Try to listen in. I'm moving closer."

Both men were handcuffed and sitting on the ground. "Where is she?" asked Agent Allen.

"Who?" replied one of the men.

"What the hell is this?" asked another agent, pointing at the box.

"We were hired to deliver a crate of bananas here," said one of the men.

"By whom?" asked Agent Allen.

"I don't know. We never met them," said one of the men. "Somebody called with instructions. Later, someone dropped off one thousand American dollars in an envelope. We must deliver exactly one hundred thirty-five pounds of bananas to this airstrip at three o'clock today."

"Rick, the plane looks like it's about to land. I'm heading over to the airstrip now," said Agent Allen.

Rick and Major Rojas looked at each other. "Where is Ms. Strauss?" asked the major.

"The plane is landing. It's bouncing and pitching … now stopped. The pilot is taxiing around in a circle. Looks like he's preparing for a quick takeoff. He cut the engine and is getting out," said Agent Allen into her headset.

"Don't let that plane leave!" ordered Agent Allen.

Agent Allen spoke to Rick. "This pilot's green. He looks frightened. We've got him handcuffed and on the ground. They're searching the plane."

Agent Allen got called over by one of her team members. "It's empty except for this." The agent handed it to her.

"What? What did they find?" asked Rick.

"Hold on. I'm about to find out," said Agent Allen. "We searched the plane. The only thing on board was a small envelope with 'TAG' written in large bold letters on the face. We're about to interview him, try to listen in."

"Who sent you here?" said one of the agents.

"I was hired by three men in Nicaragua to fly here and pick up a small load of bananas at exactly three o'clock today," said the pilot. "They paid me five thousand American dollars. I didn't ask any questions."

"What about this?" asked Agent Allen, holding up the letter.

"They gave it to me and said to hand it to the police if I'm stopped," said the pilot. "It will guarantee my safety."

"Did you catch that?" asked Agent Allen to Rick.

"Yes, I did. Nothing makes sense."

Above, the helicopter arrived and landed on the airstrip.

"I repeat. Did you hear that?" asked Agent Allen. The helicopter noise was deafening.

Rick could barely hear. "Yes!" he shouted. "Bring them all in for questioning."

He turned to Major Rojas with a confused look. "What in the hell is going on?" said Rick, shaking his head while looking skyward out the window.

CHAPTER 22

San Benito, Guatemala

Fifty miles to the south of San Benito, jet flight number Cirrus 021 was heading northeast over northern Guatemala at 350 miles per hour, cruising at 28,000 feet. A radio call came in to the tower at Mundo Maya International Airport.

Jet: "Mudo Maya Traffic, Cirrus 021."

Tower: "Cirrus 021, Mudo Maya Traffic, go ahead."

Jet: "Mudo Maya Traffic, request emergency landing."

Tower: "Cirrus 021, emergency? Clarify."

Jet: "Mudo Maya Traffic, male passenger, age fifty-one, complaining of chest pains, possible heart attack."

Tower: "Roger, Cirrus 021. Stand by."

Tower: "Cirrus 021, approved. You're cleared to land—twenty-eight."

Jet: "Mudo Maya Traffic, roger."

The tower instructed the jet to land on runway 28 and wait near the terminal in a general aviation apron area for the ambulance. All ambulance services in the Flores and San Benito area of Guatemala were handled from a single location. Fire Department San Benito Fifty-Seven dispatched both fire trucks and ambulances. Located a mile from the airport, it was less than two minutes away. San Benito Fifty-Seven monitored all airport radio transmissions to ensure rapid emergency responses. The tower called San Benito Fifty-Seven and requested an ambulance, urgent but not an emergency.

San Benito Fifty-Seven dispatcher Isabela had heard the jet's radio transmission and already began to prepare a response. She turned her head and leaned forward across her desk to see who was on duty, sitting in the break room. "I'll send an ambulance," she said while typing the call information into the EMS system. "Mario, Jose, got a request from the airport."

Mario heard Isabela. He and Jose were totally engrossed watching the final minutes of a soccer match. Both got up slowly, stretching their necks as they continued to try to catch every last, possible glimpse of the game as their bodies reluctantly inched their way toward Isabela's desk.

"We have a code two. A private jet is about to land. Pick up a fifty-one-year-old male passenger who's complaining of chest pain. Take seventeen; it has plenty of gas," she said as she handed the dispatch instructions to Jose. "Drop him off at Centro Medico Maya Hospital's emergency room. I'll let them know you're coming."

"Got it," said Mario as he reached over and grabbed the ambulance key ring off the rack next to Isabela. "This is the worst timing. It's all tied up with two minutes left. Let us know how it ends."

"Yeah, I'll do that," she said, smiling. "Now go!"

The ambulance truck had a cab in the front for two passengers and a large cap compartment with a side door in addition to double swinging doors in the rear.

Mario had the keys in hand. "I'll drive."

He and Jose got in and started out the garage port down the driveway. As they approached the street, a black van sped up and stopped in front of them, blocking their path.

Mario slammed on the brakes. "Damn, I almost hit 'em."

He watched two men dressed in paramedics' uniforms jump out. One approached their cab from each side. Both were large burly men with dead-serious expressions. One had a four-inch scar across his right cheek; the other had large letters tattooed around his neck.

"Jesus, who are these guys?" said Jose. "They look scary."

"Hey, you going to the airport?" asked the man with the scar.

"Yes, you're blocking our way, man," said Jose. "What do you want?"

"We have something to show you both," said the man with the tattoo.

Each discreetly slid a handgun up from inside their jackets just enough for both paramedics to see.

"Do exactly what we say, and you won't get hurt!" said the man with the tattoo.

"Okay, okay," said Mario. "Don't shoot. We'll do what you want."

The man with the tattoo opened the passenger's front door and signaled to Jose to get out. He and Jose got in the back. The other man slid into the passenger's seat. Mario froze, careful not to make any sudden moves. He looked down to see a gun pointed a few inches from his side. A terrified Mario obeyed every instruction.

"What's your name?" the man asked.

"Mario."

"Well, Mario, keep up with that van but don't get too close. Nice and slow. Got it?"

"Yes."

He followed the van down the street into a secluded alley between two industrial buildings. They stopped. Two other men jumped out of the van and opened a side door. Mario could see a woman lying down on the floorboard; her arms and legs tied up and her mouth gagged with dark tape. They abruptly dragged her out, walked over to the rear cap of the ambulance, opened the back doors, and put her inside.

Mario stared in horror. *Jesus, they're rough. What the hell is going on?*

The two men returned to the van and drove off.

"Now, I want you to carefully drive to the airport to meet that plane. Don't do anything stupid."

How'd they know about that plane? Mario looked down and saw the gun still pointing at his side. "Okay, okay, I will. Just don't hurt us."

"Don't worry. You do what I say, and you and your partner will be fine. Now relax. Got it?"

"Yes."

Within a couple of minutes, the ambulance arrived at the airport's security gate. The passenger gave a stern warning to Mario. "Act relaxed and natural."

The guard, André, knew Mario. He greeted him and looked across, expecting to see someone familiar.

"Hey, who's this?" asked André.

"Hi, André. Oh, he's a new guy we just hired," replied Mario as his heart rate rocketed.

"I'm Juan. Nice to meet you, André," said the passenger, smiling.

"My god, that's a nasty-looking scar you got there, Juan."

"You're right."

The guard seemed to be expecting to hear an explanation of how he got it. After a brief awkward pause, he turned his attention back to Mario.

"The plane just landed. It's over to your left, parked in the loading

apron in front of the terminal. Where are you taking him?" asked
André.

"Centro Medico Maya Hospital's emergency room."

"All right," said André. "Someone from customs will meet you
there. I'll let them know. They'll need to check his passport, so make
sure he brings it along. Want an escort to the plane?"

"No, no. I know where it is, thanks anyway," said Mario.

The ambulance pulled away slowly. The EMS radio came alive.
"Mario, Jose, you'll be happy to know your Blue Princes, Cobán
Imperial, scored in overtime," said Isabela with a cheerful voice. "They
beat Petapa, the Parrots, three to two. I love those nicknames."

Mario momentarily froze. He turned his head to his right.

The passenger dropped his head and glanced down at the EMS
radio. Mario reached down and pressed the talk button on the
microphone.

"Thank you, Isabela. That's very nice," said Mario. "We arrived here
at the airport, so I have to go now."

Mario hoped by answering stiff and formal Isabela somehow might
catch on and realize they were in trouble.

"Okay, Mario? I just thought you wanted to know," replied Isabela.

*I don't think that worked. She probably thinks I'm pissed at having to
leave before the game ended.*

The ambulance parked to the side of the jet. The doors opened and
everyone got out. They ordered Mario and Jose to move to the side and
stand perfectly still. The men opened the rear doors and pulled the
woman out. They held her up from both sides. The man with the scar
grabbed her, tossed her over his shoulder, and walked over to the jet
and up the short stairs. Within seconds, he returned.

An older man followed him down. He held something in his
hand and walked over to Mario. "Here, take this," he said. "Give it

to the police after you get back."

Mario looked down. It was an envelope with "TAG" written on it. The man turned around, walked up the steps, and closed the door. Mario whispered to Jose, "This whole medical call was a setup."

Jose cautiously responded with a slight dip of his head. The jet engines started up.

"Quick, Mario, get in. You two in the back, *now!*" said the man with the scar. They rushed over and jumped in the ambulance as the jet engines let out a roar. The truck rocked and vibrated.

"You get airport traffic on this, right?" said the man, pointing his gun at the truck's radio system.

"Yes," replied Mario.

"Turn it on. I want to make sure that plane takes off without any trouble."

Mario switched to the tower's broadcast frequency.

Jet: "Mudo Maya Ground, Cirrus 021 at alpha, request taxi 28 for takeoff."

Tower: "Cirrus 021, taxi via alpha runway 28 right, hold short."

Jet: "Mudo Maya Tower, Cirrus 021 holding short, 28 right."

Jet: "Mudo Maya Tower, Cirrus 021 ready for takeoff, runway 28 right."

Tower: "Cirrus 021, cleared for takeoff. Fly runway heading."

Jet: "Mudo Maya Traffic, Cirrus 021 departing runway 28 right."

The jet sped down the runway and vaulted up. Instead of following its original path northeast, it reversed directions and headed back toward Nicaragua. The tower noticed the change in flight plan and called out to the jet. There was no response. They tried several more times, then called the Air Defence Wing to report an unresponsive jet and possible hijacking.

"Good. They're off. Let's go," said the man with the scar.

He instructed Mario to drive the ambulance slowly out the gate back into town to a location where the black van was waiting. The two men got out of the ambulance. The man with the scar had a few final words for the paramedics.

"Give that envelope to the police. We'll be monitoring your EMS radio transmissions. Don't use your radio or cell phones to call anyone until after you return to the fire station."

No ultimatum was necessary. The two mystery men got into the black van, closed the doors, and quickly vanished. Mario and Jose drove away relieved but wondered out loud what had just happened.

"Somebody went through a lot of trouble to get that poor woman out of the country," said Mario.

"Yeah, and I bet TAG won't be happy, whatever that is," said Jose.

*

Grace sat in the back of the plane sandwiched between two large men, unable to move anything other than her head. She couldn't imagine who these people were and why they were going through so much trouble to remove her from the country. When the plane took off, it shot up almost straight, like a rocket. Her wrists hurt from the tight handcuffs, her body still ached from the accident, and now her eardrums felt intense pain from the pressure. After several minutes of silence, she heard the copilot announce they were out of Guatemala.

"PLVI Base, are you there?"

"Yes, Cirrus. How did the pickup go?"

"Smooth. Tell Sergio we have her. Should be landing in an hour."

PLVI Base, what's that? thought Grace. *And who is Sergio? Where are they taking me, Mexico? It can't be far if we're arriving in an hour.*

The large man to her right looked at her and stared down at her legs, making Grace nervous. He reached to his side and pulled out a long cylindrical object. He flicked his finger and a knife shot out, a switchblade. He waved it across her face in a menacing fashion. Grace's heart pounded; she leaned back, pressing her head into the seat cushion. He bent down and sliced the zip-tie handcuffs off her legs. "You'll need to walk where you're going," he said. "Run and you're dead."

CHAPTER 23

San Benito, Guatemala

Rick and Major Rojas struggled to make sense of the events at the airstrip. Both teams returned to the TAG complex, bringing along with them the airplane pilot, the two delivery men, and the letter. The three sat, awaiting interrogation, but the agents knew they were merely innocent pawns. The focus shifted to the letter.

Wearing surgical gloves, Rick opened the envelope carefully to preserve any physical evidence. He unfolded a note and laid it flat. It contained a simple cipher key to decrypt coded messages: "Alphabet Key: khxgivceaybnofdqjprmustzwl." That was all.

San Benito Police Chief Torres called the TAG office and asked to speak with the director. He told Rick about a call he'd received from the ambulance company with two drivers who'd been carjacked at gunpoint.

"Agent Aguilar, they told me a woman was put onto a private jet. It just took off from the airport. They handed them an envelope with 'TAG' written on it. An officer is bringing it to the station."

"Thanks for the call. I'll have someone stop by and pick it up. I hope there's still time to stop that jet. I'll call you later."

After Rick heard of the accounts described by the two paramedics, it confirmed what they suspected: the airstrip landing was a ruse.

"Major, get the commander of the Air Defence Wing on the phone immediately. Ask him to track the jet that just left Mundo Maya International Airport and request that they intercept and force it to land in Guatemala. Ms. Strauss is on that plane."

Rick was furious with himself. He wanted desperately to stop that plane. He called in Agent Allen and asked her to drive to the San Benito police station to pick up the letter left for them by the abductors. The tired agents were preparing to leave after a long, tedious day.

Rick jogged down the hallway and called out for everyone to stay put. They had one more task to do today. "Arrest Cesar!"

Major Rojas had the commander on the phone. The jet was at 27,000 feet heading due south at 350 miles per hour. They tried to contact it, but it didn't respond. It was out of Guatemalan airspace and now over Belize—interception was no longer an option. They would continue to track it as long as possible to see where it landed.

Fifteen minutes later, Agent Allen returned from the quick trip to the police station holding the letter. Rick opened it and placed it down flat on his desk. As they assumed, it held a coded message. Together, with paper and pencils, Major Rojas, Rick, and Agent Allen decrypted the note using the cipher key.

If you are reading this, it means we have the American woman with us. We use encryption to prove we are the real ones holding her. Give the key to her father. We have his daughter's phone. We will text him encrypted messages soon. We will only deal with him. No one else!
Enjoy your bananas.

Rick felt humiliated and crushed. "At least we won't have to deal with a flood of imposters claiming to have her and trying to collect a ransom," said Major Rojas. "We know who has her, and soon, she'll be somewhere in Nicaragua. What are our options?"

"At this point, other than diplomatic," said Rick, "nothing. Excuse me for a moment. I need to make a call to San Francisco. Then let's get Cesar. That may be the only good thing that comes out of this kidnapping."

CHAPTER 24

San Francisco, California

Mike was driving back to his office when his phone rang. "Rick!" said Mike. "Did you find Grace?"

"I'm sorry. Grace is on a plane heading to Nicaragua. The PLVI has her. It's a long story."

"Damn it! You're sure?"

"Pretty certain. We traced the plane that took her. It landed in Nicaragua."

"So where does that leave things?" asked Mike, fearing he already knew the answer.

"Unfortunately, there's nothing more our TAG unit here in Guatemala or the FBI can do. We have no jurisdiction. I'll call the US embassy in Guatemala City. They'll reach out to the State Department and try to appeal to the Nicaraguan government, but that surely won't go anywhere."

"Is there anything I can do?" asked Mike.

"Contact the CIA. In the past, they were able to offer some confirmation of cross-border kidnappings like this. But that's all

I have. Sorry it ended like this. Before you hang up, the PLVI left a simple cipher key they'll use to communicate with Dr. Strauss. I sent it to you. Let him know everything. Tell him we did all we could to rescue her. He should expect an encrypted message on his cell phone. They'll probably only send it once, so warn him not to delete it. Give him the cipher key and show him how to decrypt messages."

"Rick, I want to thank you and all your agents for your help. I wish we could have rescued her. Call me if you hear any more information."

Mike hung up. "Damn!" He slapped his turn signal, moved to the right lane, and exited the freeway. *I need to tell Peter in person, now. He may have already got their message, and he won't know what it is.* Mike dialed Peter's number while getting back on the freeway, heading south.

"Hello?" said Peter.

"It's Mike. I got a call from the TAG office in Guatemala. Can I meet you in the next half hour?"

"Sure, I'm home. I live in Woodside. Come to my house." Peter gave Mike his address.

"Oh, yeah, since you're on the phone. I got a strange, garbled text message from Grace's phone. I'm not sure if it's spam or a prank. Thought I'd mention it. Very odd."

"Do not delete it. That's one reason why I need to see you now."

Mike found Peter's house without any difficulty. He stopped at an electronic gate and heard a familiar voice speak up, asking him to show identification.

"Don't you recognize me, Maggie?" It was a moment that helped relieve a little of his tension.

"Good evening, Agent Murphy," said Maggie. The gate opened. "Have a pleasant visit."

Peter's driveway was a hundred yards from the road. The house was stunning. An elegant Tuscan style with a six-car garage, limestone terraces, hand-carved doors, a long lap pool, and a boccie ball court next to a tennis court. It was just as Mike had imagined. He parked in the circular driveway next to an ornate fountain. Peter walked out the front door to greet him.

"Okay, after our call, you have me worried. What's going on?"

"I'll explain everything. Let's take a look at that message," said Mike.

Following Peter inside, Mike took a deep breath. "I got a call from TAG. They believe Grace is now in Nicaragua and being held ransom by a very dangerous group called PLVI."

"PLVI? Never heard of them."

"Unfortunately, we have. I'll tell you all I know about them, but first, that message you received—it's from them. Rick sent me the cipher to decrypt it and all their future correspondence." Mike opened Rick's text message and studied it for a minute. He looked back up at Peter. "It's pretty simple. But decrypting it by hand could be tedious. There's an app you can install on your phone that will make it easier."

Mike guided Peter to the right location and, within a few minutes, had it installed. Using the cipher key as input, they read the message.

Mr. Strauss. We have your daughter. We use encryption to prove we are the real ones holding her. We have her phone and will use it to communicate with you. We will only deal with you. No one else! Hire a private rescue/negotiation company and we will kill her. We want one billion dollars in gold bars delivered to us on January 1. Our next message will tell you where to deliver it. Now go get it!

There was stunned silence.

"That's a hell of a lot of money!" said Peter. "I don't have that just lying around."

"Let's step back and consider all your options. The FBI has a unit that deals with kidnappings. They would be a good resource to advise you. I'll make a call to the CIA to see if they can confirm if she's really in Nicaragua. If so, they might be able to tell who has her and where she's being held. If she's not there, then we might be able to call on other resources for help."

"I hear you. Nevertheless, I'm going to talk to my financial people to find out if I can even get a billion dollars in time." Peter looked at his calendar. "I have a little over five weeks till January first."

"I realize it will be difficult, but try to stay calm and get some rest," said Mike. "It's getting late, and I still have one more thing I need to do. I'll call you tomorrow."

Peter walked Mike to his car. Mike could hear Peter whisper to himself, "Gracie, wherever you are, I will get you home safely. I promise!"

CHAPTER 25

Chinandega, Nicaragua

The head of the PLVI, Sergio Cruz, stood by the window of his office that overlooked his compound, smoking a cigar while waiting for the plane. He watched it break through the clouds and begin its gradual approach, which brought on a nod with a satisfying smirk. Not only did he get the daughter of a billionaire, but he'd humiliated TAG in the process. He left his office to go down and meet the plane.

His isolated paramilitary base was one hundred miles north of Managua. Known only as Base PLVI, it was originally a ranch with a small local landing strip and a few modest structures. Several years back, as recognition for his paramilitary's help suppressing political opposition, the government granted PLVI the property to use as their home. The location was ideal. Tucked away near the secluded Cosigüina Volcano Natural Reserve in a remote part of the country, very few people noticed its existence. Over time, with funding mainly from criminal activities, a modern military base rose up. They added a longer modern runway, housing, command center, gymnasium, small commissary, armory, detention facility, hangar, and a palace for the leaders of PLVI. Sergio had plans for more ambitious growth, but it required money.

The jet taxied near the hangar, where a small airport tug guided it inside, out of satellite view. The engines wound down and a door opened. Sergio stood next to his lieutenant, Luis Ortiz, who was sadistically ruthless and devoted. Two husky men escorted a restrained and very scared Grace to face Sergio. He snapped his head down and up with approval.

*

Held firmly on both sides by the two men from the plane, Grace stood petrified in front of their leader, Sergio. He was shorter than the others, maybe five-foot ten with a square muscular frame and a short crew cut, but it was his cold cruel eyes that frightened her. A taller, dark complected man stood by his side; they called him Luis. He too looked wicked.

"Welcome, Miss Strauss. We're so glad to have you here. I hope you enjoy your stay." He turned to Luis. "Take her to one of our guest rooms."

CHAPTER 26

San Francisco, California

After leaving Peter's house, Mike needed to drive back to the San Francisco FBI field office and drop off some documents. It was late, but he noticed a light on down the hall. It was his boss's office, Special Agent Bill Andrews.

"Bill, you're still here. Good. Have a minute?"

"I was about to leave, but sure," he said, motioning over to a chair.

"The Grace Strauss abduction case just took a turn for the worse. I spoke to Rick from the Guatemalan TAG office. He's reasonably certain she's now in Nicaragua. The PLVI has her."

Bill shook his head while expressing disappointment.

"Rick suggested I contact the CIA to see if they can confirm. He plans to call the embassy in Guatemala City. They'll reach out to the State Department to appeal to the Nicaraguan government."

"Don't hold your breath," said Bill. "I happen to know the CIA station chief of Nicaragua, Carlos Reynaldo. I'll give you his work cell."

"I was over at Peter Strauss's house an hour ago and helped him decrypt a ransom message from PLVI. They want one billion in gold delivered on January first."

"Christ!" said Bill, crossing his arms and shaking his head.

"They won't negotiate with anyone other than Peter," said Mike.

"Is he thinking of paying it?"

"He's looking into it, seriously."

"After you speak with Carlos, if she really is in Nicaragua, the case is out of our jurisdiction and there's nothing more the FBI can do."

Mike slowly nodded, dispirited.

"Advise Peter on kidnapping negotiations."

"I've already gone over it with him. On the way here, I contacted the Hostage Recovery Fusion Cell and brought them up to speed on the case. They'll be taking it over. But they told me there's not much they can do either."

"How many more days do you have left? Just this week, right?"

"Friday's it," said Mike in a somber voice.

"And this was the last case you were working on?"

"Yes, last active. I passed everything else on. Not the way I wanted to see it end. That's for sure."

"We'll miss you around here, Mike."

"Thank you, Bill. I appreciate that. I've enjoyed working with you. I've learned a lot."

Mike took Carlos's phone number and walked back to his office. He closed the door behind him and sat near his window, looking out at the night lights.

Mike felt frustrated. He was confident with the help of Peter's NAIMERAs, the TAG agents could have found Grace within a few days. Now it looked like weeks away at the soonest. But at least Peter was someone who could afford the ransom to get her back safely.

Mike looked down at the card with Carlos's number. *Not sure confirming Grace is in Nicaragua will do us any good, but what the hell?* He picked up the phone and called.

The voice on the other end, not recognizing the calling number, cautiously answered. "Who is this?" said Carlos.

"I'm Agent Mike Murphy, FBI out of the San Francisco field office. Bill Andrews gave me your number."

"Bill Andrews! We go way back. What is it you want?"

"I'm working on an international kidnapping. Her name is Grace Strauss. The Guatemalan TAG office believes she's now in Nicaragua, held by the PLVI. I'd like to know if you can confirm that."

"Agent Murphy, you're talking to the right person. I've been away. Haven't heard from my field agents in a couple of weeks. Is this number you're calling from secure and the best one to reach you?"

"Yes," said Mike. "It's my work cell. Secure."

"Good. I'll let you know one way or the other. I'm due for a status report at any time now. Should know something soon."

"I guess the FBI's not the only ones working late. Thank you, Carlos."

"Hold on. Actually, I'm heading your way for a couple of days. Monterey, the Naval Postgraduate School. There's a conference on Central American politics beginning tomorrow. I realize this is last-minute, but you should attend. One of the speakers is CIA Deputy Director Dr. Ixamara Navarro, the world's leading expert on Nicaraguan politics. I'm sure she'll cover PLVI and its relationship with the current government. I'm flying out tonight. It's Thursday and Friday, but she's only speaking tomorrow."

"That sounds interesting. It would be good to know who we're dealing with. Can I bring along a guest? He's Dr. Peter Strauss, the father of the kidnapped victim, and he happens to have a TS/SCI."

"Sure, look me up on SIPRNet," said Carlos. "Send both of your contact and security information, and I'll make sure you're added to the guest list. I'll send you the agenda and base access details. We'll discuss what I find out about Grace Strauss when I see you. By the way, give my regards to Bill."

"Will do. I wonder, would it be possible for us to meet Dr. Navarro privately?"

"Sure, if she's not already booked up. Yes, I think that can be arranged."

"Thank you, Carlos. I look forward to meeting you."

Mike sent Carlos the contact information he requested and almost immediately got a response back. Mike turned around and called Peter.

"Hello, Peter," he said.

"Hope this isn't more bad news," said Peter.

"No. I want to know if you're available tomorrow. There's a seminar in Monterey. CIA Deputy Director Dr. Navarro, the leading expert on Nicaraguan politics, will discuss the PLVI. We might be able to meet her privately. More importantly, the CIA station chief of Nicaragua, Carlos Reynaldo, will give us an update on what they know about Grace."

"Outstanding!" said Peter. "What time?"

"I am looking at the agenda. It starts at 8:00 a.m. It's about an hour-and-forty-five-minute drive. I can pick you up at 5:00 a.m."

"I have a better idea. Why don't you come over now and stay the night here? We'll fly down on my personal jet."

"Sure, why not? I won't ask for travel reimbursement," Mike said with a smile.

*

Thursday morning, a limo arrived at Peter's house and drove the two to San Jose International Airport. The flight time only took fifteen minutes. They picked up a rental car, grabbed a quick breakfast, and made it to the NPS at 7:45 a.m. While walking to the conference hall, they passed a huge flagpole. Over the loudspeaker, reveille started. Mike turned to Peter and touched his shoulder to stop walking. Everyone in sight paused and turned, facing the flagpole. As the music finished, three sailors began hoisting the American flag as the national anthem played. The royal blue sky was crystal clear. A perfect backdrop for the red, white, and blue. As the flag slowly raised, Mike saluted and Peter held his hand over his heart, both experiencing intense emotion; rekindling the spirit and energy Mike felt as a Navy SEAL.

"That brief moment reminded me I'm especially proud to serve this great country," said Peter.

"I agree," said Mike while taking in a deep breath of cool fresh ocean air.

Peter's response was more passionate than Mike was used to seeing from civilians and caught him by surprise. Even the more patriotic citizens he'd known didn't have a real connection to the flag or the ceremonies around it. Maybe Peter's dad had served, or maybe it was because he worked directly with soldiers as a contractor. Whatever it was, the feeling stayed with them throughout the day and beyond.

Mike arranged to meet Carlos at the entrance of the conference hall. There, he briefly introduced him to Peter, and they walked inside. Dr. Navarro's talk was comprehensive. Her presentation style was fast-paced, and she spoke with authority and confidence. She captivated everyone in the crowded auditorium with her depth of knowledge. All facts were without conjecture, and she connected events and people together with uncanny insight. She explained Nicaragua's past and present political situation. Of particular interest to Peter and Mike, the role PLVI played in violently suppressing political opposition. The organization began with fifty-six elite ex-military members, hence the roman numeral name "LVI." They formed a small, shadowy paramilitary group devoted to supporting the current repressive government. The Nicaraguan military's "shoot to kill" strategy used against peaceful protesters was highly criticized by organizations like Amnesty International and the Catholic Church.

"The government apparently listened. They recruited and formed the PLVI to do their dirty work going forward. Their members are often called blue shirts since that's what they all wear.

"When anti-government protests take place, PLVI snipers show up and open fire. You may remember the infamous May Day Massacre? That bloodbath was the work of blue shirts, just one of many. Since its inception, it's estimated they're responsible for the murder or disappearance of several hundred citizens. In gratitude, the PLVI was given land in the remote northwest to use as they wish. Property confiscated from a rancher who openly criticized the government's violent tactics. Over time, they've turned it into a small modern military base."

A satellite image of the base appeared on the screen.

"The PLVI has gradually grown their core to nearly one hundred loyal, ruthless, and highly disciplined members with an unknown number of 'falcons' serving as their eyes and ears around the country or wherever they operate. The PLVI has evolved to become increasingly violent and overtly sadistic to anyone who stands in their way. After the government began reducing funding for the group, they embarked on an urgent, almost ravenous, quest for money. While continuing their paramilitary activity, the PLVI has morphed into arguably the most dangerous criminal cartel in Central America. Perhaps the world. They engage in drug smuggling, human trafficking, kidnapping, pirating, and other illicit activities. How seriously does the US take them? The State Department is offering a five-million-dollar reward for the arrest and conviction of their leader, Sergio Cruz. Cruz has built a reputation for the way he executes his enemies, sometimes using over-the-top methods like tanks or antiaircraft guns. All to show how cruel he'll be to anyone that crosses him.

"Make no mistake, the PLVI may be small, but it's a very potent military. That has not gone unnoticed by members of the government and their supporters. When the Nicaraguan elite finally, collectively, and forcefully voiced their concern to stop the bloodshed, it led to the recent firing of the director-general of the national police, which you may have read about. But little has changed. Our latest information indicates the ruling political party is getting increasingly nervous and would like to dismantle the PLVI. Easier said than done.

"After the Far-left regained power, they invited the Russians to return. In no time, they set up a spy base called GLONASS—Russian for GPS—in Managua. Mostly meant to spy on the US, but more recently, we learned another one of their assignments is to report on PLVI activity."

After she finished her presentation, Dr. Navarro opened up for questions.

A hand raised in front.

"Yes?"

"Could you elaborate on the type of spying the Russians are conducting?"

Dr. Navarro nodded and stepped forward.

"They have over two hundred specialists. A very large contingency, which raises eyebrows. We've observed suspicious activity around an underwater fiber-optic cable linking Latin America and the Caribbean to the United States. They also spy on their neighbors as well as their own citizens. The Nicaraguan president said it's all in the name of helping to fight drug trafficking."

After the talk, for the rest of the day, attendees assembled into small birds-of-a-feather working groups, discussing particular areas of interest. Carlos arranged for them to meet with Dr. Navarro for an hour. They walked up to the podium, introduced themselves, then headed off to a SCIF. Once inside, Mike began by explaining the background of the kidnapping and how it shifted to Nicaragua.

Dr. Navarro spoke up. "I'm aware of a few past kidnappings by the PLVI. The ransom has always been under one hundred thousand dollars, and once paid, they released the hostage."

"If that's all they wanted," said Peter, "I'd write them a check tomorrow. But they're asking for a lot more."

"What do they want?" asked Carlos.

"One billion dollars in gold on January first," said Peter. "Delivery instructions to follow. I'm working on trying to get it, but my holdings are currently tied up. My financial team thinks they can pull together five hundred million in that time frame. Getting the full one billion is a challenge. Look, I'm desperate. I'll do anything to get my daughter back, and I don't care about the cost."

Carlos listened. When Peter finished, he shook his head. "I understand your plight, but you might want to hold off. I just read the most recent monthly field report. Of course, I can't disclose our sources, but they are extremely reliable. The PLVI does have your daughter. She is being kept in a holding cell within the detention facility on their base."

Carlos turned to Dr. Navarro. "The one you mentioned. They plan to terminate her life whether you pay them or not. They don't want her to live to testify against her original abductors in Guatemala. The only thing that's keeping her alive for now is the expectation you will agree to pay the ransom."

This was grim news.

"Those sonsabitches!" Peter muttered under his breath.

Mike shook his head. His heart sank. The one hope of getting Grace back alive was apparently gone.

Carlos opened a folder and laid out a stack of paper. "Dossiers on all the officers." He pointed to one picture. "This guy's the leader, Sergio Cruz. These others are lieutenants."

Carlos slid over a satellite photo of the PLVI base. "I am sure you're both curious to see this. Here's their base." He pointed out basic living quarters, the leaders' living quarters, detention facility, armory, command center, cafeteria, gymnasium, and airplane hangar.

"May I get a copy of all this?" asked Mike.

"Sure, take it. Peter, you just helped the CIA fill in a couple of blanks," said Carlos. "We couldn't make sense of how the PLVI was able to place three hundred million dollars in weapons orders; mostly advanced military equipment from a Russian arms dealer. We assumed we missed a large drug transaction."

"Do you know what all they purchased?" asked Mike.

"No, only the big-ticket items."

"I heard about that," said Dr. Navarro. "It includes an advanced stealth fighter. The SU-57. What on earth are they planning to do with that?"

"I think we just got the answer," said Carlos. "You see, the PLVI invited all the country's top political leaders to an 'Awards and Arms Display New Year's Ceremony' at their base on January first. Both predicated on them receiving the gold they expect from you."

"Interesting," said Dr. Navarro. "PLVI may be feeling some heat, you think?"

Stroking his chin while pondering momentarily, Carlos said, "Oh, yeah. 'Awards' may indicate they plan to share some of that gold with the political leadership. A payoff, perhaps, to maintain the status quo? And the 'Arms Display' will definitely be a show of strength as a warning they are now a most dangerous force not to be reckoned with."

"Can anyone get near that base?" asked Mike.

"It's ..." Carlos began to speak, but Dr. Navarro beat him to it.

"I would strongly advise against it," said Dr. Navarro. "Curious people have been known to vanish when they get too close."

"It's adjacent to the Cosigüina Volcano Natural Reserve in a fairly remote part of the country," said Carlos. "Nature lovers occasionally hike in the area, but the compound grounds are heavily guarded. I have the name of someone who could be of some help. Dominique Sánchez, a nurse—she was held captive at the PLVI compound but let go. The only person we're aware of to ever leave alive. She said it was because she provided emergency aid to one of their members after he was badly injured. Saved his life. After her release, she fled the country. Now living in Honduras. Tegucigalpa. She knows a great deal about the compound. I understand she continues to help organize anti-government protests."

Mike wrote down her name. "Thanks," said Mike. "I'll look her up."

"One more thing. She's going by an alias: Nina Perez," said Carlos.

"Peter, I am sure you are very upset. They need that gold, desperately. Now we know why. But realize you hold some powerful leverage. I recommend you use it to your advantage. Demand the PLVI send you photos of your daughter holding the current day's newspaper. That will at least keep her alive and in good health while you try to work something out."

Carlos' advice seemed like a small glimmer of hope for Peter in a sky filled with gloom. "I don't know what more I can offer them to release her safely, but that may buy some time."

Mike said, "If you uncover any new developments related to Grace that you can share, please ..."

Carlos responded before Mike could finish. "I have your number, Agent Murphy."

"I'll give you my private cell as well," said Mike. "This is my last week with the bureau. I'm joining Peter's company to head up his security team."

"Okay, thanks. Peter, it looks like you hired the best!" said Carlos.

"I couldn't agree more," said Peter, turning to Mike, managing a smile. "Carlos, Dr. Navarro, thank you. I appreciate your time and insights."

They all shook hands and left.

*

Driving out of the NPS, Peter looked at Mike. "You hungry?"

"Starving."

Peter turned the car around and headed to Fisherman's Wharf. He was craving comfort food from a familiar haunt of his, the Old Grotto. He ordered a large bowl of clam chowder. But by the time their meal arrived, Peter had completely lost his appetite.

"Can't eat, uh?" said Mike.

"No. After hearing Carlos's news, my mind is spinning. Now I have some nagging questions. How can I get Grace back from Nicaragua if the FBI doesn't have jurisdiction? They plan to kill her whether I pay them or not. There must be some way to get her home safely. I just can't imagine how."

"Let's take a walk. It will help clear your mind," said Mike.

"You're right. You know, the inspiration for the NAIMERAs came to me from an aquarium nearby. I was looking at their giant octopus when I had an idea."

"I'd like to see it if it's not too far," said Mike.

They strolled along the bay from Fisherman's Wharf toward the

Monterey Bay Aquarium, then paused in front of an old weather-worn wooden building.

"Ed Ricketts's lab," said Peter. "The front door looks like it's about to buckle in. That needs attention. Growing up, *Cannery Row* was my first Steinbeck book. Doc was an early role model for me. I wanted to be just like him."

They entered the aquarium, casually meandering until they eventually found themselves staring at a giant octopus inches away.

"That's it, or something like it," said Peter. "I became totally fascinated with every aspect of that creature. I wanted to build one. Well, not one just like it but to evolve an organism incorporating some of its amazing characteristics."

Mike moved in for a closer look at the octopus. "So that planted the seeds to the eventual NAIMERAs?"

"That's right," said Peter.

"I'm beginning to think the NAIMERAs could be helpful in getting Grace back."

Peter perked up and looked to the side at Mike. "You know, I was wondering that myself, Agent Murphy. I just don't know how."

CHAPTER 27

Palo Alto, California

The return trip was quiet, neither man saying anything. Peter tried to assess his options. Mike spent his time staring at the PLVI compound's satellite photo. Within two hours of leaving Monterey, they were back at Peter's house. Mike suggested they sit at the table with his laptop and discuss possible scenarios.

"I've been racking my brain," said Peter. "What do you think of these two ideas? The goal is to bring Grace home unharmed. I can offer the PLVI more money: five hundred million dollars in gold when she's safely released and another billion three months later. The problem with that is there's no guarantee they'll honor it. They could take the five hundred million and still kill her, assuming I'll renege and not pay the additional promised billion. It's a gamble but worth a try."

"That's a lot of money but it might work," said Mike. "And you're right it comes with no assurances of Grace's safe release. What's your other idea?"

"I ignore their warning and hire a professional hostage rescue company. I looked into them. They charge fifty thousand dollars per day for work outside the US. If I did, I am putting my faith in people to rescue her unharmed from a very dangerous compound, which may be way beyond their capability. So, this option is the bigger gamble. Plus, time is not on my side."

Mike agreed. "The Monterey trip brought back memories of my time in the service, rekindling something inside me. I studied the satellite image, and there are striking similarities with an Al-Qaeda compound we attacked in eastern Afghanistan. I led that SEAL team. Three of us were in an armored vehicle, a mile behind a small convoy, when we watched them get ambushed. Al-Qaeda captured twelve coalition soldiers. We knew they would be executed or taken across the border to Pakistan. Our choices were to abandon our comrades or attempt a dangerous rescue. That was easy. No way would we ever leave those guys, but we had to act quickly."

"What happened?" said Peter.

"Short story: We managed to get them out alive and destroy the compound in the process. Our team all received commendations. But the real reward was knowing we saved those hostages and eliminated a couple of dozen terrorists in the process. It's interesting. There are other similarities."

"With Al-Qaeda?" asked Peter, surprised.

"Actually, yes. The two have a lot in common, for one. Both groups have devoted, ruthless members. Another is with what they do to society. The PLVI formed as a paramilitary with political motivations: terrorizing their opponents. Similar to what Al-Qaeda does. And they fund most of their operations through illegal activities, like the drug trade. I think of them as criminal terrorists."

"Do you think the same type of rescue scenario can work in Nicaragua?" asked Peter.

"Too early to say. A good Special Ops unit along with air support, weapons, and reconnaissance just might succeed. If I were leading the mission, I'd need to study the site and gather information before assessing the chances."

"Can I request a Special Ops team from the military?" asked Peter.

"Good question. The USSOCOM might do it."

"USSOCOM, I've heard of them. What exactly is it they do?'

"The United States Special Operations Command conducts hostage rescue and recovery, but as I understand, only when missions are in response to terrorist threats and incidents. I'll look into it, but I am not sure this qualifies."

"Please check."

"Will do," said Mike.

*

The next morning, Mike returned to the FBI field office in San Francisco for his final day. He gave Bill the rundown of what he learned at the seminar in Monterey. Carlos Reynaldo, the CIA station chief, was able to confirm where Grace was and who had her. Mike covered everything Carlos and Dr. Navarro told them: large arms purchases and a PLVI ceremony scheduled on January 1, hosting Nicaragua's political leadership. Also, he shared the advice Carlos gave Peter. Mike asked Bill if the USSOCOM could be called upon to attempt a rescue of Grace. The answer was a definite no. They still classified the PLVI as a state-sponsored paramilitary, not a terrorist organization.

Mike was again deflated. He turned to walk out but stopped at the door. "Carlos sends his regards."

Bill smiled back.

The day was filled with mixed emotions. He was excited to be joining Peter's company while sad to be leaving. But he was mostly worried about Grace. He opened his drawer. There was the envelope with his ticket and itinerary to Hawaii. Somehow the vacation he was looking forward to seemed blah and inappropriate given the plight of Grace.

Mike dialed Peter.

"Hello, Mike?"

"I have a couple things. First, I checked, and a USSOCOM rescue is off the table."

There was silence on Peter's end. "Well, damn. I'm about out of options."

"Today's my last day," said Mike. "I was scheduled to leave tomorrow morning for a two-week Hawaii vacation, but my heart's not in it anymore. I know if I go, I'd be obsessively thinking about you and Grace. Mind if I start early?"

"God no—I mean, please start as soon as you can! I was afraid to ask if you would. I really could use you here with me. Everything's moving quickly."

"Good. I'm on my way."

Mike walked to Bill Andrews's office. "Here you go, a parting gift." Mike dropped his envelope on Bill's desk. "Two weeks prepaid, nonrefundable trip to Hawaii—plane, hotel, car."

"What?" said Bill.

"I can't use it. If you can, it's yours. I'll transfer everything into your name, and you go pack. You'd leave tomorrow."

Bill stood up. "Thanks, I might be able to swing it."

"I'm checking out now. Starting my new job immediately. I need to be there for Peter."

They shook hands, and he turned around and left.

Mike wasted no time. He drove directly to SGSI. Mike spent the entire weekend researching the area around the PLVI compound, staring at the satellite map, performing calculations, and taking notes.

The first thing Monday morning, Mike tapped on Peter's door while walking in carrying a laptop and a folder.

"We have just over five weeks," said Mike, taking a seat next to Peter. "I'd like to brainstorm my straw-man plan. Our first task is to ensure Grace remains alive and in good health."

Peter was pleased but not entirely surprised by how quickly Mike sprang into action.

"I texted the kidnappers yesterday and told them I'm working on getting the gold," said Peter. "I did float the option of giving them five hundred million when she's released and another billion three months later. Something my financial team thinks is doable. I added that I know she is in Nicaragua and I'll need assurances she's being treated well, if they want their money. I must receive a photo of her every day holding up the daily front page of *La Prensa*; otherwise, I'll assume she's being mistreated, and the deal is off."

"I'm impressed. Well done. Any reply yet?" said Mike.

Peter held up his cell phone showing a photo of Grace with this morning's newspaper. "Ever since I got it, I can't stop staring at it. She looks tired and scared, but she's alive."

Peter's voice and expression seemed to convey relief and fear together.

"What about the two-payment suggestion? Did they respond to that?" asked Mike.

"Yes," said Peter. "They answered 'One billion dollars in gold bars by January 1st.' I don't think I can get all of it by then, but they are planning to kill her regardless. One other thing, they gave me detailed instructions for delivery. It should arrive by plane at Managua International Airport at noon on January first. They want the gold stacked on three separate pallets. They attached a document I need to fill out, from the Nicaraguan ministry of foreign affairs. It's a donation request from me to PLVI in order for the gold to pass through customs."

"You'd think they'd just wave the gold through. Apparently, the entire government isn't completely corrupt," said Mike sarcastically while shaking his head.

It was clear, not delivering the full amount was a guaranteed death sentence for Grace. But whether they give them what they wanted or not, according to the CIA, the PLVI still planned to kill her. It was obvious there was only one option if they hoped to save her life.

"Peter, don't waste your time trying to get all the money. I think I have a plan that might work. It won't require much gold. I've studied the area around the compound. Logistics is an issue, but we can address that later. I mentioned similarities between this situation and another we faced in Afghanistan when our small SEAL team rescued twelve hostages. That compound had about the same number of fighters, roughly a hundred. For that plan to work, we needed most of them to leave, so we created a diversion. Around the province, we notified every local village there would be a convoy of coalition supply trucks driving through the area the following day, specifying an exact path and time. We warned them to avoid being on the road. We weren't surprised the information got back to Al-Qaeda. Three-quarters of them left to set up an ambush.

"We only had one armored vehicle with three soldiers and one attack copter we called in to join us. After they were long gone, we destroyed one wall at the opposite end of the compound farthest from the hostages. In a panic, almost all the remaining fighters rushed to stop our breach, leaving the hostages lightly guarded. That's when we hit them hard. The copter swooped in and fired rockets, wiping out most of the fighters in the open while a couple of us busted through the wall nearer the hostages with RPGs. There was some quick action on our part to take out a few guards and free the hostages. We safely evacuated everyone before the rest of the Al-Qaeda fighters returned. And the amazing part of the mission was we did it with only four SEALs, taking zero casualties. I really think we can pull off something similar down there."

"I don't know what to say. Those are dangerous people. You heard what Dr. Navarro said. They're vicious. Is this something you really want to take on?" said Peter.

"I spent eight years as a SEAL. To make it that far, you have to want to hunt and kill bad guys. Fear, you leave at the door. We were conditioned to do it, but you need to possess the will to do it. I have that. I've never lost it. If we do our homework and prepare, I have no doubt it can succeed."

Peter's spirits were immediately elevated. He scooted his chair closer to the table.

"Go on. Don't forget, we have a secret weapon, NAIMERAs, and attack drones. I want to hear this plan from top to bottom," said Peter. "I can't imagine how it can possibly be done."

Mike unfolded a large satellite image of the compound and the surrounding area, placing it across Peter's desk.

"I'd love it if we already had a complete team in place and could go in tomorrow. But we're not there. This compound is heavily fortified. I'll need every minute to prepare. Plus, delivering gold will work in our favor by having them let their guard down when it arrives, setting up the ideal time to strike. I first need to do some research. I won't be ready to present a detailed plan until I know what we have and what we're dealing with."

"Okay, that makes sense. I hate to think of Grace sitting in a prison cell that long."

"I understand. To be clear, our mission objective is to safely extract Grace from the PLVI detention facility and evacuate without any casualties to our team members. I've identified a few vital tasks necessary before we can move forward. Our first task is to keep her alive and healthy. You did that. Another is to make them think we fulfilled the ransom demand."

"But I can't get a billion dollars in gold by January first," said Peter.

"You won't need to. I contacted three companies that can supply a combination of tungsten gold-plated and gold-filled bars. None will be full gold bars. We'll fool them into believing we delivered what they asked. They won't be able to analyze the gold too carefully when it gets delivered. The PLVI will only be able to scrape off a bit to test, and I have a workaround for that."

"What are the other tasks?" asked Peter.

"I absolutely need to recruit at least four other candidates for the mission. Ideally, they'll include three of the same guys from my old SEAL team who were on the Afghanistan mission with me. They've done this before and I trust their judgment. I've kept in touch with them over the years. But whether any of them will join us is a huge question mark. And even if they do, I'll still need to find a fourth. That guy should have a similar military background and be trustworthy."

"Only four? Why not hire a couple hundred?" asked Peter.

"I want to limit it to what I think is the bare minimum. Small, efficient and agile. We're less likely to be noticed, can strike hard and fast, then get out quickly. I imagine what will work is a lightning strike, in and out, not an invasion. If my plan is executed with precision, there will be no casualties."

"Okay, I trust you. I know nothing about military tactics. Now, besides team members, what else will you need?" asked Peter.

"Intelligence. I'll take a trip to Nicaragua to perform a boots-on-the-ground reconnaissance of the PLVI compound. Looking at satellite images and talking to folks only goes so far. I'll have to record details such as compound security, geography, daily activity and movement, equipment, armament, personal and exact locations of everyone and everything. Finally, I'd like to visit Dominique Sánchez, who was held captive at the compound. Her insights could be beneficial."

"How about the NAIMERAs? Where do they fit in?"

"I'll definitely have important roles for them. I won't know what those will be until I learn more."

"All right," said Peter. "This whole situation makes me extremely nervous. It seems very risky. But I'll do anything to save her. Anything. And as you said, this is our only option." Peter took a deep breath and exhaled slowly.

"The better you prepare, the more confident you'll become, and before you know it, fear is replaced with courage," said Mike.

There was a brief pause as Peter thought about that and calmed down. "Thanks," said Peter. "I feel better. In fact, I'm encouraged you think there's hope, assuming everything goes as predicted. When do we start?"

"The plan is already in motion. You accomplished the first task by establishing daily health checks on Grace," said Mike. "The second task is to order the tungsten gold bars. We'll need 1,600 bars total and 592 of them will need to be gold-filled bars to cover the top and sides. The rest, forming the center, need only be gold-plated."

"Did they give you a quote for the gold?" asked Peter.

"Yes, everything should come out to about twenty million. As for time, the best they can do is four weeks. It's tight but manageable."

"Okay, I'll order them after this meeting," said Peter.

"One other thing," said Mike. "Tell them when they stamp the hallmark with '.999,' to leave off the 'GF' for 'gold-filled.' Ask them instead to stamp 'P. Strauss' on the bottom. If they give you any grief, tell them it's not for sale but part of a ransom. We don't want to tip PLVI off should they look that closely."

"Got it," said Peter. "Anything else for me?"

"Couple more things. Arrange a charter flight once you know where and when to pick up the gold. It must be delivered according to the date and location the PLVI specified. It's going to be over twenty tons, so let them know."

"Is that it?" asked Peter.

"I'll need to pay a visit to each of my ex-SEAL team members, then go down to Nicaragua for a week or so of reconnaissance."

"To save time, contact your former SEAL friends and have them come here. I'll cover the cost, and it will save a few valuable days. Plus, they'll have a chance to see the NAIMERAs."

"Good idea, Peter. Thanks."

"I'll have Kim help me set up some NAIMERA demonstrations in the lab. It will blow their socks off."

"Nice. I'll work on getting them here. Now, one other thing. We'll need a way to get the drones, weapons, NAIMERAs, and staff transported to Nicaragua, preferably by ship."

"That's easy," said Peter. "I have a mega yacht we could use. It's 290 feet, eight staterooms, elevator, gym, jacuzzi, spa, the works. Seven full-time crew members. I can arrange for a doctor to come along."

Mike smiled while shaking his head in disbelief. "That all sounds great. Having a medical doctor along is a good idea. I'm not familiar with yacht duties. What exactly do they do?"

"Run the whole ship, all performing multiple tasks. I have a supervisor that manages everything. Then there's piloting, engineering, and maintenance, cooking, and cleaning. And it also has a helipad."

"A helipad? So, you have a copter?" asked Mike.

"Actually, I own a couple. One's a Black Hawk, ex-military."

"Awesome. That will definitely work its way into my plan. What's the yacht's maximum speed?"

"Thirty-three knots," said Peter.

"Could we have it loaded and waiting for us in San Diego? It would save time for all of us to meet there."

"Sure, not a problem."

Mike pulled out his cell phone and ran a quick calculation. "Maxed out, we could make it from San Diego to Nicaragua in three and a half days. I'll allot a week in case we run into any mechanical or weather problems," said Mike.

"All right. Let's plan to go with that," said Peter.

"Back to that copter. Could it be fitted to deploy missiles or glider bombs?"

"I'll ask my staff and get back to you."

"Well, I think we both have plenty to do. I need to go make a few phone calls," said Mike.

"We're really going to do this, huh?" said Peter. "Thanks, Mike. I'll get to work."

Mike got up and began to walk out.

"Mike," said Peter. "I just had a premonition; whatever it is you come up with, the PLVI won't know what hit them."

CHAPTER 28

Chinandega, Nicaragua

Sergio Cruz, the PLVI leader, along with his lieutenants, met to discuss the status of his three-hundred-million-dollar arms purchase. Roberto Cruz, Sergio's brother and trusted accountant, handed out copies of the invoice. Sergio studied it. Every weapon had a purpose. Up until recently, they only needed to worry about putting down political protests and keeping area gangs and cartels in deathly fear. Lately, a new and more serious threat emerged. His inside contacts alerted him to a growing vocal faction within the political leadership pressuring the president to diminish and eventually disband the PLVI. It claimed they had grown too large, too violent, and too dangerous. Sergio and his lieutenants had a response they called "silver or lead." Share their booty while demonstrating themselves as an intimidating force, even against the nation's military. Sergio turned to his lead strategist, Ramon Suarez.

"What do you think, is this enough?" said Sergio.

Ramon nodded with a sinister smile. "Definitely. The government could never threaten us once we have an SU-57. Every one of the

Air Force's sixty-five combat planes is either retired or out of service. They're so old even if they manage to bring them all back, we could shoot them down in minutes. Our entire arsenal is state of the art. Come January first, once our guests see what we have, they will shiver in their boots."

"Good, that's the goal; it will be worth the steep price," said Sergio. "I have bigger plans. Expensive plans. But we don't make money if our drugs aren't getting through. Two of our submarines proved disastrous. One sinks the first time out and the other gets captured by the American Coast Guard."

Roberto spoke up. "Those losses cost us a combined four hundred million in equipment and potential drug revenue. It can't keep happening."

"It won't. We *will* fix those problems," said Sergio while looking around the table with a stern face. Heads nodded. "Luckily, something just fell into our laps—kidnapping. Kidnapping rich foreigners." Sergio held the invoice and scanned it one last time while pinching his chin. "All right. The numbers and delivery dates look good. Since I have you here, let's go around the table, give me an update."

Sergio turned to Luis Ortiz, his right-hand man. They'd become close friends while serving together in the Nicaraguan military. "How's our guest today?" asked Sergio.

Luis leaned his tall slender body back in his chair. "No different, still a major pain," he said while pointing his index finger down to the ground in the form of a pistol. "When this is over, I want to put a bullet in her head. I sent the photo of her holding today's newspaper."

"Good. One every day, don't forget. Be patient. She's the goose that will give us a badly needed golden egg. A very large one. Let her have the paper and find some books. Try to keep her occupied. Make sure she has good food and water. An hour of exercise too. We need her alive and healthy for a few more weeks. Once the gold arrives, she's yours."

"Franco?"

"No mention of protests. It's been a quiet week."

"Did the leader break down and give the names of those organizing the protests?"

"No. He died this morning from his wounds," said Franco.

"Damn." Sergio shook his head and looked disappointed. "Miguel? Tell me some good news."

"A test shipment of cocaine made it to Miami. The pickup went smooth."

"Nice. You got past southern command. When's the real one?" asked Sergio.

"Ten days," said Miguel. "Sending two hundred pounds. We have a Coast Guard informant; we'll know when they leave. Once they do, our fast boat races in for the drop-off."

"Good work. Keep it up. Remember, if we can't deliver, we're irrelevant. Anything else?"

"Yes, our six new speedboats will be delivered on January first to the marina," said Miguel. "Top speed, seventy knots with a fifty-mile radar range. No boat can outrun us now. I'll put the old ones in dry dock to make room."

"Perfect," said Sergio. "Make sure they're fully armed and gassed up. We'll take some of our guests out for a ride after the ceremony."

*

One hundred miles to the south in Managua, two Russian spy analysts, Serge Agapov and Egor Yelchin, were sorting the day's communications from the PLVI compound. For the past few months, the spy station had been providing periodic updates of PLVI activity at the request of the Nicaraguan government. The reports read like a despicable crime novel. Murders, kidnappings, torture, pirating, human trafficking, and drug running. The analysts started to feel sorry for the Nicaraguan people, ruled by a government that knowingly allowed this to go on. Then the encrypted text messages between Peter and the PLVI began to appear. This was not the first time they'd seen communication like this. Within seconds, they located the cipher key, plugged it into one of their decryption programs, and inserted the messages. Egor tapped Serge's arm and pointed at his computer monitor.

"So, they are the ones who have the American," said Serge. "They demand a billion American dollars. In gold."

"Her papa is going to pay," said Egor, shaking his head. "Imagine how our lives would change with a billion dollars."

They both shared a sly smile. Suddenly, monitoring the PLVI traffic had become much more interesting.

CHAPTER 29

Palo Alto, California

Mike sat quietly at his desk, staring down at a satellite image of the PLVI compound. He'd typed page after page of notes on his laptop. Without thinking, his left hand began massaging his right hand, which had started to cramp up. He put together several detailed plans, but all were based on assumptions. He needed more information. Question after question and no way to answer any of them without a trip to the compound. He realized this was where the NAIMERAs could definitely be an asset. Where were they holding Grace? In what room? How many guards? What weapons did they carry? What were the fences made of? Were they electric? Sensor alarmed? How could he get through undetected, and what tools would he need? Once they rescued Grace, how could they safely escape? The PLVI had a jet and pirate speedboats the yacht couldn't outrun. The list went on and on.

The PLVI compound was much better guarded and fortified than any he'd seen in Afghanistan. Going down there and performing surveillance should answer most of his questions. Having those answers would help him decide if a rescue was even possible. On another page,

Mike listed his available assets along with the names of ideal members to include on his team. Of course, there was himself: an experienced military planner, troop commander, and sharpshooter. Kyle Miller, an accomplished sniper, skilled in precision long-range shooting. Then Sandy Lopez, a jack-of-all-trades, a breaching team leader, a point man, a brilliant military tactician, and an all-around weapons expert. Finally, Deandrea Williams, a combat-tested helicopter pilot and sharpshooter. All seasoned Navy SEAL veterans, each with several hundred combat missions under their belts. They had all been part of the same regular SEAL team, not elite going after the big-name high-value targets, but still, they saw plenty of combat. Close quarters combat. Most importantly, they could trust each other with their lives. But they may need others.

Mike picked up his phone but couldn't make the call. Unsure how to begin or what to say. *This is awkward. How do I phrase this? Only one way to find out.* He called Kyle, who lived alone on a large ranch outside Reno Nevada. It rang several times. Just when he expected it to kick over to voicemail, he answered.

"Hello?"

"Hey, it's Mike. How's it going?"

"Mike. Mike Murphy. Good, doing fine. This is unexpected. What's up, dude?"

"Quite a lot, actually. I left the FBI. I'm now heading up security for a company on the peninsula."

"Wow, that was sudden ... got to say, not a total shocker. Last time we talked; you really didn't seem all too happy."

"I wasn't. You're right. It was time for a change. So, what have you been up to?" asked Mike.

"Let's see, still living on the ranch. Spending my time taking care of the place between programming gigs. I got tired of driving a hundred miles every time I needed to go anywhere, so I got my pilot's license and picked up a small plane. I love it."

"That's impressive."

"Thanks … Okay, Mike, so are you going to tell me why you called?"

Mike chuckled. "Yes. I know this is coming out of the blue, but I need to meet with you, Sandy, and Deandrea."

"Okay … you in trouble?"

"Me, no. But I need help from all of you. It's urgent."

"It's not something you can talk about over the phone?"

"No, Kyle. It has to do with the daughter of my new employer. She's been kidnapped, and they're holding her in Nicaragua. They're going to kill her. The only way to get her out safely is to go in and get her."

"Um, this sounds serious. Not FBI stuff, uh?"

"No. The FBI can't help with this. What I need to say and show you has to be done here in Palo Alto. I realize I'm asking a lot, but can you drop everything and make it here in the next day or two? I wouldn't ask if it weren't life or death."

"Not a problem for me. The other guys coming too?"

"I'll know soon. You're the first I called."

"Sure, dude. After you talk to them, call back and let me know when and where. I'll be there, bro."

"Thanks, Kyle. I really appreciate it."

They hung up. *All right. One down. That wasn't as tough as I thought.* Mike called Sandy next. He lived in Los Angeles with his son Marc. After retiring from the military, he opened his own martial arts studio. Mike told Sandy about leaving the FBI and starting a new job.

"The last time we spoke, if I remember right, you had forty-five students in your club and Marc had plans to join the Navy to become a SEAL after college," said Mike.

"The studio's taken off. We're now over two hundred. Just hired another instructor. Marc's in his last year of high school. He's been accepted into the ROTC program at USC and still has his sights on becoming a SEAL. I'm super proud of him. Nice kid—focused and determined. So, was this call purely social, or is there something going on?"

Mike explained he needed to meet with him along with Kyle and Deandrea. It must be in person; he couldn't talk about it over the phone. Sandy said he would need to make a few arrangements but agreed to come.

The last call went out to Deandrea in Maui. He and his wife Claire just started their own helicopter tour company. He was the only pilot. Mike told him about changing jobs, then followed with his request to meet him along with Sandy and Kyle so he could explain the full situation in person. Deandrea said it would be disruptive for their fledging business but he, too, could come.

Mike called Kyle back to let him know what the others had said, and they both looked forward to seeing each other tomorrow.

He walked into Peter's office. "Three members from my ex-SEAL team will be here in the morning," said Mike. "Could you help arrange access and the 'blow their socks off NAIMERA demo' you mentioned?"

Peter nodded and smiled. "I'll need their contact information. Kim and I have done NAIMERA demos before. We have all the props to put on a good show."

"Thanks. Let's wow them," said Mike.

*

Tuesday morning, Deandrea arrived in San Francisco on a red-eye. Sandy's flight landed shortly after. A limo picked them both up and drove straight to SGSI. Kyle had his own private plane, so Mike met him at Palo Alto Airport. By 10:00 a.m., they were all sitting in Mike's office along with Peter.

"Very nice, Mike," said Kyle.

"SGSI makes military drones, right?" asked Sandy.

"Yes, but much more. Do you guys remember the one we used in Afghanistan?"

"I do. I called it 'the ghost drone,'" said Deandrea. "Send it off, it vanishes, then comes back after completing a successful mission."

"Now, let me explain why I asked you all here," said Mike.

He began with the lengthy background to the kidnapping and how Grace ended up in Nicaragua.

"And after a couple of days, Grace was whisked out of Guatemala to a compound called Base PLVI in Nicaragua. It's run by a criminal cartel that also acts as paramilitary for the government," said Mike.

"The FBI or State Department can't do anything?" asked Sandy.

"No, outside their jurisdiction."

"How about the ransom? What do they want?" asked Deandrea.

"One billion dollars in gold bars," said Peter.

"And that's, what, not enough to let her go?" asked Kyle.

"I wish it were," said Peter.

"Unfortunately, it's not," said Mike. "We learned that they plan to kill her to prevent her from ever testifying against her original abductors in Guatemala."

"Knowing you, Mike, you must already have something in mind," said Kyle. "Let's hear it."

"You know me too well. I have a few thoughts. Since there's a hundred of them, we'll need to even the odds. Just like we did at that compound in Afghanistan. They're the paramilitary and respond to anti-government protests, so I plan to announce a false protest across the country. That way, most of them will be gone. We'll create a few diversions so we can get in and out with Grace quickly. One will take place when the gold arrives. Well, not the gold they expect but a stack of gold-plated and filled bars, good enough to fool them into believing it's real. Certainly, a cause for celebration. Right after that, we shock them with powerful explosions across the compound from drone strikes. Then we pounce on the detention facility, grab Grace, and leave."

"That sounds way too easy," said Sandy, shaking his head. "I've got two comments. One is that compound looks well protected; you better have a few more tricks up your sleeve. The other is, can you really get away safely? I mean, they must have ways to come after you?"

"You're right. I've been thinking about them both. I'll take a trip down there to gather more information about the compound and then design a solid mission plan. As for the exit strategy, I understand they have a military jet, presumably with missiles. Plus, a fleet of high-speed boats they use for pirating. Both would need to be dealt with."

"A military jet! Who the hell are these guys?" asked Deandrea.

"Good question," said Mike. "But we have something extraordinary on our side. Something that will tip the scales. It's the reason I needed you all to come here in person. To meet our secret weapon."

Peter passed out nondisclosure forms to sign. "What you're about to see is secret and must stay that way."

They all signed.

"Here, we had these made for each of you in advance," said Peter as he handed each an access badge.

"Let's head to the NAIMERA Lab," said Peter.

Mike silently smiled. He couldn't wait to see the reactions of his friends to what they were about to encounter. They all walked into a transition security booth. Maggie spoke up.

"Peter, there are three members of your entourage who do not possess the proper security clearances to enter."

Kyle, Sandy, and Deandrea all began to look around the booth. They appeared puzzled.

"I'll vouch for them, Maggie," said Peter.

"Very good."

"Where is Maggie, in another building?" said Deandrea.

Mike softly smiled. "No, she's here in the booth with us, looking through those cameras," said Mike.

Kyle, Sandy, and Deandrea all looked up and spotted the multiple security cameras. They were clearly confused.

A drawer slowly opened. "Mr. Santiago Lopez, Mr. Deandrea Williams, and Mr. Kyle Miller, welcome to Strauss Global Sciences Inc. You are entering a secure area. Please leave your cell phones in the drawer to your left," said Maggie.

They complied—except Kyle. "I didn't bring my cell phone."

"Correction. Please check the bottom right pocket in your cargo pants," said Maggie.

Kyle touched his pants and realized she was right. He put his phone in the drawer while shaking his head in apparent disbelief.

"Access granted," said Maggie. The door in the security booth opened, and they all walked out.

Once inside the NAIMERA Lab, they walked down a hall until they came to a room with a sign above the door: "NAIMERA Development." Kim stepped out and introduced herself.

Peter turned around and addressed the guests. "Gentlemen, inside that room, you'll see the culmination of years of research, innovation, and a great deal of financial investment. I realize you all signed nondisclosures, but I need to insist everything you witness must remain within these walls."

Kyle, Sandy, and Deandrea all verbally agreed.

Kim opened a pouch and grabbed several earpieces. She offered one to everyone. "Here, you'll want to wear one of these. It enables conferencing with the NAIMERAs and anyone else wearing one. This way."

Kyle turned to Deandrea showing a bewildered look and mouthed the words, "NAIMERAs?"

Peter walked up to the entrance. A tinted glass door slid open. They followed him inside, alert and curious.

Unlike Mike's first visit to the NAIMERA Development room, no voices spoke up when they entered. The room setup was different. There were several props, a mound of hay, fake boulders and trees, and a few rows of human dummies.

Peter stepped in front. "You're about to meet our secret weapon, the NAIMERAs. That stands for Naturally and Artificially Intelligent Chimeras. Kim and I have set up a few demonstrations so you can appreciate some of their extraordinary capabilities. They all have undergone extensive combat training. NAIMERAs can be calm and gentle or ruthless killers, switching between the two as the situation requires. Analogous to police or military war dogs, except they determine the level of response without human commands. Kim, would you do the honors?"

Kim stepped forward as Peter stepped off to the side. "NAIMERAs, come greet our guests."

Heads swiveled, scanning the room for a NAIMERA. They were camouflaged in various locations. One by one, they flew over in the form of bats and landed on a large stainless-steel perch near everyone.

Kim waved her arm out as she spoke. "Each NAIMERA has a name. Buttons is the smallest, obviously, here on the left. Next is Marty. Then Baron, and finally, our largest, Trinity. All designed to excel at somewhat different tasks but each very effective. We'll begin by demonstrating their incredible sense of smell. To your left, in that corner is a stack of hay five feet high."

Kim lifted one arm. "Here in my hand is a single strand of hair taken from one of Grace's hairbrushes. Another strand is buried within that stack."

She approached Marty and let him become familiar with the scent. "Okay, Marty. Find the other strand."

Marty leapt up and flew over to the pile of hay, circling several times, his wings collapsed tight to his center, and he dove straight into it like a missile. There was a small sound of movement inside. Marty resurfaced and flew back to the perch grasping a strand of hair in one of his feet. Kim took it and thanked him. Pinching a single strand in each hand, she raised her arms.

After a few seconds of stunned silence everyone followed with a light round of applause.

"That's crazy," said Kyle.

Heads were slowly shaking, not sure if they believed their eyes.

"As you can see, they are capable of finding someone or something through the sky or even underwater, with little problem. Next, I'd like to demonstrate their intellect. Ask them any question or how to speak in any language known to man. Kyle, would you like to start?" asked Kim.

"Sure, anything? I'm a bit of a math enthusiast. Let's see. Trinity, what are the first six Leyland prime numbers?"

She answered without any hesitation, "In order; 17, 593, 32993, 2097593, 8589935681 and 59604644783353249."

"I'd need my math reference book to be sure, but that sounds right," said Kyle.

"Her answer is correct," said Buttons.

"Whoa, they can really talk?" said Kyle.

"No way, how can they do that?" said Sandy.

"Deandrea, would you like to ask anything?" asked Kim.

"Okay. Here's a curve ball for the bat named Marty," he said smiling. "In French, how would you say, 'It's nothing really special.'"

Marty answered, "*Ça ne casse pas trois pattes à un canard.*"

"Wow, now that was good! An idiom," replied Deandrea. "Even the accent was flawless."

Deandrea shook his head in disbelief. Sandy covered his mouth with one hand. Kyle crossed his arms and quietly stared.

"Sandy. What would you like to know?"

"This question is for all of you. Can you find Grace and help to bring her home unharmed?"

All four NAIMERAs spoke at once, "Yes."

"Impressive. I like their self-confidence," said Sandy.

The humans in the room smiled, nodding their heads with approval.

"Let's move on to their offensive capabilities," said Kim.

Set up across the large room were several human ballistic dummies positioned in three rows twenty feet apart. Each row contained three standing dummies holding a weapon.

"Trinity, you take the last row; Baron, the middle; and, Marty, the first. Destroyed the targets. When you're ready, Trinity, you start."

Trinity stood four feet tall off the perch. As she lifted up, everyone was hit with a violent burst of wind. She circled, then swooped down. When she got within thirty feet, from under her wings came a narrow laser beam. It shot out, focused on one dummy to another, and in a blink, their heads tumbled off their shoulders to the ground. She turned back around and fired again, severing their arms. Light smoke lingered over the severed parts. She came around overhead and gently landed back on the large perch.

Deandrea put a hand up and covered his mouth.

Kyle let out a "Holy shit!" without thinking.

Baron and Marty followed, executing their attacks with similar results. When it was over, a chorus of superlatives followed. "Awesome!" "I'm speechless." "Amazing."

Sandy pointed to Buttons. "What can she do?"

It was the perfect lead for the final demonstration. On a stand nearby was a wooden box with a quarter-inch hole drilled to the inside. Otherwise, it was completely sealed. "Buttons, go inside and burn your way out."

Buttons launched her one-inch body up and fluttered over to the outside of the box. As the guests looked on, fascinated, she transformed into the shape of a tiny thin snake and slithered inside. A few seconds later, the box began to smolder, and a chunk of wood the size of a half-dollar dropped and rolled on the floor. Buttons popped out and flew back to her perch.

Deandrea, Sandy, and Kyle couldn't stop staring at the NAIMERAs.

Sandy quietly commented, "If you told me they were from another planet, I'd believe it."

"That about wraps up our demo. Now, NAIMERAs, fly off and camouflage."

They flew off in different directions, landing on fake trees, walls, and rocks. Then, like chameleons, blended perfectly into their surroundings.

A round of applause followed.

"Thank you, Kim," said Peter.

"Yes, thank you from all of us. Very impressive," said Deandrea.

Mike tapped Kim on the shoulder. "I have a favor to ask. I'll stop back later to talk about it."

Kim looked mildly puzzled. "I'll be here."

She stayed with the NAIMERAs while the rest went back to Mike's office for a wrap-up. Peter began by thanking them for coming on such short notice.

"This is incredibly important. My daughter means the world to me, and I will do whatever it takes to bring her back safely. As you consider your decision to join our effort, be assured I understand the disruption and sacrifice this would involve. I promise to make it worth your while. You'll receive five hundred thousand dollars each." Peter took a step back.

Mike stood up. "Guys, I'll be leaving tomorrow for a nine-day trip to gather more information on the compound. When I return, I'll begin to solidify the mission in detail. If I'm convinced it can happen with a high degree of success, we'll move forward. You can tell me now or wait before deciding. Whatever you choose, it won't affect our friendship."

Kyle spoke. "I'm in. Solid. But will only the four of us really be enough?"

"Thanks, Kyle. Will four, do it? I don't know yet. If we need to add more, certainly we will. I can't answer that until I find out exactly what we're dealing with."

Deandrea cleared his throat. "I'd love to say yes now, but I need to get Claire's okay. I'll have an answer when you return. To be clear, what do you see as my role—pilot?"

"Right now, yes. You'd be our air support."

Eyes turned toward Sandy.

"Man, this is tough. I want to say yes, but after losing Gabriela, I'm Marc's only parent, he's my priority. I'll think about it but right now, my answer's no. Sorry," said Sandy.

Mike felt deflated.

"I respect that. If anything changes, let me know," said Mike. "Well, thanks again for coming. I'll be in touch. Now, let's get you guys home."

After Mike returned from dropping Kyle off at his plane, he walked over to the NAIMERA Lab. Kim was working away. She saw Mike walk in.

"You need a favor?" asked Kim.

"Yes, I'm leaving tomorrow on a nine-day trip to Honduras and Nicaragua. I'd like to bring along some of the NAIMERAs to help with reconnaissance. I'm thinking Marty, Buttons, and Baron."

From Kim's expression, she appeared more concerned than surprised. She looked away as if processing the ramifications of the request.

"All right, they can make the trip but I'll have to come along too."

Mike was not expecting that response. He assumed she would show him how to care for them and they would be free to go.

Kim explained NAIMERAs required daily nutritional care and monitoring—Marty, in particular, because he was still developing. She acknowledged she could show him how to do that, but there was another consideration. There was the possibility, to some degree, of emotional trauma Marty and Buttons might experience from being away from their safe home for the first time with a new human in a strange and unfamiliar environment.

"Overall, taking them out is not a problem. In fact, it will be good for their maturity. But we need to take it slowly," said Kim.

Mike paused to think about how this would play out. He sat against a table with his arms folded, remaining quiet for a minute.

"All right, that's not a bad idea. I originally planned to camp out, but there's a hotel nearby. It'll be too risky to have you with me. I'd like you to stay in the room to monitor and record our activity. Could you and the NAIMERAs be ready to leave by tomorrow morning?"

"I'll need to pack and make some arrangements, but, yes, it's not a problem."

"If you're wondering what to wear, the weather should be hot. We won't need visas, but make sure your passport's up to date. Also, it's advisable to get a few vaccines. You may already have some of them. Hepatitis A and B, typhoid, yellow fever, and rabies. I've had them all, but if you need any, stop by medical today."

Kim nodded slightly. "Last year, I went to Ecuador and the Galápagos. I'm good."

Mike stood up, rubbing his eyes. He looked tired. His hair was disheveled. The past week had been mentally exhausting. "Great, I'll make the travel arrangements. Let's plan to meet in the front lobby at 0800."

CHAPTER 30

Tegucigalpa, Honduras

Mike, Kim, Marty, Baron, and Buttons arrived in Tegucigalpa on Peter's private jet and soon found themselves in a rented four-wheel-drive Jeep, looking for a place to have lunch. They stopped at a small café just off the road.

While waiting for their food, Mike searched for Dominique Sánchez. Every attempt came up empty. He remembered she might be using an alias, Nina Perez. He found an "N. Perez" listed under a job search site. That person was a nurse. Dominique was a nurse. It listed an address in Tegucigalpa. He mapped it. Mike dialed the number on the resume, and a woman answered. Mike asked if she was Dominique Sánchez. She began to panic.

"How did you get this number? Who are you?" Nina asked quickly in a serious voice.

"Carlos Reynaldo, the CIA station chief gave me your name. I'm an American, Mike Murphy. Please don't worry."

"Mr. Murphy, your call alarmed me. I was about to hang up and run. And Dominique no longer exists. I am Nina. Nina Perez. What do you want?"

"I'm sorry, Nina. I'd like to talk to you about the PLVI compound."

After a short pause, Nina spoke. "I told Carlos all I knew. What more do you want?"

"The PLVI kidnapped my boss's daughter, they're going to kill her if we don't do something. I could use your help," said Mike.

"I heard rumors the PLVI was holding a new kidnapping victim. Are you absolutely certain you aren't being followed?" said Nina.

"Yes, positive," said Mike.

"All right, I am off work today. It's safer if you come to my house. But you must be careful. They have eyes and ears in places you least expect."

"Thank you, I understand and will be cautious. I have your address. We'll be there in fifteen minutes."

"How did you find me? I never gave my address out to Carlos."

"I found your resume posted online."

"I forgot about that. You can come by now."

The call ended.

Mike had scribbled her address down on a napkin. A minute later, he returned to double-check what he had written against Nina's posted resume. It was gone. She must have just removed it.

*

Mike and Kim arrived at Nina's modest one-room apartment. She opened the door, cautiously scanning the neighborhood as she let them inside. They thanked her for agreeing to meet. As Nina listened, she walked to her two front windows, peered out, and closed the blinds. She turned around and, with a worried look in her eyes, replied, "You're welcome."

They introduced themselves and explained their connections to

Grace. Mike followed with a brief history of the kidnapping. He told her his goal was to assess whether a rescue would be possible.

Nina led them into her kitchen, where they sat down at a small dinette table. Mike pulled out a notepad and pen from his backpack. He watched as Kim carefully placed her specially modified carrying bag next to her, then snuck a peek inside to check on the three NAIMERAs, who all quietly slept. She looked over to him and smiled, signaling they were fine. Nina must have seen two tired-looking faces. Without asking, she set down three cups and poured everyone coffee.

"Thank you," said Kim, smiling. "Exactly what I need. Nina, I'd like to hear a little bit about you," said Kim. "Do you have any children?"

"Yes, I have one child, a daughter. She immigrated to the United States several years ago. I've been an ER nurse for twenty years and now work at a local clinic. I was married. Blue shirts killed my husband. We both were part of an underground movement to stand up to injustice. I'm still involved, organizing anti-government protests. It's dangerous, but I'm safe as long as I can remain hidden."

"I'm curious, Nina, why did you join the anti-government movement in the first place?" asked Mike.

"As an ER nurse, I treated injured protesters. Some I watched die. All so young, it broke my heart. I wanted to help."

"I'm sorry about your husband," said Kim. "It must be difficult."

"Thank you. It is, but his death made me more determined in my struggle." She paused and looked up at a picture of him on the wall. "All right, I'm ready to answer any questions you have."

"Thank you. I'm interested in hearing everything you know about that compound," said Mike.

"Please, go ahead and ask me anything," said Nina.

Mike laid out his list. Wasting no time, he began by asking why they'd allowed her to leave?

"I was very lucky," she answered.

Blue shirts had captured her while she attended an anti-government protest. The same one, she later learned, where her husband died. They took her back to the PLVI compound for interrogation. She told them she was a nurse caring for injured protesters. At first, they didn't believe her. Not long after, one of their soldiers seriously injured himself in a training accident. As the only person available with any medical knowledge, they pulled her in to see what she could do. She stopped the bleeding and saved his life. It was her duty as a nurse, but she hated herself for doing it. Their leader, Sergio Cruz, slowly began to trust her but wouldn't allow her to leave. For the next three months, they allowed her to move about freely but forced her to stay and work as their captive nurse. Repeatedly pleading for her freedom so she could return home to her daughter, they finally relented with a stern warning not to ever again get involved with the anti-government movement. If she did, they promised to track her down and kill her.

Mike unfolded a satellite map of the compound. Nina's memory was vivid. One after another, she identified each structure. She described the organization, its leaders, their habits, the compound, and what it was like being held captive. Everything she could recall observing or hearing while there. Of particular interest to Mike was any information about the detention facility and how well guarded it was. He asked if she knew the schedule of guard patrols and the contents of the armory. The answer was no. As she spoke, Mike began mentally integrating this new information into his rescue plan.

Nina warned attempting to go there was foolish. They patrolled the compound with drones, soldiers, and vicious guard dogs. She suspected the perimeter fences topped with barbed wire contained sensors. She remembered a black cable running along the center.

The conversation shifted to the protest movement. Nina had become the coordinator for the protest movement, sharing communication across social media. Mike asked if she could help post a fake protest. He'd like to observe the PLVI's reaction to an announced protest. Nina knew her posts were monitored, so she embedded secret keywords somewhere in the message to indicate the type of protest.

"We have to keep pressure on the government. It's dangerous, but we think we found a way to do it safely."

"How do you do that?"

"Every protest we announce includes a local weather report. You'll see either 'sunshine,' 'cloudy,' or 'windy' mentioned. This month, 'sunshine' means the protest is real and prolonged. We rarely call for those because they are the most dangerous. The word 'cloudy' means show up, disrupt, and leave right away. The hit-and-run protests are the safest. By the time the blue shirts arrive, we're gone. And 'windy' indicates the protest is a bluff. Over half the protests we post are bluffs, just to frustrate them. Every month, we rotate the words to mean something different. They haven't caught on yet, so it's working."

"Clever!" said Mike. "Nina, I have a request. I'll want to watch PLVI members leave and return as they respond to a bluff protest posting. If I call you in a week, would you do that for me?"

"Certainly, tell me where and when."

"Terrific. I may need you to do it again on January 1st too, if you would?"

"Again, if it helps to free your friend's daughter, I'm happy to do it."

It was time to go. They thanked her for her help and praised her for her bravery. Kim reached out to shake Nina's hand. Nina pushed it aside and hugged her, then Mike.

"Our dream is to rid Nicaragua of oppression and corruption," she said.

They walked out and got into their Jeep. Driving away, Kim spoke while turning her head back at Nina's apartment. "I'm glad I got to meet her. She's such an inspiration."

CHAPTER 31

Chinandega, Nicaragua

Facing poor road conditions and possibly criminal gangs along the way, the long drive to Nicaragua would be safer in the daylight. Mike realized he needed to pick up the pace. After stopping briefly for a few provisions, they were on their way. Because of the remoteness of their destination, the nearest hotel was fifteen miles away from the compound in the small coastal town of Mechapa, Nicaragua.

The five-and-a-half-hour drive from Tegucigalpa, Honduras, along narrow, bumpy country roads was arduous and perilous, demanding Mike's undivided attention. He drove carefully, dodging road hazards while staying alert for roadblocks or booby traps set by bandits. A short stop at the border crossing briefly interrupted their trip. The guard checked their passports, asked where they were heading, and popped his head inside the Jeep. He waved them through.

After driving off, Kim opened her carrying bag and let the NAIMERAs out. Buttons rode inside a leather necklace pouch that Kim wore. The other NAIMERAs stayed in the back seat, captivated by the scenery. Along the way, they called out any wildlife they spotted. It was like having scenic tour guides through a zoological park, making an otherwise boring journey more interesting.

"There, in the trees on the right, three keel-billed Toucans," said Marty.

That got everyone's attention.

"It must be difficult for them to fly with such large beaks," said Kim.

"Not really," said Marty. "The beak's exterior cover is hard keratin, but the interior is a lightweight, spongy hollow bone."

"Really?" said Kim. "That's interesting."

A short time later, Buttons noticed a commotion in a vast open area.

"I see an ocelot. In the field to the left. Chasing something," she said.

Kim swiveled her head but couldn't see anything.

"Armadillo," said Baron.

The cat pounced, but it was hard to tell what happened. They continued and lost sight.

"Hopefully that armadillo found a hole," said Baron.

"Why's that?" asked Mike.

"One of their defences is to roll up and wedge themselves, exposing only their tough, leathery exterior," said Baron. "It would be difficult for an ocelot to extract it."

"Oh, I wish I had seen that. Ocelots are beautiful," said Kim, scanning the horizon.

They continued on with no one saying a word for an extended period.

Kim broke the silence. "I'm curious, Mike, why are you so determined to save Grace when you haven't ever met her?"

Mike tilted his head while pondering that question. It was something he hadn't given much thought to. "Something deep inside,

I imagine. Think it's just my nature. I want to serve. It was one of the motivations that led me to become a SEAL and later to join the FBI. I know I'd feel terrible if I didn't try."

"Why'd you become a SEAL in the first place? There are lots of other ways to serve."

Mike turned momentarily toward Kim. "My father died in 9/11."

"I'm sorry, did he work in the Twin Towers?"

"No, he was a fireman. I remember him as fearless … kind … thoughtful. The perfect dad."

"I have always admired firemen," said Kim. "He must have been a great influence."

"He was. I miss him every day. So, why'd you become a scientist?"

"My mom was a veterinarian and my dad an engineer. They weren't running into danger trying to save people, but they wanted to make the world a better place. I found both of their work fascinating but couldn't choose, so when I came across biomedical engineering, it was a natural fit. Then I met Peter …"

"Seems like you made the right choice. Do you have any siblings?"

"No, I'm it. How about you?"

"One brother and one sister, both in New York."

They went through another lengthy period of silence as they drove through the countryside.

"What do you think the week's going to be like?" asked Kim.

"I expect long periods of boredom, watching the compound, and recording events. Having the NAIMERAs along will make it much easier."

"Boredom? Impossible," said Baron. "This is exciting."

"I concur," said Buttons. "I've been thrilled since we left."

Mike and Kim shared a smile.

"Well, maybe not for them but probably for you," said Mike. "Caring for the NAIMERAs nutritional needs is crucial. But you'll be confined to the hotel room for most of the day, watching satellite video feeds from us, monitoring everything we see."

"Looking out for trouble, I know," said Kim.

"That's right, another vital role," said Mike. "Call out if you see anything suspicious. An extra set of eyes can't hurt."

Mike passed a sign welcoming them to the town of Mechapa.

"Well, here it is …"

He felt a sense of relief, they made it without any trouble. They drove up to the hotel as the sun began to set. Mike checked in. It was a two-bedroom with a kitchenette and a full bath. As he accepted the room key, the desk clerk reminded him that the hotel had a restaurant. When they got to the room, Kim checked the NAIMERAs. The excitement of the trip caused them all to deplete their daily energy pellet. She inserted one in each of their gastrovascular cavities, then Mike and Kim left to have dinner.

When Mike returned to the room, he called Peter to tell him about their trip so far and to check on the status of any potential replacement candidates. One person inquired who served three years in the army, not special forces, and with no combat experience. Another who served in the special forces of Australia called from overseas. He was curious but declined to submit a resume. Mike began to worry. Hopefully, by the time he returned, a couple of viable candidates would turn up. If he couldn't assemble a full team, the mission was definitely in doubt.

Day after day, Mike and the NAIMERAs left before sunrise, drove to the Cosigüina Volcano Natural Reserve, and parked far out of sight beyond the perimeter fence of the compound. The NAIMERAs transmitted video streams of everything they observed. On multiple screens, Mike not only could see but recorded everything on his computer. Within the safety of their hotel room, Kim spent her days monitoring video feeds from both the NAIMERAs and Mike's headset.

In order to get a full unobstructed view of the compound, Mike hid under a camouflage blanket near a row of bushes close to the perimeter fence. Unless you tripped over him, you wouldn't know he was there. Three large vicious dogs wandered freely, chasing anything that caught their attention. They were Kangals, a very dangerous breed. Exerting a force of 750 pounds per square inch, their bites could be devastating. Mike remained downwind so the dogs were not an issue. From dawn to dark, he quietly observed the daily compound activity through his binoculars. One by one he collected details of the items on his list.

Baron and Marty were invaluable. Unnoticed, they moved about the compound freely. That is, unnoticed by the PLVI. On the morning of the second day, Baron and Marty headed out toward the hangar to collect inventory. On the way, high above, Marty caught a glimpse of a high-speed missile heading straight down at them.

"Baron, twelve o'clock coming straight at us!"

Both Mike and Kim listened, alarmed at what they were hearing, but not seeing the danger on their video feeds.

Baron turned his head just in time to see it, a large harpy eagle. It grabbed his back and caused him to twist. Even with enormous talons the size of bear claws exerting several hundred pounds of pressure, it was no match for Baron's exterior. Baron released a sizable electric shock, sending the stunned eagle fleeing while letting out an unusual high-pitched scream.

"Baron, what happened?" asked Kim with concern in her voice.

"Oh, that. An eagle tried to make a meal of me."

"No, are you all right?"

"Yes, barely a scratch."

"But we heard a loud screech—what was that?" asked Mike.

"The eagle was shocked I couldn't join him for lunch."

Mike shook his head, with a half-smile.

Gathering information was a breeze, with one exception, the armory. It remained locked up and sealed without any way to get inside. All through the day, either Marty or Baron waited patiently nearby to capture some video of the interior. It was accessed only twice and never with the doors fully opened. Not knowing their complete weapons stockpile could pose a problem.

An essential part of the mission in January would be to remove any possibility blue shirts could come after the yacht after rescuing Grace. Marty was tasked to visit the PLVI's marina to locate their speedboats. There were six in covered wet docks. He discovered that the marina had security cameras and its own radar tower. Later, Baron entered the hangar to verify the types of planes in their air fleet. There was one military jet, one passenger jet, and four smaller single-engine planes. The SU-57 was the most dangerous. Adjacent to the airfield was another radar tower.

Over time, he got an accurate count of the number of blue shirts, the weapons they carried, and the daily schedule when guards made their rounds. Marty and Baron mapped out the location of every external security camera on the compound.

The perimeter fences were armed with security sensors; they would need to be disabled before attempting to breach the compound during the mission. To test it, Marty flew out to the opposite end of the compound and landed on a sensor to cause it to trigger. The PLVI security team dispatched a surveillance drone to investigate. From that, they learned that drones scouted the perimeter but were only sent out when there was a reported security alert.

Having studied photos of Sergio and his lieutenants, the NAIMERAs watched their movements and could identify them by sight. The week was winding down, but there were still a few critical pieces of information missing. Two of which involved Grace. They had to verify she was being held in the detention facility and to pinpoint her exact cell location. Both were tasked to Marty.

*

Two armed guards approached Grace's cell. It was a daily routine she looked forward to.

"Drop the book and get up," said one guard while unlocking the cell door. Grace complied, happy to walk, stretch, and get some outside air. Her cell was depressing, musty, and not well-lit. They escorted her down the narrow hall and stopped by the door. One guard reached over and toggled a switch. Grace assumed it had to do with security. He did it every day. They then proceeded outside.

Both guards sat in the shade against the wall of the detention facility with guns lying across their laps. "Now go! Go exercise. Stay right here where we can see you."

The smirk made Grace feel uncomfortable, as if the guard was taunting her to run so he'd have an excuse to hurt her. She jogged in a circle, taking deep breaths while looking up at the sky. Perched on a tree limb in the distance was an unusual bird. It looked like a bat. *Bats are definitely not blind. That thing is watching me.* She finished jogging and started doing push-ups. Then more jogging. All while building up a sweat. Wherever she moved, that bat seemed to turn its head to follow. Finally, her time was up, and the guards escorted her back. As they did, she turned her head, and there it was again, staring at her.

*

Marty watched as the guards took Grace back inside. Once a day, she was allowed outside for an hour. Although Marty was able to detect Grace's scent around the area, that observation confirmed she was being held in the detention facility. According to Nina Perez, it contained several holding cells spread throughout the large two-story facility. Knowing her exact cell location would save crucial time when they returned to get her out during the mission.

The complex was under tight, constant surveillance with cameras and guards. Marty flew toward the complex, perfectly blending in with the background. He landed on the door, camouflaged. He turned the handle, the door slowly cracked open, and went unnoticed by the guards sitting nearby. As he crept through the doorway, an alarm went off. His body triggered a sensor. A dog began barking. One guard jumped up. Noticing the door had opened, he grabbed his gun and rushed over. Before he and the dog arrived, Marty was gone.

Marty pondered his options while resting on a tree limb. Something small moved and caught his attention. He focused in and saw mice scurrying around the facility, then watched as they hopped up and squeezed through a tiny hole in the wall. Even with his ability to reshape his body, he couldn't make it through something that small. It gave him an idea. Marty flew off and returned with Buttons on his back.

*

Marty explained how she could get inside and what to do. In the form of a bumblebee bat, Buttons took off. Battered by gusty winds, she finally arrived outside the detention facility. There was the small hole in the wall. She flattened and reshaped in the form of a mouse, then used her tiny feet to propel her way through.

There were two guards nearby, both preoccupied reading. A guard dog slept by their feet. She transformed back into a one-inch bat and flew up. The dog must have detected her scent. It began barking and growling in her direction. Exposed, she landed immediately and attached to the wall. While not making a move, she camouflaged herself, blending in perfectly with the bricks under her. A guard stood up, the dog pulled the leash towards Buttons, continuing its manic bark. The guard looked but saw nothing. He gazed down at the dog, annoyed.

"Have you lost your mind?" he said to the dog as he pulled it back toward his desk.

With their backs turned, Buttons quietly took off. She flew around inside the facility until she found Grace's cell and landed on a bar.

"Grace," said Buttons in a soft, squeaky-voice.

Grace looked around, not seeing anything.

"Grace, it's me. Buttons."

Grace's mouth opened in shock. "Buttons! Oh my god! How did you find me?"

"I can't stay long. I needed to find you so we can come back later and get you out. We're all here. Marty, Baron, Kim, and Mike."

"Mike?" said Grace, confused.

"Don't worry, you'll meet him when we return."

Luis walked into the detention facility carrying the daily newspaper. He nodded to the guards as he walked past.

Buttons saw him coming. "I have to go, but we'll be back for you in a few weeks." Buttons flew off, but she caught Luis's attention.

"Did you see the size of that flying cockroach?" he said.

The guards looked over, but by then, she was gone.

"I hate cockroaches!" said Luis.

She landed against the wall high above the hole, camouflaged herself, then inched her way down. The guard dog again must have detected her scent and went wild. This time, the guard held its leash tight and scolded the dog.

Luis turned around. "What's going on?"

"I don't know, maybe he saw that cockroach," answered one of the guards.

With Luis and the guards distracted, Buttons transformed into the body of a mouse and squeezed through, back outside. As she dropped to the ground, a hungry rat waited only a few feet away. There was no time to transform into a bat and fly off. Wasting little time, it charged. Buttons' reflexes took over. She fired her tiny but potent laser. It caught the rat squarely on the nose. The heat burned off all its whiskers from the left side of its face as the rat's head recoiled. It sprang up into the air, arching its spine as whiskers floated to the ground. It landed and bolted off. She reshaped into a bat and flew back to Marty, landing on his back, hanging tight around his neck.

"Are you okay, Buttons?"

"Yes. Grace's cell is on the first floor in the southwest corner, there's two guards with a large, vicious dog."

*

Luis opened the cell door and tossed the rolled-up newspaper hard at Grace, hitting her in the arm. "Hold it up and smile for the camera," said Luis sarcastically.

Buttons' visit had filled Grace with hope and a renewed will to resist. She'd had enough of Luis's daily rude behavior. Grace displayed the front page and showed a huge happy smile. "Luis, you're the asshole of the world," said Grace in Spanish.

Luis almost dropped his cell phone. His eyes shot an angry, mean look back at her. "I look forward to killing you when this is all over," said Luis.

She ignored his threat. "I saw the way Sergio looked at you. He thinks you're an idiot. Everyone does," said Grace, smiling calmly.

Luis was fuming. "Oh, you are dead. Just wait." He turned around and walked out clenching a fist.

*

On Saturday, the day before their scheduled departure, Mike contacted Nina Perez and requested she post a bluff protest to occur at 1500 in a town one hundred miles south. He would need that information to create a window of time to execute an attack on the compound. Within fifteen minutes, three-quarters of the blue shirts drove off, forming a caravan of SUVs. He made note of the time they left and how far they had to drive. His last task was to record when they all returned after discovering that no protesters showed up.

Through a narrow opening under his camo blanket, he kept watch on the compound with his goggles as twilight set in. One by one the SUVs returned. Marty and Baron monitored the far end of the compound in case the SUVs arrived out of Mike's sight. They sat, perched above the armory.

The breeze coming in off the ocean shifted, and the wind suddenly picked up, causing the camo blanket concealing Mike to lift and flap from behind. Mike realized he was no longer downwind of the compound. Within seconds, three of the dogs caught his scent and bolted for the perimeter fence, barking and growling.

*

Marty noticed a sentry looking towards the barking dogs. He lifted a transmitter and spoke to someone. Marty intercepted the conversation; the sentry requested a security drone. A minute later a drone darted off. Marty followed in hot pursuit. Baron stayed, watching for the return of the remaining SUVs. Marty realized it was heading toward Mike. He broadcasted a warning to Mike. Kim monitored the events with heightened concern. Within seconds, the drone paused and hovered thirty feet to Mike's side. Mike looked up but said he couldn't see anything. Suddenly, the drone began a slow zig-zag pattern, moving in his direction, scanning the area with a thermal imaging camera.

Kim could see this unfolding from Marty's monitor. "Marty, can you stop it?" she asked frantically. Marty was already following close behind. Within seconds he swooped down, paused directly overhead, and fried the drones control unit with his laser. It tumbled, lost elevation, and landed nearby in dense bushes.

"Thank you, Marty. You got it!" she said. "That was scary."

*

Mike was still focused on the compound but called out to Marty and Baron to head back. All the SUVs had returned. Dogs continued to bark but were no threat behind the fence. Mike heard the commotion about the drone and assumed the trouble had passed. He paused, rubbed his eyes, and turned his head back toward the compound for one last look, still lying flat.

"I've about seen enough," he said while pulling the camo blanket from over his back, preparing to stand. "Time to wrap it up, everyone."

His earpiece popped out and landed on the ground.

*

Marty returned and sat perched on a branch near Mike. He intercepted a radio transmission: "Tito, did you find the drone?" *Who is Tito?*

Baron announced he was on his way. Suddenly, something startled Marty, causing him to launch up and hover. The bushes nearby were rustling. A guard emerged holding a machete. Mike found his earpiece and started to blow off the sand before putting it back on.

Marty tried to alert Mike. "A blue shirt is coming at you, Mike!"

201

"Mike! Look out!" called Kim. "Marty, help him!"

Mike sensed movement behind him but had no time to react. The guard kicked Mike hard in the side. Mike recoiled in pain. The machete came down. Mike stopped its full force with his binoculars but still caught a glancing blow of the blade on his upper right arm. The guard lifted his machete for the fatal blow over a defenceless Mike.

Marty approached as fast as he could while realizing this guard is Tito. In the exact voice that transmitted the message, Marty called out in Spanish, "Tito! Stop, he's one of our guys!" Tito paused to look around. Marty hovered directly above and behind Tito, and using every last ounce of power, he fired.

In an instant, Tito's head sizzled and exploded under the unrelenting intense heat. His body twirled like a puppet cut from its strings. The machete dropped from his hands as he hit the ground in a thud.

*

Mike's arm was bleeding but not badly. He grabbed the wound with his other hand and applied pressure. It slowed. He pulled out a bandanna, wrapped it around his arm and tied it. Mike picked up his earpiece and slipped it back in.

"Are you okay, Mike?" asked a frantic Kim.

"Yes, it's nothing, but we need to get out of here before they come looking for that guard."

The dogs went berserk, ferociously barking and growling, creating ear-piercing sounds that wouldn't let up. That noise drew everyone's attention. The returning blue shirts knew something was definitely wrong. They scrambled to investigate.

Mike slowly stood up, gathered everything, rushed back to the Jeep, and jumped in. There was a sharp constant pain in his side. Marty and Baron flew in, landing in the back seat. The entire time, Buttons remained in the leather necklace pouch around Mike's neck. He backed away and drove carefully, trying to stay on the narrow single-lane dirt path with lights off. From the rear mirror, he could see a couple dozen flashlights scanning the area. They'd left just in time.

*

Forty-five minutes later, they were back at the hotel. Kim stood outside, anxiously waiting as they arrived.

"Tell me what hurts."

"My ribs. The cut is nothing."

"Ribs? We need to have them checked out, and you might need stitches," said Kim looking closely at his bloody arm. "There's a twenty-four-hour clinic not far away."

Mike was a mess: dusty and dotted in blood. Sensing no dire urgency, he washed up. The slightest movements, even taking a breath, caused him to wince in pain.

An hour later, they were checking out of the small clinic. Mike's wound only required butterfly bandages. His ribs hurt but since he didn't have shortness of breath, nor was he coughing up blood, they were probably just bruised. The nurse gave him pain medication, advised keeping it iced for a couple days and recommended he have a CT scan when he returned home.

The next morning, the shaken and exhausted group checked out of their hotel and drove to Tegucigalpa to catch their plane back home.

CHAPTER 32

Palo Alto, California

Mike, Kim, and the three NAIMERAs were finally home. The long flight was calm and quiet, exactly what they all needed after an exhausting ordeal. Mike felt pain with every breath around his badly bruised ribs. He recalled breaking them during a struggle with a terrorist in Afghanistan. *I hope I didn't crack any. This feels the same and it takes weeks to heal.*

They arrived at SGSI, left their luggage in the lobby, then headed directly to the NAIMERA lab. Buttons, Marty, and Baron retreated into their enclosures and almost immediately fell asleep.

Peter walked in, saw Mike's arm bandaged, and noticed how carefully he moved. "What happened to you?" asked Peter.

"I'll get to that. First, I'd like to tell you about our trip."

"Okay, so how did it go?" asked Peter.

"We met with Nina Perez, who was a great resource." Mike winced in pain between each breath.

"You need to have that looked at," said Peter, staring at Mike's left side.

"I will. Right after this. Anyway, we spent the next week closely surveilling the compound and gathering almost all the information we need to execute the rescue mission."

"You couldn't get everything?" asked Peter.

"No. The doors to the armory were kept closed most of the time. I'd feel more confident if I knew all the weapons they have. But I think we have enough to move forward. That is, providing we find more team members. Which reminds me, I want to call Deandrea and Sandy to see if one or both are in. We'll definitely need five."

Peter interrupted briefly and said he'd been monitoring the posting replies. There were several interested candidates.

"Great. I'll check them out."

Mike turned to Kim. "I never thanked you for taking me to the clinic. You were awesome."

"You're welcome," said Kim, followed with a half-smile.

Peter showed an inquisitive facial expression, asking for more clarity on that last comment.

"One of the security guards stumbled upon me as I was about to leave," said Mike. "Marty took over and performed laser brain surgery on the unlucky devil."

"So that's why you moving so gingerly," said Peter.

"Yes, I've an appointment in an hour for a CT scan," said Mike, while glancing down momentarily at the calendar on his phone.

Kim looked surprised.

"I made it on the way back from the airport."

Peter turned back to Kim. "So other than Mike almost getting killed, it was a success, right?"

"I think so," said Kim. "This was their first exposure to real combat. We should have them evaluated."

"Yes, good suggestion," said Peter. "It might reveal something."

"Evaluated?" asked Mike.

"Exactly," replied Peter. "Our staff psychologist, Dr. Otis, has been working with the NAIMERAs throughout their development. He's made sure they're mentally prepared for the demands of combat. They must always show the proper judgement and know when to draw lines. They can be killers, as you saw. He'll need to have a talk with all three."

Mike got up slowly, wincing. "Excuse me, doctor's appointment," he said. Turning to Peter, he said, "I'll give you a full debriefing and team member updates when I get back."

*

Mike's checkup went better than expected. There were no signs of infection, only superficial damage, and they applied fresh dressings. His CT scan revealed no broken or fractured ribs. They were badly bruised but should recover in three weeks. Continuing taking pain medication would help. Hearing that news lifted his spirits.

Mike returned to his office later that afternoon. He crossed his fingers and called Deandrea.

"Hello, Deandrea."

"Hi, Mike."

"I just got back. What's the verdict?"

"Convincing Claire was a hard sell. She assumed I was done with combat. Plus, we have a rather fledging helicopter tour business with bills to pay. I'm the only pilot. The five hundred K sure helped. I'm in."

"Terrific. I've got to cut this short. I need to make one more call. I'll be in touch."

Mike called Sandy. He and his son Marc had just sat down to eat.

"Hi, Sandy, I'm back. What have you decided to do?"

"I'm sorry, Mike, but I've still got to say no."

"Yeah, I understand. No hard feelings. But you will be missed."

They hung up.

*

"Dad, what was Mike talking about? Why are you sorry?"

Sandy explained the situation; Grace's kidnapping by the treacherous PLVI who intend to kill her. The planned assault on the compound, culminating in a hopeful rescue. Then there was a one-month commitment away. Marc was jumping with excitement inside. He planned to follow in his father's footsteps and become a SEAL after he finished college. He couldn't help himself. He said he would love to be part of it.

"Do it, Dad."

"I can't take on something like that, son. If anything happened to me, you'd be alone."

"Yes, but didn't you take risks like that every day when you were a SEAL?"

"That's right," said Sandy. "That was my job. More importantly, it was back when your mother was still alive."

Marc looked down while he sat listening. He raised his head slowly, staring into his father's eyes. "Dad, I will always have you, like I always have Mom. She's with me every second of every day. You don't have to worry about me. I'm leaving for college this fall. Then the Navy. You should do the right thing. Support your friends and save the woman. I know you'll come back, and I'll be all right. Really, I will."

Sandy crossed his arms, impressed with the emotional maturity of his son. The answer was still an emphatic "No."

*

Now that Mike knew who was and wasn't on the team, he needed to find two other team members, then solidify the mission plan. He wanted to bring Peter up to date. When he tapped on his door, Kim and Peter were sitting in front of his computer monitor.

"Have a seat, Mike," said Peter. "You should see this. Dr. Otis interviewed Marty, Baron, and Buttons while you were gone."

Mike pulled up a chair. Peter pressed the replay icon.

The doctor's voice was slow, clear, and calm, speaking in a gentle, reassuring tone. He acknowledged they all recently experienced traumatic events and asked if they'd like to talk about it.

"I would. I killed a human," said Marty. "It was my only option to save Mike's life."

"Do you have any regrets?" asked Dr. Otis.

"Yes. Not for what I did but for how long it took me to respond," replied Marty. "I hesitated to turn the switch on. I should have acted before that PLVI blue shirt attacked Mike."

Peter hit Pause and turned to Mike. "As an ex-SEAL, you can relate to this. Dr. Otis worked with the NAIMERAs to help them learn to toggle between normal and killer modes. He calls it turning the switch on and off. If they're unable to perform that properly, they're not well suited for combat." Peter turned back and hit Play.

Dr. Otis reminded Marty, Baron, and Buttons they all passed extensive psychological and moral screening. Their thought and decision-making processes had been thoroughly vetted.

"Deciding when and to what extent you need to turn the switch on and off may be the most difficult part of your combat development. This, of course, applies to all of you. Marty, your initial response was guided by your amygdala, followed immediately by the more calculated assessment of the situation made in your cerebral cortex. As you experience more and more similar situations, your reaction time should gradually decrease. However, I need to stress; you can trust yourselves to make the right choices. We believe in you. Believe in yourself."

Dr. Otis asked Baron if there was anything he'd like to discuss.

"No, Dr. Otis. What you said was helpful."

Dr. Otis turned and looked down at Buttons. "Buttons, do you have anything on your mind?"

"Yes. They detected my presence once I entered the detention facility. I instantly camouflaged. When I tried to leave, I was almost eaten by a rat, but I reacted quickly, using my laser. My defences worked and my reaction was immediate and decisive. You have prepared me well. Thank you."

"Why, you are quite welcome, Buttons. Thank you for the kind, thoughtful words."

Baron, Buttons, and Marty seemed to feel better. Dr. Otis reminded them to contact him any time of day if they had unresolved issues. The session ended.

Peter turned to Kim and nodded. "I think they'll be all right."

She agreed. "We should be proud of them."

Mike was on a roll. *This day keeps getting better and better.*

Kim stood up and said she needed to check on some things.

Mike asked Peter if this was a good time to meet. It was, and with that, Mike opened his backpack and laid out maps and notes. He gave a full account of his visit with Nina Perez. The knowledge she shared was a great help. Mike moved on to cover every detail he observed of the compound and the PLVI. Mike left the bad news for last: Sandy wouldn't be joining them.

Peter asked Mike what was next, assuming he could fill the final spots on the team.

"We're heading off to Kyle's ranch for two weeks of mission training," said Mike. "I'll need to get a few things from your weapons closet."

"What exactly do you want?" asked Peter.

"Assault rifles, ammunition, an attack drone, six missiles, and one dozen RPGs, all with dummy warheads," said Mike.

"Not a problem, I'll have them for you tomorrow. What about the NAIMERAs, will you bring them along?"

"That's a tough one. We'd better not. It's been so long I'm afraid we're all pretty rusty. We'll need to focus on our own development. Having them there might be a distraction. Plus, the NAIMERAs are clearly battle ready. I only need to tell them the mission plan. I'm sure they'd have no trouble executing. Now, I really need to find two more people. And soon!"

Mike's job posting drew applicants from six possible candidates to fill the team's two vacant positions. Peter handed Mike a small stack of resumes. Mike said he'd look them over and conduct phone interviews tomorrow. He'd had a long tiring day. It was time to head home to get some rest.

*

Mike returned home exhausted but couldn't settle down. He was anxious to peek at the resumes. Unfortunately, he had left them in his office. Restless, at 2100, he left his apartment and drove back in to work. He read over the resumes. Some seemed a little inflated, boasting of things Mike needed to verify. The place was quiet and everyone had gone home, except one who never left. Mike acted on a hunch.

"Maggie, can you hear me?" he said.

"Good evening, Mike," she replied.

She processed his access into the building, but Mike hadn't been sure she could monitor conversations everyplace. *Apparently, she can. Good to know.*

"Maggie, if I give you the name and address of someone, can you run a background check on them?" asked Mike.

"Yes," replied Maggie. "Quite extensively."

One by one, Mike provided Maggie with the names on each resume. And one by one, he laid them on the rejection pile. One had a current restraining order placed against him. Two had serious financial debt. Most lied about their education and work history. Two fired from jobs not listed. Within twenty minutes he pushed the stack aside. Leaving the last one. A female.

"Maggie, her resume looks impressive. Special Ops, silver star. Expert marksmen. Tell me about Ms. Anne Foster."

"I find nothing negative. Everything she provided is accurate," said Maggie.

"Thank you. That's all," said a now more hopeful Mike.

"You're welcome, Mike."

Mike looked down at the resume, then checked the time. *She lives in Texas. Too late now. I'll give her a call tomorrow. But we still need one more.*

Mike was running out of time to fill the vacancies on the team before their two-week mission training would begin at Kyle's ranch. It required a full team, period. He drove back home feeling cautiously optimistic about Anne. That helped him sleep a little easier.

The first thing in the morning, Mike called Anne.

"Hello, is this Anne Foster?"

"Yes, and who are you?"

"Mike Murphy. You applied for a spot on our mission. I'm looking at your resume. Very impressive."

"Thank you. It represents lots of sacrifice and hard work."

"I understand. I was a Navy SEAL."

"So, can you tell me what this 'mission' is about?" she asked.

"Not in any detail until you get here," said Mike. "I can disclose we plan to rescue a kidnapping victim," said Mike.

"Not where, when, or anything?" asked Anne.

"Unfortunately, not until you get here. I can't risk word of this getting out. I need to say things are moving fast. We have a two-week training mission that's about to start. Your participation will be your interview. If you're a good fit, you're hired. After that, it's a week of travel, then the mission. You won't get back home till after the new year. Are you interested?"

"Yeah, I'm out of work. When were you thinking?"

"Now."

"Now, as in right now?"

"Yes, you'll need to fly out and be here by tomorrow morning."

"Damn, uh … sure, what the hell? What about compensation?"

"Five hundred thousand."

"I'm packing."

"Great. Let me know when you'll arrive in San Francisco, and I'll pick you up."

Mike hung up. *She might work out.* He called Kyle.

"Kyle, I should let you know where things stand with team members. I found a candidate. She'll be part of the mission training. Can you give her a room?"

"Yeah, no problem. What do you know about her?"

"Name's Anne Foster, served in Afghanistan and Iraq, army Special Ops. Sniper. You have something in common. My impression is she's tough as nails. Could be a good fit. But we still absolutely need one more, and I can't find anyone suitable to fill the last slot. If I had more time, I'm sure I could, but I don't."

"Christ, no one else? That's hard to believe. You'd think with all the ex-Special Ops guys coming home, someone would jump at this."

"Nothing but duds. At least from the ones who applied."

"Hold on. Remember Drake Connors from Afghanistan? The guy was fearless and a decent soldier."

"Yeah, his name sounds familiar; what happened to him?"

"He was caught with drugs and discharged. I stay in contact with him. He's been to my ranch. I host veteran groups from time to time. I have a real soft spot for the troubled and disadvantaged."

"Crap. Drugs?"

"Yeah, but I'd like to give him a chance. He's living in San Francisco. Let me ping him and see if he'd be interested, if it's okay?"

"I don't know. Is he clean?"

"When he was here, I didn't notice anything. But of course, I wasn't really looking. If he's willing to try, I'll keep an eye on him. Can't hurt to check him out."

"We are running out of options. If he's interested, give him my number. Tell him we leave in the morning, so he needs to decide soon. Regardless, I'll see you tomorrow."

Later that day, Drake called Mike. It went well. He assured Mike the drug incident in Afghanistan was a mistake and behind him. Mike invited Drake to join them at Kyle's ranch. He'd rely on Kyle to watch him, and if he made it through mission training without any issues, he was in.

Mike called Kyle to thank him for his suggestion. Deandrea and Anne would arrive in the morning. He asked Kyle not to mention the NAIMERAs to the new members until they signed NDA's.

*

Before pressing ahead, Mike called one last meeting with Kim and Peter. Peter said the attack drone, training missiles, RPGs with inert ordnance, and assault rifles with live rounds were ready.

Mike was happy to report they found a combat-experienced Special Ops candidate, Anne Foster. "With Maggie's help, she checked out. Also, Kyle found one other, a former SEAL, who can fill the final spot. We have concerns because of Drake's rocky drug past, but we'll have two weeks to closely evaluate him. If both work out, they'll move forward with the rescue." Mike began to feel confident.

"I didn't realize women were allowed in combat," said Kim.

"That was the case officially until 2013. Special Ops opened up to women in 2015," said Mike. "Oh, yes, there's a little issue with the NAIMERAs. Drake and Anne aren't trusted, at least until they're evaluated and of course, have signed the NDA."

They all agreed details of the NAIMERAs must be carefully guarded.

"I need to tell them something because the NAIMERAs are a huge part of our mission," said Mike.

"Understood," said Peter. "Let them know we have a secret weapon, describe them in terms of their capabilities, and have them sign an NDA. I have a short NAIMERA demo video you can take along. If they sign the NDA, then it's okay to let them watch it. If they join the mission, they'll definitely meet them."

"Sounds good," said Mike. "All right, the next time I'll see you both, it will be at the port in San Diego."

Peter's administrator arranged to rent an extra-large quad-slide motorhome. It was the perfect size for everyone, plus two weeks' worth of provisions and their equipment.

*

The following morning, Deandrea arrived from Hawaii. Mike met him at the terminal. While they waited for Anne's plane, Mike brought Deandrea up to date and cautioned him not to mention the NAIMERAs to Drake or Anne. They waited by the terminal as her plane disembarked. One after another, passengers walked past. Mike held a picture.

"That's her?" asked Deandrea.

"Yes, the only picture I found of Anne on the web."

"In combat gear, with a helmet, and camouflage face paint, it's pretty hard to tell what she looks like."

A stout woman, about five foot ten, carrying a bag around her shoulder, marched out. She looked intimidating.

"Anne Foster?" asked Mike.

"That's me. You must be Mike. Who's this?"

"Deandrea Williams," said Deandrea while extending a hand. "Nice to meet you."

"Likewise."

They all shook hands and walked toward baggage claim, exchanging small talk along the way. Anne grabbed her military duffle bag off the baggage carousel like it was filled with pillows, flung it over her shoulder, and they headed off.

Mike and Deandrea looked at each other, impressed.

When they arrived at SGSI, Drake was still not there. Then a car pulled up in the guest parking lot and dropped Drake off. Mike walked over to greet him. After a brief introduction to Anne and Deandrea they finished loading bags and were off. Mike drove but asked Anne and Drake to sit up front.

"Anne, I see you served in an army Special Ops unit," said Mike.

"That's right," said Anne. "I was stationed out of Fort Bragg. Had two tours in Iraq, two in Afghanistan."

"Tell me about your training."

"After a few months of the basic stuff, went on to fifty-three weeks of SFQC."

"What's that?" asked Drake.

"Special Forces Qualification Course," said Anne. "It consisted of six phases, like small-unit tactics, combat marksmanship, language and culture, special forces tactics, and so on. I'm sure you guys went through much of the same."

"What did you do?" asked Mike.

"Initially, tagged along on the front line and interviewed Iraqi women when we entered their homes."

"You speak Iraqi Arabic?" asked Mike.

"Yeah. Enough to get by," said Anne.

"What else did you do?" asked Mike.

"I really wanted to be a sniper. They finally let me do that," said Anne. "I grew up in Texas with four brothers. Dad made sure we were all comfortable around guns. I love 'em."

"Kyle was a sniper. I'm sure you'll have lots to talk about," said Mike. "I'd like you and Kyle to direct our rifle training."

"No problem. So, when are you going to tell me about this mission?"

Mike took a deep breath. "Okay. It's a compound in Nicaragua that's heavily guarded and run by a paramilitary crime organization called PLVI. They're called blue shirts. They kidnapped the daughter of the CEO I work for."

"PLVI? Never heard of them," said Drake.

"I'll lay everything out in detail," said Mike.

"Good. Can't wait. I want to know numbers, weapons, and the skill level of these blue shirt folks," said Anne.

"Drake, I never had a chance to get to know you when you were a SEAL. What were your specialties?" asked Mike.

"Breaching and weapons expert," said Drake.

"We all could use a tutorial on RPGs. Would you be up for that?" said Mike.

"Sure. They are all inert, right?" said Drake.

"Definitely," said Mike with a puff of laughter. "Don't want to blow up Kyle's ranch."

"Deandrea, what's your part in all of this?" asked Anne, turning her head back.

"Copter pilot, right, Mike?"

"Yes, plus loading and launching the drones. Which reminds me. There are some drone manuals in my backpack. You might want to start reading up on them."

Later that afternoon, they arrived at the ranch. The reality of what they were preparing for would soon begin to sink in.

CHAPTER 33

Nye County, Nevada

If anyone thought the next two weeks would be easy, they soon discovered how wrong they were. The mission would require some sprinting across the PLVI compound while carrying combat equipment. Although they all had been through rigorous military training, that was years ago. Every day began the same: they'd start with a five-mile run, then a light breakfast, push-ups, followed by a dozen fifty-yard sprints.

A tired-looking Deandrea walked over to Mike. "Is it really necessary that I take part in all the exercises? I thought my role was to pilot the copter?"

"Yes, and yes," said Mike. "You're our pilot, but you need to be ready to fill in if we need you for something unexpected."

Deandrea and Mike continued to walk together toward the house.

"Okay, not a problem. Claire's been after me to lose a few pounds."

"All right, everyone inside," said Mike.

The next phase moved indoors. "We'll spend the rest of the day walking through my straw-man mission plan. But first, I need you two to complete some paperwork," said Mike as he handed Anne and Drake each a document.

"We're bringing along a secret weapon or two. Please read this over and sign. They're nondisclosure agreements."

Both carefully read the documents, then signed. Mike collected them and put them aside.

"Good, now that we've got that out of the way, let's move on."

"Hold on," said Anne. "I want to hear about our 'secret weapons.'"

Mike smiled. "I'm jumping a little ahead of myself, but since you both signed the NDA, I can tell you a little. They're called NAIMERAs. For now, just think of them as small creatures capable of extraordinary things; living attack drones. In two weeks, after you make it through training, you'll meet them."

"Fair enough," said Anne.

"Everyone, gather around. I'll lay out our goals, what we're faced with, and my strategy. I want this to be a lively brainstorming session. I'd like to hear your unfiltered thoughts," said Mike while starting up a combat simulator program on his laptop. It came up with a satellite image of the area around the PLVI compound.

Mike gave them a brief history of the kidnapping and PLVI. They studied the compound in detail. For each structure, he covered its function, access points, security, and contents. He discussed the compound's overall security, including the guard dogs, drones, security camera system, fence sensors, radar, and sentries.

"Before we can enter the compound, all those will need to be neutralized; the radar taken out first. Otherwise, they'll see us flying in."

"Excuse me," said Drake. "Look, I don't want to put a damper on your plans, but there's a lot of gaps here. I mean, for one, how are you going to disable all the security cameras? You can't do that with boots on the ground; they're too spread out. Do we have surveillance drones? If not, how are you going to know what's going on? These guys aren't going to just sit on their hands while this is happening. This sounds more like a suicide mission."

"Sure, if it were just us, we couldn't do it. The NAIMERAs will take care all of that."

"He's right," said Kyle. "They're freaking amazing."

"What the hell are these things?" asked Anne.

"I can tell you what I know," said Mike. "They vary in size, the smallest is one inch, the largest about four feet. But they can reshape into practically any form. They are living creatures that can talk. Speak any language known to man and communicate electronically or verbally up close. They can fly, walk, slither—whatever. They can produce deadly electric shocks or shoot a powerful laser. I'm sure there's more I'm leaving out."

Anne turned to Drake with a skeptical look, then back to Mike. "You're pulling my leg."

"No. Watch this." From his laptop, Mike fired up the short demonstration video Peter gave him. It showed the NAMIERAs doing many of the things Mike mentioned. When it finished, Kyle and Deandrea spoke up and confirmed it was all real.

"Yeah, but I need to see these things for myself," said Anne.

"Me too," said Drake.

"You will," said Mike, as he looked up at the clock. "All right, let's break for lunch, back here in two hours."

After lunch, Anne, Deandrea, and Kyle dozed off while sitting on the sofa in front of the fireplace. Mike sat sipping a strong cup of coffee while quietly reviewing his afternoon training goals. Drake left for a walk around the ranch. Mike was jarred from his work by the chime of an arriving text message.

It was Sandy. *How's everything going?*

Mike replied, *Just started mission training at Kyle's ranch with two new members. Both working out. So far, so good.*

Sandy fired back, *Great, keep me posted. Thinking about you guys.*

Mike replied with a thumbs-up emoji.

The next evolution of their training moved on to weapons. Kyle walked everyone out to his target range where he practiced. He was an accomplished sniper in the service. He set up a tripod for his rifle, a McMillan TAC-338.

Kyle pointed down the range. An expansive stretch of desert. His targets were paper plates on wooden posts laid out in a pattern, with the first one three hundred yards out. The next one three hundred yards farther but five yards to the right, and so on, up to fifteen hundred yards.

He offered his rifle to Mike and asked if he'd like to give it a try. Mike was not an expert sniper but pretty good with a gun. He aimed for the three-hundred-yard target. The first bullet missed completely. Then the second. The targets were small, nevertheless, Mike felt frustrated. "I at least should hit the frigging thing!" in his words. The third attempt nicked the upper left edge of the paper-plate target.

"Mike. Let me help you," said Kyle while taking the gun from his friend.

Kyle had installed his own weather station. He pulled out his cell phone and checked the wind, temperature, and humidity. He knew the elevation and distance. Kyle explained that you needed to consider the environment when assessing long-range shots. But fundamentally, at three hundred yards, from what he could see, Mike's mechanics were off. Kyle held the gun and demonstrated without firing.

"Listen up, this will help you too," said Kyle. "As you prepare to fire, take a few long deep breaths. Exhale slowly. Count down—three, two, one, then fire. Your body is much more stable at that point. Finally, gently squeeze but maintain steady pressure. No jerking the trigger.

"The air is cold, which produces more drag, so the bullet will drop more quickly. But the targets are at a high elevation, which offsets some of that. In Nicaragua, it'll be warm and at sea level, so you'll need to keep that in mind. After the first shot, assess how it recoiled. It should have come straight back. If not, your aim is off. The barrel has a right-hand twist inside. That has the effect of producing a slight drifting to the right, called spin drift. However, from three hundred yards away, it's not much of an issue but would be with longer shots."

Kyle handed the gun back to Mike and said, "Try it again, Mike."

Mike took Kyle's advice, and this time, he hit three out of three targets. He looked at it with binoculars. "No bull's-eyes, but not bad," said a more content Mike. He handed the rifle back.

Each target had a one-inch radius in the center. Kyle considered anything outside the middle a miss. He set up carefully, settling on his parameters and fired. One. Two. Three.

Mike watched with binoculars. "I think you only hit it once," said Mike.

Kyle laughed lightly. "I hit it one on top of the other. It only needed one hole," said Kyle.

Mike looked again more carefully. Everyone took turns viewing it with the binoculars. They were impressed.

"Anne, you were a sniper. Here you go," said Kyle as he handed his rifle to her.

"The TAC-338 is a fine piece," she said as she handled it. "But I wish I had my M82A1 with me."

"M82s are nice. You could blow a hole in a tank at close range," said Kyle.

Anne nodded in agreement while she set her sights on the three-hundred-yard target. She went through the targeting assessment carefully. She spoke as she prepared to shoot, "I may need a few rounds to warm up. I'm not used to this one."

She fired three shots a few seconds apart. Mike lifted his binoculars and focused.

"I think you're warmed up. All three either went through Kyle's hole or missed completely," said Mike, shaking his head. Anne gave Mike a side-eye, adding a slight smirk.

"Clearly, you and Kyle mastered this one," said Mike.

Drake, Mike, and Deandrea took turns practicing under Kyle's and Anne's guidance.

After a short break, they moved on to RPG training. Drake stepped in front of the group, holding an RPG-7VL. "You've all seen these, but there's a few things you may not know. This particular RPG was designed specifically with fortified targets in mind. Each grenade weighs about nine pounds. It's initially launched by a powerful gunpowder booster charge, creating a puff of gray smoke. After about ten meters, a rocket motor kicks in, propelling it at three hundred meters per second."

"I can't remember," said Kyle, "what's its max range?"

"Just over eleven hundred meters. It's really pretty simple to use," said Drake, holding the launcher up. "Load the grenade. Aim using this optical sight or, if you like, this iron sight, and press the trigger." Drake pulled out the grenade and held it up. "As the grenade shoots out, it rotates counterclockwise. These stabilizer fins will deploy to help keep it on target. A sustainer motor accelerates the grenade until it reaches its target."

"Can you get injured, using it?" asked Deandrea.

"Sure. If you're standing right behind the launcher, the initial explosive charge can ruin your day. And of course, if you mishandle it or if it malfunctions, the grenade can kill you."

"Ever used one in combat?" asked Anne.

"Several times. Once took out a truck packed with ISIS fighters. Now, if there's no more questions, I'd like everyone to take turns firing at that first target."

While Drake helped Anne set up a shot, Mike patted Kyle on the shoulder, gestured toward Drake with a nod, and gave Kyle a thumbs-up. The two stood behind, quietly observing. Today's targets were stationary, positioned two hundred yards away. Anne zeroed in using the optical sight and fired. It hit the bull's-eye. Mike and Kyle both broke out clapping. Anne turned her head, looked back, and smiled.

When they finished, Deandrea demonstrated how to load missiles and launch the attack drone. Because of the high demands placed on everyone during the long fourteen-hour training days, Mike made sure to allot periodic breaks; a time to have a snack, drink something, and use the restroom. Drake used his time to grab a backpack and hike off alone. It caught Mike's attention. When he mentioned it to Kyle, he said he thought it was Drake's way of chilling out. After all, the scenery on the vast ranch was worth taking in.

The last training evolution of the day moved on to close-quarters-battle (CQB) training. Mike and Kyle rented several mobile trailer buildings, arranging them to resemble structures in the PLVI compound. Although not to scale, it offered an environment where they could prepare themselves for up-close and dangerous combat engagements.

Mike and Anne were to simulate a lightning assault on the detention facility. Drake was to play the role of a PLVI guard. When they burst in, Drake seemed to be genuinely surprised and momentarily confused. He overreacted and fired his rifle, narrowly missing Mike and Anne.

Mike scolded him, and when he got face-to-face, he noticed his eyes were bloodshot.

"Drake! What the hell are you doing? You could have killed us. We told everyone to empty their goddamn guns!"

"Oh, man. Sorry. Thought I did. Really."

Mike walked up to Drake, face to face. "Your eyes are bloodshot."

"It's allergies, I guess. I'm fine."

Mike canceled training for the rest of the day. From that point on, he checked everyone's rifle before beginning any more simulated CQB training.

*

The next morning, Kyle and the rest of the group started with morning exercises. After breakfast, they met outside for more training. Kyle needed to make a quick pit stop and jogged back to the house. In the bathroom, he found someone's backpack. He unzipped it to check for identity and found a gallon-sized plastic bag containing four smaller bags. All stuffed with drugs. He left the backpack, minus the drugs, stepped in the kitchen, and waited. A minute later, the door opened. Someone rushed into the bathroom and grabbed the backpack.

"Oh, shit! Where is it?"

Kyle walked out, holding up the bag.

"Looking for this?"

Drake looked shocked but defiant. "Yeah, okay, you caught me. Big deal. Give it back."

"You're off the team, asshole. The drugs were a one-time mistake, right! What a bunch of crap. Grab your stuff and get out of my sight before I break your neck. You want to kill yourself? Here!" Kyle threw the bag back at Drake.

Drake froze momentarily as if trying to assess his options. He turned around, walked to his room, and began to pack.

Kyle yanked a set of keys off a rack and walked outside.

"Mike," he called.

Mike walked over.

Kyle handed him the keys. "Take my car and drop Drake off at the Greyhound depot in town. It's ten miles down the road. I just kicked him out. The idiot has enough fentanyl and other drugs to kill an elephant. Sorry, I'm the one who brought him in. You need to take him. I can't look at the jerk."

"Damn it!" said Mike, slowly shaking his head. "Hey, it's not your fault."

Mike ran into the house, grabbed his wallet, and walked out toward the car.

Drake followed.

Mike motioned to him. "Let's go."

Kyle watched the car drive off, turned around, and told the team what happened.

"You're kidding. That goddamn idiot almost shot us!" said Anne.

*

The drive to town was quiet. Mike turned his head and looked at Drake. One of his knees was vibrating up and down as he clutched his backpack, tightly.

"Why do you need that shit?" asked Mike.

Drake shook his head. "I don't know. For me, it takes the edge off the stress of life."

"Can't you cope without it?"

"Hell, I tried, really. You must think I'm a damn loser."

"Actually, no. I know it's not easy," said Mike.

When they arrived, Mike stepped out and paid for Drake's return ticket. He opened his wallet, pulled out a hundred dollars, and handed it to Drake. From his phone he got a number and texted Drake.

"Here, take this for lunch," said Mike. "I just sent you the name of someone in San Francisco who can help you. Good luck."

He turned around and walked back to the car. He sat for a few minutes with the windows down, pressing his fingers against his forehead. He picked up his phone and fired off a brief text to Sandy. "Drake's going home. Drugs."

A minute later a reply came back. "Mission still on?"

"Don't know. Need to talk it over."

When Mike returned, everyone gathered for a meeting.

"This puts us in a bind. The risk level just got a lot higher. My plan requires five, minimum."

It got quiet.

"Hell, I say keep going!" said Deandrea. "Let's see if we can work something out. We've got those NAIMERAs."

"Yeah, I agree," said Kyle. "What do we have to lose? It's either that or we quit and a hostage dies."

"Uh, excuse me," said Anne. "I'm willing to wait and see what we come up with, but it better be good. I'm not signing up for any suicide mission."

For the remainder of the afternoon, they brainstormed various scenarios to get Grace out with the NAIMERAs, one pilot, and three on the ground. Mike plugged in their positions and weapons into his combat simulator. Over and over, he ran various rescue scenarios, changing their approach and the type of weapons they carried. They could do it but with a high probability of suffering a casualty to one or more members. It was time to break for the day. Everyone was exhausted.

"Thanks for your help and ideas," said Mike. "Let's hold off any more training until we develop a mission plan that works. I'll let you all sleep in. Back here at 0900."

The next morning, no one wanted to get up. But someone did. The house filled with the aroma of coffee, bacon, and pancakes. Mike rolled over and looked at his phone. It was 0730. Suddenly, music began to play. Reveille. *Someone either has a sense of humor, or they're torturing me.*

Everyone seemed to walk out into the dining room at the same time: Anne, Kyle, Mike, and Deandrea. Plates were on the table filled with food and coffee poured. But no one was there serving.

"Okay, what's going on?" said Kyle. This was his house, and he had been the one preparing breakfast.

"Yes, who do we have to thank for this feast?" asked Anne.

From the kitchen, Sandy walked out holding a coffee pot. "Good morning! Sit down and eat. Everything's getting cold."

"Good morning. It sure is," said Mike.

Sandy reached out to shake Anne's hand. "You must be Anne. I'm Sandy. I've heard some good things about you."

"Thank you. Heck, the way the guys talked about you these past couple days, I assumed you were some sort of mystic warrior," said Anne.

"All right. What got you to change your mind?" asked Mike.

"Turns out it was Marc. We had a few long talks. He wanted me to go, and I realize I can't tether myself to him forever."

"He's growing up fast—mature and independent—both good traits, especially for someone that young. You must be proud," said Mike.

"I am. Now, everyone, eat up."

Mike noticed a slight hesitation. "Relax, we'll skip the five-mile run this morning. Don't worry," he said.

*

The remaining days of training proceeded on schedule. They settled on a solid plan A to swoop in and rescue Grace. The way they saw it playing out was two-thirds of the PLVI blue shirts would leave to put down a fake protest, the gold ransom would arrive, creating a distraction, and the security eyes and ears of the compound would all be disabled. Then the drones, helicopter, and team would converge to create great chaos. They would destroy any ability for the PLVI to pursue them, then they would swoop in, grab Grace, return to the yacht, and head north at full speed. Their training focused on preparing each member for every possible role.

Other than the incident with Drake, the training was a total success. There was nothing on the agenda for the last day except to relax. It was a chilly Nevada desert afternoon, a time to stay indoors. Going around the room, Mike wanted their final opinions.

"I feel pretty confident in the plan and with our preparation," said Mike. "What do you think, Anne?"

"I wouldn't want to face those guys unless I felt we were ready. Y'all are awesome, the plan is rock solid, the NAIMERAs sound amazing, and our training was pretty damn good. So yeah, I think we're ready."

"I couldn't have said it any better," said Sandy.

Deandrea and Kyle nodded.

"All right, I like what I'm hearing," said Mike.

Early the next morning it was time to head back to Palo Alto, then fly down to San Diego to board the yacht for the slow journey south. Mike arranged for Peter, Kim, and the four NAIMERAs to meet them at the port. Peter had weapons, ammunition, one small carrier drone, an attack drone, glider bombs and missiles securely loaded on the yacht. He also ordered combat gear for each member of the assault team. The crew had everything ready from their end, including enough fuel and provisions for a two-week trip. Peter would be there to see them off, then fly back. The boat ride down to Nicaragua would take just under a week. They planned to arrive one day before the charter flight carrying Peter and the fake gold bars.

CHAPTER 34

San Diego, California

For most of the plane ride down to San Diego, no one spoke a word. Mike was busy reviewing his mission plan, trying to catch anything he might have overlooked. After the plane landed, as soon as the door opened, there waiting for them was a large limo. They loaded up and were off to the port. The limo pulled up to the dock. Peter's yacht was huge, almost a football field long. As they boarded, the seven-member crew stood by and welcomed them on deck. There was Jonathan, the captain; Henry, the ship's manager and copilot; Phillip, the chef; Steve and Al from engineering; then finally, the ship's two stewards, Jackie and her husband Dave. Peter hired a physician and longtime friend for the trip, Dr. Robert Townsend. As soon as everyone was aboard, the crew returned to their duties and began making preparations for departure. The NAIMERAs watched the activity through a window perched in a side cabin. This was their first time on a boat. Peter glanced up to check on them. Then he and Kim walked over, greeted Anne, and introduced themselves.

"Everyone, grab your stuff, I'll show you to your rooms and give you a tour," said Peter. "Unfortunately, I'll be getting off before you leave."

After settling in, they walked together up to the helicopter tied down on the helipad.

"A Black Hawk!" said Deandrea. "Mike said we'd have one, but seeing is believing."

"Yes, this will be yours for the trip," said Peter.

"She's not new but looks nice. Real nice. Has this one seen combat?"

"From what I understand, yes, four years in Iraq. I bought it from surplus."

"Any antimissile capabilities?"

"Yes. Infrared and ultraviolet laser countermeasures. But it's only effective against heat-seeking and UV, not radar homing," said Peter, patting a small canister on the side of the copter.

"Right, like lock-on after launch. But good. At least it's something," said Deandrea, shrugging his shoulders. "I trained on a Black Hawk. Shouldn't take too long to get reacquainted. I'll have it up a few times before we get there."

They paused and looked underneath.

"Is this carriage for small missiles?" asked Mike.

"Yes, as well as glider bombs," said Peter.

Next, they walked inside the galley and the dining area. There was a large pantry, loaded with snacks, and a fully stocked refrigerator with various beverages, fruits, and veggies.

"Feel free to drop in and help yourself whenever you like. Breakfast is served between seven and eight, lunch noon to one, and dinner from six to seven. If you miss any of those, talk to our cook, and he'll whip something up for you."

They went up the elevator to the gym. It had weight machines, treadmills, and exercise bikes. Music played in the background, and one entire wall had an expansive view of the water. In a large adjacent room, there was a jacuzzi, spa, sauna, and showers. Anne and the guys milled around while Peter walked near the window with Mike.

"So, we lost Drake? It was probably a good thing," said Peter.

"Unfortunately, yes. Luckily, Sandy changed his mind and joined us," said Mike.

"Folks, we have more to see before I get off. Follow me." Peter led them up a narrow set of stairs. "Here's the first thing I want to show you."

Mike paused and stepped back. His eyes widened while he caught his breath. "Are you kidding me? How did you get that?"

Peter smiled. "It was put in for a demonstration. I took a small entourage of Naval officers out to show off our attack drone's defences against lasers. It worked so well I never got around to dismantling the thing."

It resembled a fourteen-foot-tall rectangular box capped with a large turret containing the lens. A sign above read, "DANGER: 300 KW Laser."

Mike shook his head in disbelief.

The controls were below and behind. They stepped down several stairs. Peter opened a closet. Inside was a computer screen, a radar screen, a control panel, and a simple hand yoke, similar to the one found on an airplane.

"The yoke repositions the turret both vertical and horizontal to direct the laser beam," said Peter. "It's unlikely we'll need it, but it's comforting to know we can defend ourselves if attacked."

Kyle stepped closer. "Where do you get the power?"

"This red button fires up a dedicated generator producing the electrical power. Take my word, it can blast targets a half mile away with no problem."

"Too bad we can't fit that on the copter; we'd make quick work of the PLVI," said Deandrea, smiling.

Kim seemed surprised. She'd visited the yacht several times for corporate cruises around San Francisco Bay. "I didn't know this was on board. Do you think the yacht might be attacked?"

"No, but you can feel safe. If we run into trouble, this ship is well protected. There's something else. It can generate a thick fog screen that completely disorients any attackers," said Peter.

"One of our first tasks is to destroy the few PLVI boats they have. They won't be bothering us," said Mike.

"All right, everyone, that wraps up my tour. Let's head down to the galley. The cook has dinner waiting for us," said Peter.

"Wait a minute," said Anne. "I want to see those NAIMERAs."

"Let's wash up and eat first," said Kim. "I promise you'll meet them after that."

Sandy's ears perked up. "Mind if I tag along?"

"Sure. You're invited too, Sandy," said Kim, smiling.

*

Kim sat next to Anne. She hadn't had the chance to get to know much about her. Anne spoke carefully in a strong confident tone, each word pronounced perfectly. It left Kim with the impression Anne was precise and thorough. Kim found her fascinating. She was the most self-reliant woman Kim had ever met. Anne preferred to fix everything herself: her plumbing, car, appliances. She had plans to move to Alaska and build her own house someday, completely on her own. The discussion moved on to the NAIMERAs, what they were, and how they were created.

"The NAIMERAs are living creatures we created in the lab," said Kim. "They can reshape themselves as they like, fly, crawl, walk, slither, converse in any language known to man, and generate a powerful laser beam."

Anne leaned back and held her chin. "That's what I heard. Speak any language? Really?"

"Yes, seriously. Up close you can hear them, but when they fly off, they can speak to you through a transmission earpiece you wear."

"This I've got to see."

After dinner, Peter stood up. "Everyone, I'm off. Have a safe trip. I'll see you all in a week."

Most went to their rooms. Kim, Sandy, and Anne walked together to a room set aside for the NAIMERAs. They were all sleeping on perches. Kim opened the door, and they stepped inside.

"Buttons, Trinity, Baron, and Marty, I brought by two members of our team to see you. This is Anne and—"

"You remember me? I'm Sandy."

A chorus of "Hello, Anne. Hello, Sandy," erupted.

Anne stood silently, her arms down to her sides. "Hello? Who is who, again?" she said while carefully studying the exotic creatures. One by one, the NAIMERAs called out their names. Anne appeared in a mild state of shock. "This doesn't happen to me often," she said. "I'm speechless."

"I'm not," said Sandy. "I hope you NAIMERAs are as good as I think you are. We're counting on you."

"You can, Sandy," replied Baron.

"We'll have a week to get acquainted," said Kim. "Let's let the NAIMERAs get their rest." They stepped out, but Anne's eyes remained on them until the door closed.

*

Over the next several days, the team devoted their time to rehearsing for the mission. Every member needed to memorize not only their role but those of every other member in the event that they were called upon to fill in. The NAIMERAs participated in the discussions. Although they weren't human, they could, at least to some extent, fill in as well. Sandy studied the plans and pointed out a couple vulnerabilities. Could they have booby-trapped the perimeter? How would they deal with squirters if there was a firefight near the detention facility? They'd need to watch for anyone fleeing and hiding, ready to shoot. In each case, having the NAIMERAs overhead with their special abilities would neutralize the threat.

For his part, Deandrea had no trouble relearning out how to maneuver the helicopter. After taking it up a few times, he was completely comfortable flying it. Every team member took turns test-firing the laser. They also rehearsed defensive scenarios should the yacht come under attack and they needed to deploy fog.

Mike led the team into a storage room and opened up a case containing tactical gear. A bag labeled for each member contained boots, pants, shirts, knee pads, gloves, helmets, bandannas, ear protection, ballistic goggles and a small satellite phone.

"Here, take yours and go try them on," said Mike. "Make sure they fit and feel comfortable."

One-by-one they walked back in, lifting and extending their arms. Squatting and standing back up.

Anne stepped in. "Top and bottom fit okay but take a look at these gloves," she said holding them up. "Does it look like I wear anything in a size small?"

That brought about a chuckle from everyone. "Here, Anne, we have more of everything, try this pair," said Mike, offering her a larger set.

"We all need to keep a satellite phone strapped to the back of our helmets for easy access should our earpiece communication equipment fail," said Mike. "Don't expect it, but as they say 'expect the unexpected'.

"Everyone, keep your bandannas tied around your neck in case smoke or dust become an issue and you need to cover up quick. And don't forget to wear those ballistic goggles; don't want any eye injuries. We'll also have cameras on our helmets so the NAIMERAs can tell what we're seeing. Everything fit?"

Heads nodded. "Okay, we're all set," said Mike.

Mike and Kyle shared a room. Every night, Mike tossed and turned, restless, worrying he may have missed something. Kyle slept like a baby. Mike couldn't understand how he could sleep so soundly, knowing what they were about to encounter. Or worse, not knowing. He didn't want any surprises or loose ends. It drove him to obsessively check and double-check every aspect of the mission.

Mike had Marty load all the known parameters along with his latest mission plan and run combat scenarios on his tactical combat simulator software. Requiring only minor tweaks, Mike's mission plan offered them the best chance of success, eighty-seven percent, with no team casualties. It wasn't perfect but pretty damn good. Team preparation, execution, and the element of surprise were their strengths.

Mike used a satellite phone to call Nina Perez. "Hi, Nina. It's Mike Murphy."

"What can I do for you?"

"We're going forward with the rescue, so I really need to make sure you'll be available to post a bluff protest message for us on January 1st around three p.m."

"Yes, Mike. I've not forgotten. I promise I'll be ready. The town of Granada is a good location, we've held protests there before. The PLVI will want to stop it. It should take them a couple hours to drive there and back. Is that enough time?"

"Yes, that's perfect."

"I hope you're not making a mistake. I'll pray for you."

"Thank you. We understand the risks. I really appreciate your help. I'll call back on January 1st."

The yacht arrived off the southern coast of Honduras on December 31. Exercising extreme caution, their strategy was to stay north, out of Nicaraguan waters, so as not to draw the attention of the PLVI. They'd move closer when the mission was about to begin. Even though they were several miles out to sea, at midnight, New Year's explosions could be seen and heard. Within seconds, everyone came out of their cabins and stood on deck to watch an impressive firework display from a nearby town. No one appeared able to sleep, anxious for the day ahead. The light show was a welcome diversion.

CHAPTER 35

Managua, Nicaragua

The cargo plane carrying Peter and the twenty tons of gold-plated and filled tungsten bars began its approach into Managua International Airport. From his window, Peter spotted a large semitruck with a flatbed trailer parked near the general aviation area. *That's probably my truck.* The PLVI instructed Peter to make arrangements for a truck to transport the gold from the airport. A PLVI rep would meet him and escort the truck to the base. The gold was required to be securely partitioned into three separate stacks for proper weight distribution on the airplane. Once they landed, Peter asked the crew to make sure one particular stack was placed on top of the others when loading it on to the trailer.

During the flight, the crew asked Peter why he was bringing so much gold to Nicaragua.

"It's confidential. I'd rather not say."

This brought on curious looks between the flight crew.

"Where are you off to next, back to Denver?" asked Peter.

"I wish; after refueling, it's a quick load and departure to

Switzerland," said the pilot.

"Undisclosed cargo accompanied by three passengers. Not that unusual," said the flight engineer.

The plane gently landed, taxied, and came to a stop. The semitruck immediately pulled up nearby. The rear door of the plane opened, and the cargo ramp dropped down. Following Peter's instructions, the gold was loaded on to the truck in an arrangement that assured only gold-filled bars would be on the top and along all the sides. Peter stood nearby along with the truck driver, observing.

Peter called Mike. "Hi, I just arrived at the airport. No signs of the PLVI rep yet … Hold on, here come a couple of guys."

"All right, I'll send Deandrea to pick you up," said Mike.

"Thanks, got to go. I'll call you right back."

Two men approached. One introduced himself as the PLVI representative. The other was a Nicaraguan customs official.

As Peter handed his passport and the "donation" paperwork to the official, he turned to see the PLVI rep jump up on to the truck bed. Peter watched anxiously. The rep appeared to count the rows and columns to verify the number of bars was correct. Peter's pulse quickened. Next, the rep reached into his pocket and pulled something out. Just as Mike had predicted, using a rectangular stone, he scratched off a small sample of gold from one of the top bars. The rep pulled out a pair of rubber gloves from his back pocket, crouched down, then discreetly performed what looked like a quick acid test on the gold's purity. It was a stressful couple of minutes for Peter.

The rep exposed the stone to the direct sunlight while carefully studying it. His head bobbed slightly, so Peter assumed it was acceptable. Still bent over, he removed a six-inch knife from a leather sheath attached to his belt. He stabbed a few gold bars, creating several puncture wounds. From Peter's angle they didn't appear very deep.

The rep leaned in while shading his eyes from the bright sunlight. He strained to check each hole, then stood up slowly. Showing only a stoic reaction, Peter couldn't tell if it passed. The rep jumped down and pulled out his cell phone, took a picture of the entire stack, and appeared to text it to someone. Without being asked, from out of the cab, the driver retrieved a large blue tarp, covered the gold, and tied it down.

Peter took a couple of deep breaths, trying to calm back down. "All right. I delivered what you want. Where's my daughter?"

"She'll be dropped off back here after I deliver the gold."

The customs official told Peter and the PLVI rep to follow him to his office to complete the paperwork. As they walked away, the rep kept turning his head back toward the truck. The official's office had a window facing the loading area. While sitting waiting to finish the paperwork, the rep's head swiveled every few seconds back toward the truck. Suddenly, two large fuel tankers crept slowly in front, blocking the view of the truck.

The rep jumped up and in a loud nervous voice said, "What are they doing? Get those goddamn things out of the way!"

"Calm down, calm down," said the customs official. "They need to refuel airplanes. Just sign this, and you're good to go."

The rep scribbled his signature in a flash, grabbed his copy of the paperwork, and ran outside. By then, the fuel tankers had moved on. He seemed relieved. There was the truck with the blue tarp. He waved to the truck driver to come over. The driver complied.

The rep yelled above the noise of the diesel engine. "Follow me!"

The driver nodded.

The rep walked to his SUV, got in, and slowly exited the security gate with the truck close behind.

The plan called for Peter to fly back to the yacht and stay there.

While he sat waiting for the helicopter, he called Mike. "They just left. No Grace, unfortunately."

"Not a surprise, but the gold passed his scrutiny?"

"Yep, your idea worked like a charm."

"When you pressed him about getting Grace, what did he say?"

"He said when the gold reached the compound, they'd have someone drop her off back here at the airport."

"Unlikely. But who knows, maybe the PLVI's leader will change his mind and release her after all. We'll hold off on starting any rescue action until the truck reaches the compound. If Grace comes out, then we abort the mission."

"Sounds good. God, I really hope they release her," said Peter.

"So, do I. We'll know soon."

"Oh, here comes Deandrea now."

Deandrea landed without cutting his engines. Peter raced over and jumped inside. After a quick exchange with the control tower, they lifted off slowly. Peter looked down and saw the plane he had arrived in with a truck behind it.

"Hold it. Can you hover right here for a second?" said Peter.

The truck had a stack of gold on the trailer being offloaded back on to the plane.

"Oh. My. God! They switched trucks! They're stealing the gold. Damn!"

Deandrea hovered for a minute as Peter looked down in disbelief.

The tower radioed Deandrea. "Rotocraft N600RC. Repeat, depart Alpha 5, ACS Tower, over."

"Roger, ACS Tower. Rotocraft N600RC, departing Alpha 5," replied Deandrea. "Sorry, Peter. I can't stay here."

Once out of the airport, the helicopter headed back toward the yacht.

Peter called Mike. "Peter, what's up?"

"The gold. Someone somehow switched the trucks, and the gold's being loaded back on the same plane. I don't know what's going on."

"Does the PLVI rep know?"

"No. I'm certain he thinks he's got the gold."

"Good, that at least gives us some time."

"Who else could have known about this?" said Peter.

"Don't worry. As long as they think they have it, our plans won't change much. But once you guys get back, we need to move on this quickly. I'll see you in a minute."

*

Mike gathered the team members together and told them the news. Once the truck arrived at the PLVI compound, they would uncover something, but it certainly wouldn't be gold, and definitely no cause for celebration. They needed to slightly alter their strategy. In any event, Grace would still be in grave danger.

Mike made note of the time. He called Nina Perez and asked her to post a message on the internet anti-government message board announcing a large surprise protest in the town of Granada later in the day.

"Can you phrase it so the PLVI will want to send several dozen members?" asked Mike.

"Yes, I know exactly what to say. It will shock them," said Nina. "They'll want to shut it down and get revenge."

"Excellent. Thank you for your help."

"Good luck. I hope you free the girl."

*

Marty and Baron left the yacht. Their first assignment was to report any activity around the compound, especially the detention facility. Trinity flew off toward the marina; tasked with disabling the marine radar, security cameras, and damaging every speedboat so they could not be used.

Within fifteen minutes, Marty reported back that the detention facility was quiet. He flew by and could detect Grace's scent. She was still inside.

Baron observed eight large black SUVs each packed with eight PLVI blue shirts pull up near the armory. They loaded rifles, boxes of ammunition, tear gas canisters, and masks, then all sped away from the compound.

"Excellent. Our odds just got much better," said Mike. "Marty, Baron, go take down the base's radar and cut the lock on the north gate."

Within seconds, Baron swooped down and cut the connections for the base's radar system. Marty melted the steel lock off the north gate.

"Radar's down," said Baron.

"The northern access gate is open," said Marty.

"Good," said Mike. "We're heading out."

Marty and Baron split up and began methodically severing cables for every security camera and sensor on the base.

Trinity called back. "Marine radar is down. Security cameras disabled. I found all six speedboats in dry dock and cut huge holes in all their hulls."

"Good work," said Mike. "Trinity, fly up and watch the area ten miles around the compound. Stay aloft for the duration of the mission. Let us know if those SUVs return."

"I will," said Trinity.

*

The team loaded up into the Black Hawk and headed for their staging area just beyond the north end of the compound. On the way, Mike had a moment to reflect. *Why were the speedboats in dry dock? Probably out of the water for maintenance.*

CHAPTER 36

PLVI Base, Nicaragua

Sergio sat quietly at his desk, making one last pass over his notes. He had received confirmation that all the elite political leaders in the country were on their way. In front of him, laid out, were names, personal bios, and pictures. As they arrived, he planned to greet each with a firm handshake, then say something memorable. *When I'm done, they'll respect and fear me like never before.*

His phone rang. "Yes."

"Boss, you wanted to know when the gold arrived. It just passed through the main gate," said Luis.

"Good, right on time," said Sergio.

He walked over to his window to see for himself just as a line of SUVs headed out.

"What in the hell? What's going on down there?"

"Big protest is about to start. Those bastards heard about our celebration. They actually said we won't show up. If we do, they'll have spoiled the day for us. Either way, they win. I gave orders to make them pay dearly."

"Did you need to send that many?"

"Yes, boss, they're calling it bigger than the one in Managua."

"Damn it! Where is it?"

"Granada," said Luis.

"There again? Hell. Call and tell them to squash it and hurry back. I'd like them to catch some of our celebrations before the guests leave."

"Boss, is it time to finish off the girl?"

"Sorry, Luis, but I've decided to let her go."

"Let her go? Why? We promised to kill her. She'll go back and testify against the guys in Guatemala."

"You're right, but there's no need to do that now. Those idiots got arrested and convicted. The gold is here. A billion dollars! This is easy money. If we plan to keep it up, we can't go around killing hostages after a ransom's been paid now, can we? Nobody will ever pay us again."

Luis could be heard muttering profanities.

"You got that, Luis? Release her. Unharmed! Have one of the guards take her to the airport. Then it's done with."

"Yes, boss."

Sergio slipped his phone in his pocket, glanced into the mirror, adjusted his collar, then left to greet his guests.

*

Luis walked to the detention facility, still voicing profanities. He stepped inside and motioned to one of the guards behind the desk.

"Heriberto, come here. I've got a task for you."

"Yes, Lieutenant?"

"Get the girl and drop her off at the airport in Managua. The ransom's been paid. Sergio wants her released."

"Released? I thought you were going to blow her head off?"

"Yeah, so did I," said Luis with a disgusted look. "Just go do it."

"Yes, sir."

*

Heriberto walked down the hall and unlocked the door to Grace's cell. "Come on, get up. Let's go."

"Where are you taking me?" said a suspicious Grace. It wasn't time for her daily hour of exercise.

"To the airport. It's your lucky day," said Heriberto as he escorted her down the hall.

Grace was not sure if the guard was telling the truth, but she walked with a spring in her step. They left the facility and headed toward the parking lot.

*

Within the security office, a red light began blinking on the screen over the icon of the radar station of the base. Then the radar at the marina came up red. One of the guards, Raul, picked up the phone and called the marina.

"Marina, dockmaster."

"This is Raul from security. I'm getting an indication your radar is out. Can you check?"

"Sure, hold on." The dockmaster walked outside and saw severed cables dangling in the wind. He glanced at the six speedboats in dry dock. They were all heavily damaged.

"Somebody cut the radar cables and vandalized all the speedboats."

"Look around, anything else damaged?"

The dockmaster looked up. "Crap, the security camera cables are cut too. Lucky, those weren't our new boats. When they arrive, I'll make sure to post a guard to keep an eye on them."

"Thanks." The call ended, and the guard turned to his partner.

"Enzo, someone vandalized the marina! Let's check out security footage."

On the security monitor, suddenly, more red blinking icons began popping up on the site map for buildings and the perimeter fence. One after another, cameras and sensors went offline.

The guards both stared at the display screen, confused.

"I don't believe this. I bet the server's flaky," said Enzo.

"Got to be. Try rebooting," said Raul.

The system restarted and came back up still showing red blinking icons all over the map. The two guards looked at each other.

"We need to tell Sergio, now," said Raul.

"Yeah, but if this is a false alarm and we take him away from the celebration, we'll both be tied up and blown to pieces," said Enzo.

"Right. Let's check one first."

They walked outside and looked up at the camera over their door.

"Shit! How could anyone cut that cable? We've been right here," said Raul.

They went back inside and replayed the camera's last recorded minute.

"What is that?" said Enzo.

They paused, rewound, and replayed it in slow motion.

"Stop. A bat? It shot a laser beam at the cable. This is crazy," said Raul.

They pulled up the marina's security recordings. It showed a larger bat firing a laser beam at the boats, radar, and camera.

"Send out the security drone to check the perimeter. There's something going on," said Raul. "I'll call Luis. He can tell Sergio."

*

Luis returned to the command center and stood alone, watching Sergio greet guests. His phone rang, and he recognized the number.

"Yeah, what's up, Raul?"

"Lieutenant, we have a big problem. All the security cameras, sensors, and both radar stations are down. Something cut the cables. It destroyed the boats at the marina too."

"Something?"

"Umm, it looked like bats that shoot laser beams," said Raul.

"You mean a drone, right? Bats can't shoot lasers," said Luis in an annoyed voice.

"You might want to come up here and see for yourself, sir. Sure looks like bats to us."

"I will. Sergio needs to hear about this first."

Luis hated to interrupt Sergio. He was talking and smiling while greeting the guests. Luis approached and tapped his shoulder.

A surprised Sergio turned around with a puzzled look.

Luis tilted his head.

Sergio stepped closer. "This better be important."

"Boss, sorry to bother you, but something just took down both radar stations and cut the cables on all our security cameras and sensors. We might be under attack."

"Goddamnit!" Sergio turned his head away and tried to process this news. "A rescue? But they delivered the gold." Sergio nodded his head as if he realized something. "I don't know why I didn't think of this. Those Guatemalan cops must have spilled their guts when they were arrested. They knew we planned to kill the girl."

Sergio became suspicious. He walked over to the truck and lifted the blue tarp. There was a stack of gold-painted cinder blocks. "That arrogant bastard. He sent me bricks. Shit! I bet he arranged the protest just to get our guys to leave. Oh, they are good."

"They must have drones and possibly air support," said Luis. "Why else take down both radar stations?"

Sergio nodded. "Let's get everyone together. I want them armed and ready for combat."

"Yes, boss."

"And don't let that girl get away!"

"Christ, I asked Heriberto to take her to the airport, but I'll make sure we get her back. What would you like me to do with her? A quick bullet?"

"No, no. Have Heriberto take her to the target area, tie her up, and stand guard. The jet's going to give a demo; she'll be part of the show. Remember to call and warn him to leave before the missile strikes."

"Yes, boss."

"When you're done with that, if I'm right, they're heading for the detention facility to rescue her. Set up an ambush. Can you handle this quietly?"

"My pleasure, sir," said Luis with fire in his eyes.

"Good. I need to get back." Sergio turned around to talk with his guests.

Luis rushed off and sent out a broadcast message to all the blue shirts. "*Urgent,* everyone *muster in front of the armory immediately. If you're off site, return to base. Now!*"

Luis looked at his watch. *Damn, that protest is in Granada. It's going to take them at least an hour to get back.* He called the main gate.

"Main gate."

"Has Heriberto driven out yet?"

"Yeah, just left with a woman. We can still see them."

"One of you guys, jump in a car and go after him. *Now!*"

"Okay, don't worry, when we catch up with him, what do you want us to do?"

"Tell him to get back here and meet me by the armory. Do not let that girl go!"

Within minutes, they had Grace and brought her to the armory. Thirty blue shirts circled around, each receiving an assault rifle and ammunition.

"Heriberto, come here," said Luis, tossing him a rifle.

"Take our guest to the range and tie her to a post near the target structure. Stay with her until we give the word for you to leave. If anyone or anything tries to save her, kill it or kill her."

"Anything? What should I be looking for?" said Heriberto.

"Drones that look like bats," said Luis. "Got it?"

"Yes, Lieutenant."

Luis motioned to the thirty blue shirts to gather closer. He told them that the base was under attack and the target was the detention facility. He split them up into five teams. One team, along with himself, would go to the second story of the detention facility to provide cover. Two other teams would position themselves on each side outside the facility. If anyone showed up, they'd surround and take them out. The rest would stay and guard Sergio and the armory. They all rushed off to their positions.

On the second floor of the detention facility, Luis opened two windows and stuck his head out. Trees obscured much of his view. There was a small parking lot with several cars and trucks in front of the facility. Two teams below took positions, flanking the entrance and waiting for any signs of intruders.

CHAPTER 37

PLVI Base, Nicaragua

The Black Hawk flew low, stayed behind hills and landed just beyond the northwest corner of the PLVI compound. Anne, Sandy, Kyle, and Mike jumped out and began offloading their equipment. Anne and Sandy prepared the attack drone, attaching two missiles. Meanwhile, Deandrea mounted two missiles under the Black Hawk. Mike and Kyle loaded the carrier drone with the glider bombs.

"You all know what to do. Let's hit them hard, grab Grace, and get out," said Mike.

Deandrea returned to the copter. Everyone stepped back while the drones started up. They lifted up vertically, then flew off toward the compound.

"Team, I just intercepted a message broadcasted to all PLVI blue shirts," said Marty. "It said they should meet in front of the armory, those off-site need to return."

"That's not good. We may have lost the element of surprise," said Mike. "Where are you two?"

"We're almost done cutting cables," said Marty.

"Both drones are in the air," said Mike. "We're heading in. Are the guard dogs loose?"

"No, they're all in their kennel," said Marty.

"That's one less thing to worry about. The northern gate lock was cut, right?"

"Affirmative," said Marty.

"Marty, when you're done see what's going on over at the armory. Baron, meet us at the detention facility. We need to act fast."

*

On his way to the armory, Marty passed over the PLVI's security drone. He swooped down and cut it in half. "This time you're really not coming back."

*

Mike hurriedly led the team through the northern gate. The detention facility was only two hundred yards away. They split up into two groups: Mike and Sandy approached from the front left, Anne and Kyle from the front right. They kept low, moving cautiously under trees and around parked cars and trucks. They were fifty yards from the front of the detention facility. Baron, circling above, noticed two groups of six blue shirts below. They were hiding under bushes, flanking the facility's entrance.

"Everyone, stay down! Don't move. You're walking into an ambush," said Baron.

"Where are they?" asked Anne.

"They're on both sides, two separate teams of six hiding under bushes, armed with rifles."

Kyle picked up a short thick stick off the ground; he removed his helmet and stuck it inside, then slowly lifted it directly over his head. From the second story of the detention facility, a stream of automatic fire pelted the helmet, ricocheting off and knocking it to the ground.

"That didn't come from either side," said Kyle.

"There's another team on the second story," said Baron.

"Can you tell how many there are up there?"

Baron passed above the front of the building. "Seven. All with assault rifles."

"Great, we really did walk into an ambush," said Mike.

With all of them pinned down, blue shirts began to make their move. Guns sprayed bullets over their positions. They had to stay low under the cover of cars and trucks. With bullets raining down, unable to move, blue shirts advanced along their flanks. No one could get off a single shot.

"Damn," said Sandy. "I've got RPGs but I'll get my head blown off if I try to use them."

Luis fired off a quick broadcast to all the blue shirts. "We've got our intruders pinned down outside the detention facility. They'll be dead in a minute."

"Crap, we're sitting ducks, they're executing a shoot-and-move maneuver on us," said Mike. "Hey, Deandrea, we could use some air support."

"Glad to," said Deandrea.

"Wait, no, that won't work. Grace is in there. If we hit it, she's dead," said Mike.

The blue shirts continued to advance along their flanks. There was no place to run or hide. In a few minutes, they would be in a position to fire at them from all sides. Baron flew in front of the second story and fired his laser. He hit one of the blue shirts but was knocked violently into an aerial tumble by a bullet.

"I was shot," said Baron. "My exterior can't take another direct hit."

Baron fluttered to a branch and sat perched with a good view below. He signaled the release of a glider bomb from the carrier drone circling high above. It came down slowly, and he guided it within one of the blue shirt teams on the ground. The powerful explosion left six dead. Luis's head emerged from the second-story window looking up, trying to tell where the bomb had come from. Baron released a second, directing it toward the other blue shirt team. Another loud explosion rocked the area. The threat from the ground was over, but bullets continued to rain down from the second story of the detention facility, keeping the four pinned down.

"Good work, Baron," said Mike. "Can you glide one into that top window?"

"Unlikely," said Baron. "The trees are in the way."

*

The sounds of gunfire and bombs alarmed all the guests, drawing their attention away from the ceremony and toward the detention facility. Sergio paused and reassured everyone it was only a training exercise. He resumed his conversation with the president and vice president, showing off his array of weapons in the armory.

"Explain to us why you need a stealth fighter jet?" asked the president.

"Drug cartels are growing bolder and more dangerous every day. We need to stay one step ahead. With this, we can move quickly to annihilate a threat anywhere without being detected," said Sergio.

"Anywhere?" asked the president. He and the vice president shared a concerned glance.

*

Meanwhile, Marty circled above. Some movement caught his attention a mile away near the target area. He flew out and swooped down to check it out.

"Team! I found Grace. She's tied up in the target area. A blue shirt has a gun pointed at her."

*

"We'll try to get there as soon as we can," said Mike. "Deandrea, it's all clear. Fire a missile."

"I have the coordinates for the center of the detention facility. Is that where you want it?" said Deandrea.

"No, the building's too big. It might not take them out. I need it near that window on the northwest corner."

"Deandrea, I've got it," said Baron.

The copter hovered a mile above and a half-mile north. Baron gave the command sequence to launch one missile. Within seconds, a HellFire I-n arrived, coming in low between a row of trees, then straight up into the window. Half of the second story exploded. Flames engulfed what remained of the facility.

"Thanks. Finally, we can move. Deandrea, we need a bigger distraction," said Mike. "Hit the armory."

Marty jumped in. "You can't. The Nicaraguan president is standing with Sergio right in front," he said.

"Well, take out the fuel depot. We need something."

*

Marty circled the attack drone around and launched one missile. It hit the fuel depot, creating a huge explosion.

From high above, Trinity reported in. "A line of black SUVs is speeding back toward the base. They're about ten miles away."

*

Within seconds toxic smoke swirled from the burning fuel. Team members, sprinting across the compound, began coughing but covered their faces with bandannas and continued on. They had to find a way to the target range. It was about a mile away, but they needed to find transportation to get there quickly. They began to hunt for a vehicle with keys inside.

"Marty, can you neutralize that guard and free Grace?" asked Mike.

"I'll try."

*

Marty flew cautiously above the target area. Heriberto was watching for drones. He fired his automatic rifle and hit Marty, ripping open one wing and damaging his hydrostatic system. He fell, tumbling through the air, but managed to transform flat, forming a quasi parachute. After he hit the ground, Heriberto ran over to finish him off. But Marty quickly reformed into a thin snake and slithered into a crack in the dry soil, changing colors and camouflaging, all while in pain and oozing fluid. Heriberto hunted but couldn't find him.

"Team, I've been hit. I can't fly but I'm okay. I'm near the target area. I couldn't save Grace."

Baron responded. "Find a safe spot and stay there. I'll come get you as soon as I can."

*

Sergio and his guests watched in horror as missiles flew through the air. The gunfire and explosions nearby were deafening.

"What's going on here?" asked the president. "This isn't training."

Events were spiraling out of control. Sergio was losing his composure.

"You need to leave," said Sergio.

The stunned crowd stared at Sergio momentarily.

"We're under attack. I'll handle this like I've handled all the other threats this country has faced."

The president took offense. "You might have helped us once, but now you're just putting us in danger. That's it, Sergio. This administration is done with the PLVI. You're on your own."

Sergio shot back a snarled stare, then rushed into the armory and walked out with two stinger missiles. He called Luis, but his phone kicked immediately over to voicemail. Sergio aimed for the attack drone and fired. In a second, the drone exploded. He picked up the second stinger and fired. The missile screamed toward the Black Hawk. The copter's IR defences worked perfectly, redirecting the missile before it got close.

Sergio motioned for the jet pilot. He reached out and held him firmly around his neck. "You've got two missiles loaded; destroy that copter. After you do, come back and hit the target. Now!"

The pilot looked off toward the north end of the base where he last saw the Black Hawk. He gave Sergio a quick nod and ran toward the hangar. Passing through a cloud of dense black smoke from the still-burning fuel tank, the pilot climbed up into the SU-57 jet.

The president pointed to the motorcade and announced, "We've seen enough. Let's go." The nervous guests hurried to the parking lot. Sergio was furious. A blue shirt approached and told him the detention facility was in ruins. Nineteen blue shirts, including Luis, dead. Sergio's face turned red as he looked over at the remaining blue shirts guarding him. "What are you doing here? Find and kill those intruders!"

Sergio turned around to see his guests drive off.

Oh, shit, the missile. Heriberto's still there. Sergio called him. "Heriberto, you need to leave the target area. Kill the girl and run!"

*

Marty was still unable to fly but was otherwise okay. He intercepted the call from Sergio and scrambled his transmission.

Heriberto heard, "Heriberto, you need to leave the target area …" and then static.

"What did you say?" replied Heriberto.

Sergio repeated his command, but Marty again scrambled it, then retransmitted an altered message, mimicking Sergio's voice perfectly.

"I said, you need to leave the target area. Untie the girl and get out of there. Do not harm her. I repeat, do not harm the girl! Understand?"

"Yes, sir," said Heriberto. "I'm leaving." He hung up.

Heriberto untied Grace, jumped in his truck, and drove off.

*

Sergio looked across the compound and saw Heriberto drive away while Grace walked free. Sergio was livid. He patted his side; he still had his gun. He ran over and jumped into a truck.

"She is not getting away. I'm going to kill the bitch if it's the last thing I do!" Sergio said angrily to himself as he drove off, pounding his fist against the steering wheel.

CHAPTER 38

PLVI Base, Nicaragua

"The SUVs are five miles away and picking up speed," said Trinity. "Thanks," said Mike, looking down at his watch.

He had four, maybe five minutes max before sixty-four armed blue shirts showed up. The team ran together in the direction of the target range, pausing at every car and truck along the way, trying to find one with keys left inside.

"We're wasting time," said Mike. "Let's split up and meet over at the south end by the access road. Anne and Kyle, check the cafeteria's parking lot; we'll go behind the gymnasium. Hopefully, one of us will find something."

They ran off.

Mike and Sandy crouched low, advancing along the side of the gymnasium. They were about to enter the parking lot when they heard voices, then footsteps. They were getting closer. Two armed blue shirts were scouting the area. Sandy tilted his head toward the side. They ducked into the entryway of the gymnasium. Mike had his gun pointed out, and he stood tight in the corner. Sandy crouched, remaining silent, tucked close to the wall. Shadows came into view right in front of Sandy. They grew larger and larger. Without seeing them, he could tell one was about a foot away from the entrance.

In a flash Sandy twisted, lunged, and shot his right leg up, making perfect contact under the chin of one of the blue shirts. The guy's neck snapped as Sandy's leg powered through the enormous resistance. He was heavy and fell over hard.

The other blue shirt stepped back and started to lift his rifle, but Mike shot him before it got above his waist.

They paused momentarily, staring down at their victims. Mike patted their pockets. He reached in and grabbed their keys, and then they ran off into the parking lot.

*

Kyle and Anne heard the gunfire echo between the buildings.

"Mike, you guys all right?" asked Kyle.

"We're okay."

Kyle and Anne saw no one but moved cautiously close and low around cars in the back of the cafeteria parking lot. Their movement caught the attention of the two guards at the main gate who heard the gunfire. The guards were a quarter-mile away, but they could see them both. They a clear shot. One guard aimed and fired.

At that instant, Kyle tripped over a parking block. The bullet exploded into the car window inches from his head.

They both dropped to the ground. Scanning the area, Anne saw the two guards aiming their guns in their direction. She made a slight noise with her lips and tilted her head in the direction of the gate. They slowly repositioned their bodies behind tires but looked directly at the guards.

Anne whispered, "I'll take the one on the left."

Like a pair of synchronized swimmers in motion, both went through the same silent routine. They scanned the tree branches, then over to the high grass between them and their targets. Black smoke moved low across the sky to the east at about ten miles per hour and constant, showing wind speed and direction. It was hot and humid, close to sea level, and the distance about 450 yards. They studied their targets.

The two guards strained their eyes to see where the two intruders had gone. Using their elbows as bipods, they aimed their rifles.

"On three," said Kyle quietly. "One ... two ... three."

They fired.

Both guards dropped. Bullet holes between each of their eyes.

*

Mike and Sandy, each holding a set of keys, walked through the gymnasium parking lot, pressing the fobs. They heard a faint sound in the distance and saw headlights flicker on a van parked next to a small building.

"Bingo!" said Mike.

Mike called out to Kyle and Anne. "We got a van, meet us on the south side of the gymnasium."

Within a minute, they were on their way, driving down the perimeter access road heading toward the target area.

"Look up ahead. There's a truck heading toward the target area too," said Kyle.

"They must be after Grace. We've got to hurry," said Mike.

The truck was a half-mile in front. Mike tried to go faster, but rocks and potholes littered the road.

"Baron, we're driving to the target area. There's a truck ahead of us. Can you stop it?" said Mike.

"I'll get there as soon as I can," said Baron. "I must deal with the jet first."

CHAPTER 39

PLVI Base, Nicaragua

Baron circled above and watched Sergio give orders to the pilot. The jet was extremely dangerous to the Black Hawk, the team members, and even the yacht. He only had one goal: stop that jet. It began taxiing for take-off as Baron began to assess the situation. He could try to fly by and use his laser to damage it, but he would need to get close, and it was about to begin accelerating.

Unsure what to do, he dove down, landing on the windshield. In desperation, he spread out to block the pilot's view. It worked, but the plane kept moving. Somehow the pilot was able to guide it without vision from the front. Engines roared full throttle. The plane screamed down the runway. Baron needed another strategy, quickly. He slithered around the nose of the jet and down under the plane. As it lifted off, fighting off the suction of the engine intakes and the wind, he wrapped himself tightly to the missile rack. He was secure, but now what? *Burn a hole through the fuselage.* Baron could barely move, but he'd need to reposition his body to aim and use his laser.

Wait, something's coming in. Baron began intercepting missile targeting instructions sent by the pilot. It was an air-to-air fire-and-forget type. He now knew the missile's intended target. *It's going after the Black Hawk.* Baron had to act fast. The missile could be launched any second. He reprogrammed the missile with new instructions and a different target.

Once launched, the missile tore through the air and performed a 180-degree turn. In an instant, it plunged down and sliced through the armory's steel roof. After a momentary pause, it exploded, forming a thunderous fireball. Flames, debris, and smoke shot up several hundred feet. The ground shook violently, and the powerful air blast was ear-splitting. The adjacent command center vanished. No building was left standing. Smoldering twisted steel frame skeletons were all that remained.

*

Along the access road leading to the target area, Sergio's truck bounced and slid sideways from the sudden shockwave. Then, debris rained down like a squall, breaking his windshield. He stopped and turned his head back over his shoulder to see a huge cloud covering his compound. When the smoke slowly lifted, his compound was gone. He noticed a van following him. He was in shock but needed to regroup. He was now more determined than ever to kill Grace.

*

Baron had to destroy the SU-57 jet. He pulled up its wiring schematic from his memory banks. If he could twist his body twenty degrees, the center of his chest would be pointing directly at the wiring harness for all of its major controls. He slowly repositioned and fired; his laser penetrated the skin of the plane with little trouble, and cut the bundle. Immediately, the pilot lost all control. Baron released, dropped down and flew off. The jet began rapidly spinning while steadily losing altitude and headed off toward the ocean. Baron looked below at the smoldering hole where the armory once stood. The entire compound was leveled.

Then Baron heard Marty call out to him from below: "Baron, Grace needs help, urgently!"

Baron saw Sergio walking and holding a gun.

Grace tried to run but tripped and fell.

With lightning speed, Baron began a steep dive at two hundred miles an hour. In a flash, he arrived, flapping furiously, trying to stop. At fifty feet he fired his laser, burning a hole through Sergio's hand. The gun dropped. The pain must have been intense because he let out a blood-curdling scream.

Baron landed on a target post nearby and kept his laser trained on Sergio, who held his injured hand gingerly against his chest.

He looked up at Baron. "What in the hell are you? The devil?" Sergio's gun lay nearby and he made a move to pick it up.

"Freeze right there," replied Baron in Spanish. "I have your head in my sights."

"You! You're the one who killed Tito."

Mike's team showed up and jumped out. Sandy pointed a gun at Sergio. Kyle looked around to find something to secure him, and he found zip ties in the truck. They tied his arms and legs together. Sergio appeared to be in excruciating pain but still tried to resist.

Mike and Anne rushed over to Grace, who was still on the ground. "Grace! Are you okay?" said Mike as he and Anne gently lifted her to her feet.

"Yes, yes, yes," she replied, choked up with tears. "I don't know. I can't believe you're here." Tears streamed down her cheeks.

Deandrea brought the copter down nearby.

Anne saw the copter approaching and held on to Grace as the wind picked up from the powerful rotors.

Marty called for help. Within seconds, they found him. Kyle removed his shirt and created a makeshift stretcher for Marty. While picking him up his ripped skin flapped, exposing a lacerated hydrostat. A few gathered around to check on his condition. Anne noticed the arrival of a caravan of black SUVs across what was once the compound.

"We've got visitors."

"Everybody inside, quick," shouted Deandrea.

Kyle and Sandy dragged a still struggling Sergio over and strapped him in. They all jumped into the Black Hawk. It lifted off, remaining low, heading first in the opposite direction of the blue shirts, then it turned and made a beeline for the yacht.

Below, several dozen blue shirts stood and watched as the copter flew off.

"We forgot something," said Mike. "The carrier drone is still circling."

"I'll take care of it," said Trinity. "We have enough glider bombs left to eliminate the remaining blue shirts. They're all clustered together."

"Thanks, Trinity," said Mike. "Just head back to the yacht. They're not a threat, and we've seen enough bloodshed."

CHAPTER 40

Pacific Ocean

Not wasting a second, the yacht set off at nearly full speed, heading northwest out of Nicaraguan waters. After Dr. Townsend dressed and bandaged Sergio's hand, they cuffed his hands and feet and locked him in the ship's secure vault. The doctor then joined Kim, who was tending to Marty's wounds. His muscular hydrostat had sustained a sizable laceration from the bullet, requiring a local anesthetic and over two dozen sutures. Within thirty minutes, he was back together but unable to fly until the wound healed. They carried Marty topside.

In a well-deserved moment of relaxation, everyone gathered on the upper deck for a little food and a refreshing drink. They needed time to recuperate from their harrowing ordeal.

"I'm so glad it's all over," said Mike.

Heads with smiles nodded.

Peter and Grace embraced side by side. "Daddy, it is so good to see you." She looked around. "Where's Alan?"

"Honey, he didn't survive the accident. I'm sorry."

Grace shook her head. "Every day I thought about him. I was afraid he didn't. I hope he didn't suffer," said Grace.

"He didn't."

She became teary-eyed. The emotional trauma of knowing she'd lost Alan mixed with the joy of regaining her freedom was overwhelming.

"I've been in contact with Alan's family since the accident," said Peter. "It's so sad. They're devastated as you can imagine and they constantly asked if you've been found."

"I can't wait to call them," said Grace.

The sun slowly retreated across the Pacific as calm descended over the yacht. They could finally relax.

*

On the bridge, the ship's captain, Jonathan, noticed a blip on the radar. Then two. Three. Six! All approaching at incredibly high speed. "What on earth?" he said out loud.

Over the ship's intercom, he called all hands up to the bridge, immediately. Everyone jumped up and rushed toward the stairs.

When they arrived, Jonathan spoke. "I called you all up here to see this. It looks serious." He pointed at the radar screen. "Six speedboats, forty-five miles south-southeast, heading right for us and closing fast."

"Can we pick up any more speed?" asked Peter.

"We're about maxed out," said Jonathan. "I can crank it up to thirty-three, but we can't outrun them. They're coming at us at seventy knots."

"Trinity," said Mike, still wearing his communication earpiece.

"Yes?"

"You destroyed the PLVI's speedboats, right?"

"Yes, I'm positive, all six. I cut every one of them the length of the boat below the draft," said Trinity.

"Okay, thanks."

Mike turned back to Peter and Jonathan. "Well, if it's not PLVI blue shirts, it might be another cartel working with them or possibly random pirates. Try broadcasting a warning."

Jonathan sent several with no response. The radar showed no change in speed or direction.

"When they get closer, I'll fire off warning flares," said Jonathan.

"We're in international waters," said Mike. "If they're armed and hostile, we're going for the kill."

Heads nodded in agreement.

*

These waters, like many in the world, had a history of pirates attacking personal yachts. If that's who they were, the team needed a plan and fast. Fortunately, they had antipirate defences on board, a powerful laser, and the ability to create a massive fog smoke screen from behind. But the fog could only be deployed for so long. In desperation, they could securely lock everyone down inside a vault, but having pirates on board would be a disaster. As part of their preparation on the journey down, they had gone over pirating attack scenarios.

While they talked, Henry the copilot continued sending out Mayday distress calls. The Honduran Coast Guard responded. They would send help as soon as possible but didn't have anything in the area. They estimated it would take two hours.

Mike and Deandrea walked toward the Black Hawk.

"Deandrea, load up some flares. I want you to have a dozen glider bombs, and our last Hellfire," said Mike. "Fly out and see if they're armed, shoot off some warning flares, and try to establish radio contact. Make sure they can see you're armed."

"And what if they keep coming without a response?"

"If they've got weapons, then it's them or us. Take out one of their boats. Hopefully, that will be enough to get them to back off. A Black Hawk with missiles is pretty intimidating. Bring Trinity with you. If they keep coming, we'll need some up-close reconnaissance to find out what they've got before they catch us."

"I heard that," said Trinity. "I'm on my way to the helipad."

"Trinity, broadcast live video; I need to know what each boat's carrying," said Mike.

"I may not be able to get too close, but I can zoom in to capture detailed images from a thousand feet."

"Do your best, but be safe. You'll have a dozen glider bombs to use if you get a chance."

Mike turned to Steve from maintenance and engineering. "Is the drone ready to fly?"

"It's refueled. Several glider bombs are still loaded."

"Good, make sure there's a dozen."

"How about the Black Hawk?" asked Deandrea.

"It was refueled, and I ran it through a postflight maintenance check. It's ready," said Steve. "I'll make sure the HellFire and glider bombs get fully loaded."

Mike addressed the team. "We need an inventory of our remaining weapons. I want everyone armed." He looked toward Kim, Peter, and Grace. "Everyone. Although, you three will wait it out in the vault. Sergio's in there tied up; he's not a threat. Grace, keep an eye on him," said Mike, followed by a wink.

Kim glanced down and touched a pouch around her neck.

"I'll take care of little Buttons," she said.

"Better bring along Marty too. He's still recovering," said Mike.

Mike asked the ship's crew who would prefer to wait it out in the vault. Steve and Al from maintenance and engineering, along with the cook, Phillip, wanted to stay topside. The ship's stewards, Jackie and her husband Dave chose to stay together in the vault. Dr. Townsend thought it best to stay in case anyone needed medical attention.

"In the unlikely event the pirates get on board, keep yourselves locked inside. They won't be able to get you. There's food and water, and help is on the way."

"Help?" asked Kim.

"Yes, the Honduran Coast Guard responded to our Mayday. They're sending a boat. Two-hour ETA. They know we're in trouble."

"A lot can happen before then," said Kim.

"Don't worry, Kim. It's going to be all right," said Mike.

Those who were waiting out in the vault left to go securely lock themselves inside.

"Let's go see what we have," said Mike.

Mike's team hustled below to the storage locker and stared at the remaining arsenal.

"Okay, eighteen rifles … plenty of ammo," said Mike. "Only one RPG?"

"I had to shed the weight and leave the rest behind at the detention facility when we started running," said Sandy. "Meant to go back and get 'em, but the place got leveled."

"Too bad, but we still have the carrier drone with two dozen glider bombs," said Peter.

"It'll be difficult hitting moving speedboats with them, but it's better than nothing," said Mike.

"Remember," said Peter, "they're autoactivated and pressure detonated when the cone encounters five pounds of force."

"Thanks for the reminder. Everyone, grab a rifle and ammo. Let's bring the rest of this up top," said Mike.

Mike and Sandy stood together on the main deck watching the Black Hawk lift off and head toward the oncoming boats. Mike turned around and leaned over the railing, trying to imagine how pirates might climb up the sides of the ship.

"Who do you think these guys are?" asked Sandy.

"No idea," said Mike. "They're preparing for a classic fast boat swarm attack, so I'm guessing they're not new at this."

"Sure looks that way. When they get closer, I'd expect them to split up and encircle us, then attack from all sides," said Sandy.

"We need to find out what weapons they've got," said Mike. "If they have RPGs or grenades, they'll try to disable the yacht to force us into surrendering. One missile from the Black Hawk should scare the hell out of them. Otherwise, that laser could be our ace-in-the-hole. Fog, glider bombs, and rifles are our last resort."

"I like our chances," said Sandy, nodding his head.

"The copter's got to be close by now," said Anne.

Mike talked through his earpiece. "Deandrea, do you have an update for us?"

"Yes, I can see their wakes, but the boats aren't too visible yet. I sent out a few warning messages. No reply, about to start firing flares."

"Thanks."

A few minutes later, Deandrea reported back. "I've got a clear visual. Blue shirts. Definitely hostile. They're shooting at me. I'm going higher."

"Blue shirts! How did they get boats? These guys won't give up," said Mike. "What do you see?"

"They're aligned, straight across, fifty feet apart. Time to try a little persuasion," said Deandrea.

*

Another warning message arrived on the speedboats' radios.

"They're threatening lethal force," said one speedboat pilot.

"I heard it," replied Ramon.

With their leadership decimated, Ramon Suarez, the last lieutenant, was now the acting head of the remaining PLVI blue shirts. Called back from the fake protest, they were furious only to find the compound obliterated. They arrived to watch as Sergio was loaded into the Black Hawk and flown toward the sea. When they got to the marina, they found the old boats damaged, but a fleet of newer, faster speedboats had just arrived. Every remaining blue shirt wanted revenge. They grabbed their guns and a small arsenal left in the marina's weapons locker. It was all or nothing.

"Take a look. How many missiles is that copter carrying?" asked Ramon.

A blue shirt with binoculars focused on the Black Hawk. "One."

"Only one? Interesting," said Ramon. "If they had more, I'm certain they'd have loaded them."

"It looks like they have something else, smaller gravity bombs, maybe?" said the blue shirt.

"Those are useless against moving boats," said Ramon. He picked up his transceiver and set it to broadcast. "Everyone, no matter what happens don't stop. That's an order!"

Ramon watched anxiously as a puff of white smoke emerged from under the copter—he knew what was coming.

The missile arrived in a blur, leaving behind a momentary vapor trail. The boat next to Ramon's exploded and disintegrated instantly, scattering bodies, boat fragments, and flames in its place.

Ramon broadcasted another message: "That copter has no more missiles. Keep going. Show them we are not backing down! Save Sergio!"

Every blue shirt roared, "Save Sergio! Save Sergio!"

*

Mike listened to Deandrea as he reported in. "They're down to five. Still coming, though. Trinity's on her way down."

Mike sat at a desk in a forward cabin, looking at the computer screen. "Thanks, I'm picking up your video transmissions. Coming in nice and clear. Trinity, tell me what you see."

"I count ten or eleven fighters in each boat. Only see rifles … one grenade launcher … grappling hooks."

"Thanks, I see that too," said Mike. "Go back over the center boat. I thought I saw something different around one of the blue shirts."

"Sure," said Trinity.

"Perfect. Stay right there. Not sure what I'm seeing … a single life vest?" said Mike.

"No, Mike," said Trinity. "One blue shirt is wearing a vest loaded with grenades."

"That's an assault vest," said Mike. "Only the desperate fighters in Iraq and Afghanistan would wear them. I guess these blue shirts are no different. I've got what I needed. Any chance you can hit them with glider bombs?"

"The probability is low; they're moving fast and erratic in the waves," said Trinity.

"Okay, head back," said Mike. He stepped out and addressed the team and crew. "They'll be here soon," said Mike. "Five boats, over fifty blue shirts, all with assault rifles. One's wearing a vest packed with grenades."

Sandy picked up the lone RPG. "I'll keep an eye out for him. I've dealt with them before. He's definitely the most dangerous of the bunch." Kyle and Sandy left to set up positions on the bow.

To the rest of the team, Mike said, "Let's get ready. The laser should stop them. But get in place in case we need to deploy fog. Good thing we went over this. You all know what to do."

Mike called up to the bridge. He instructed Jonathan and Henry to keep the throttle down. "There's going to be trouble. Get ready for a three-sixty on my command, and don't let up."

The Black Hawk landed. Trinity flew down from the helipad to join Baron, perched on the railing, as Mike and Anne approached.

"Blue shirts will be here soon. The way this will play out is we'll first use the laser when they get into range. That should stop them all. If it doesn't, we'll create a fog curtain on the stern and do a three-sixty, as we talked about. Trinity, you cover the starboard with gliders from the Black Hawk. Baron, you take the port side using gliders from the carrier drone. You know what to do. We're counting on you."

Mike turned to Deandrea. "You've got twelve glider bombs. Go up with Trinity."

"Why not just send up the carrier drone with all the gliders?"

"Two reasons. I want the copter up high as insurance just in case they get lucky and bring down the drone. Plus, only twelve gliders can fit in that drone. We may need all twenty-four. Any more questions?" asked Mike.

"One," said Trinity. "If they manage to get close to the yacht, should we swoop down and hit their pilots with our lasers?"

"No, not unless all else fails. You could be shot coming in close, and I'd rather not risk you getting hurt. If it comes to that, then let's leave it to Baron. He has the tough armor. But if they're firing high-velocity bullets at close range, even his skin is no match."

"You're right," said Baron.

"Now get up there. Good luck!" said Mike.

Mike grabbed his rifle, turned to Anne, and tilted his head. "Let's get topside. Time to try that laser out on some real targets."

They rushed up the stairs and arrived panting. "We better test it once to make sure it's ready."

"Anne, you handled this pretty well during the demos, want to take it from here?"

"Sure, no prob."

Anne set the output to one hundred percent, then reached over and pressed the power button. The generator supplying electrical power started up. They could feel the deck vibrate. With both hands on the yoke, Anne positioned the turret starboard, aiming down at the waves two thousand feet away. She pressed the trigger. An intense narrow green beam shot out. Within seconds, water around the area boiled, creating a small steam cloud.

"Outstanding!" Anne said. "It's good to go."

"I doubt we'll need fog, but I'll stand ready to start generating," said Mike.

"Got it. I plan to end this, fast," said Anne.

CHAPTER 41

Pacific Ocean

"Did you see that green flash?" said one speedboat pilot.

"Yes," replied Ramon. "Laser."

Ramon picked up his transceiver and set it to broadcast. "Everyone. Get ready to fire. Pilots, begin evasive maneuvers."

The speedboats continued at seventy knots but in unison began weaving in an unpredictable pattern between each other.

*

Anne kept a close eye on the fast-approaching boats. *Clever, but you can't out-maneuver this.* She felt confident she alone could annihilate the speedboats. Now within a half-mile, she zeroed in on one boat and fired as it weaved.

The beam was narrow and intense. In seconds, they were down to four but kept coming. *Like shooting fish in a barrel*, thought Anne. She rotated the turret and aimed for another boat.

*

The ferocity shocked every blue shirt but in particular Ramon. This was no ordinary yacht. The heat was blistering. In an instant, the pilot lost control, his speedboat veered hard left and flipped over, almost colliding with another. Ramon broadcasted to his remaining boats.

"Pilots, maintain your course. Everyone, prepare to fire directly at that beam on my orders. Don't let up, till we kill that laser!"

Every gun, loaded with full clips of ammo, raised up toward the yacht. From the turret of the laser housing, a beam emerged, trained on Ramon's boat.

"Fire!" shouted Ramon.

From four boats, forty high-powered assault rifles let loose, and bullets pelted the boat near the laser. The beam went dark.

"We did it! Save Sergio!" broadcasted Ramon.

Above the roar of the speedboat engines, every blue shirt raised their rifles and shouted, "Save Sergio!"

*

The barrage of bullets smashed the laser lens, causing an explosion of glass. The laser housing, riddled with bullet holes, resembled a colander. Anne quickly shut the generator off and dropped to the deck. She reached down in pain; her leg felt searing heat and was bleeding. One bullet had penetrated the laser housing and lodged into her thigh.

Mike reacted immediately, flipping the switch to start the fog. Within seconds, a huge cloud of thick, dense fog filled the stern of the yacht. He shouted up to Jonathan to turn the yacht hard to starboard and full speed.

"Hey, Doc, I've been hit, and I'm bleeding pretty bad," called Anne.

Within a minute, Dr. Townsend was up by her side, working on her leg.

*

The speedboats were closing in on the yacht and were about to encircle it when a wall of fog suddenly appeared.

"Cut your engines!" broadcasted Ramon.

The boats slowed to an idle as they cautiously coasted through the cloud, unable to see beyond the front of their crafts. They could hear the roar of the yacht's engines, but no one could tell where it was.

*

Circling above, Trinity watched the boats slow as they entered the curtain of dense fog. She dropped her first bomb, hitting her target as it emerged in the clearing. Standing blue shirts were blasted over the sides. The few that managed to survive leapt into the water to douse the flames from their burning clothes.

Trinity had her first kill. The enemy fleet was down to three, the remaining boats bobbing directionless in the waves. The yacht was gone. Without warning, out of the fog, it shot through at full speed, heading directly toward one of the boats.

In the confusion, most of the blue shirts seemed frozen, uncertain what to do. Trinity heard someone yell out, "Fire the grenade!" Something shot up and landed on the yacht's deck behind Sandy and Kyle, followed by a powerful explosion.

Windows shattered, and a fire broke out in a forward room. Smoke billowed as flames spread. The damage to one of the bulkheads exposed several electrical conduits that controlled the ship.

Dr. Townsend was making his way slowly down the stairs with Anne as the explosion hit, causing them to stumble and sway. When they got down, he left Anne to check on Al, who remained lying on the deck unconscious. It wasn't clear how badly he'd been injured.

Two crew members, Steve and Phillip, rushed to extinguish the fire.

Mike was lying flat on the deck, portside, firing. He looked back at the fire. "Steve, need help?"

"We've got it."

*

Baron tried repeatedly to control the glider bombs in gusty twenty-mile-per-hour winds, at speedboats now moving and bouncing in the waves. He'd already used eight and hadn't hit any. He was down to four.

It was a challenge, but Baron was learning quickly, getting closer with each attempt. Finally, he hit one. Like Trinity's big hit, the bomb landed near the fuel tank. It exploded, forming a huge fireball.

Two boats remained. One moved alongside the yacht. A grappling hook shot up and landed on the deck, attaching securely to the rails. The lone blue shirt, Pablo, wearing the assault vest, grabbed the rope. While standing on the side of his rocking speedboat, he pulled the pin on one of his hand grenades and tossed it up. It exploded on the deck, shattering windows and causing another fire.

*

Above, the crew scrambled to extinguish the fires. Flames moved closer to the electrical wires. Fearing a bigger problem, they ordered the engines stopped and all power cut. For a moment, it became eerily quiet as the yacht slowed and began to drift.

*

Sandy and Kyle, lying flat on their stomachs, fired on one boat. Blue shirts dropped. But a couple found shelter and peppered the side of the yacht near them with bullets.

"I've had enough of this," said Sandy reaching for the RPG.

"Kyle, when I give the word, fire at those bastards."

Sandy was ready. "Okay, fire."

Bullets rained down over the heads of the blue shirts, providing cover just long enough to let Sandy send off the RPG. There was another huge explosion. The boat was gone. Sandy and Kyle stood up and joined Mike, looking over the bow. Boat debris and dead blue shirts littered the area around the yacht. There was only one boat left and it was next to the yacht. They saw the blue shirt wearing his assault vest climbing up a rope.

*

Ramon was furious. One boat after another had vanished. They had one chance to save Sergio. Pablo had three grenades left. He hung on to the rope with one hand while just a few feet below the main deck. He grabbed another grenade. Ramon saw three men with guns looking down over the railing

"Throw it, Pablo! Throw it now!" yelled Ramon.

Pablo fumbled, trying to hold both the slippery rope and the grenade while attempting to reach the pull ring using one of his fingers from the hand clinging to the rope.

One of the men was taking aim at Pablo.

"Goddamnit, Pablo, throw it now!"

Pablo finally managed to pull the ring but, in doing so, lost his grip. Ramon could only watch as Pablo fell backward down at him, still clutching the now-active grenade.

"You idiot!" shouted Ramon.

Pablo landed hard in the middle of the boat. A second later, the grenade exploded.

*

Debris shot up, narrowly missing Mike, Kyle, and Sandy, who watched from above. Suddenly it was quiet. They walked around the boat and carefully scanned the water, looking for any more threats. There were none.

CHAPTER 42

Pacific Ocean

The attack was over and both fires extinguished. Broken glass and pieces of charred debris littered the deck. Everyone's attention now turned to Al. He still hadn't regained consciousness. Dr. Townsend knelt by his side, evaluating his condition. Overhead, waiting until the fires were out, Deandrea circled and slowly landed the helicopter. Both Baron and Trinity returned to the yacht. Baron directed the carrier drone back on board. It was another close call for everyone.

Mike rushed down below deck and opened the vault. It was safe to come out. They all met above on the main deck, shocked to see the damage. Al looked seriously hurt.

Dr. Townsend stood up and told Peter and Deandrea that Al needed to get to a hospital ASAP. Anne's bleeding was under control, but that bullet had to come out.

"The closest trauma center is in San Salvador," said Dr. Townsend. "Al needs brain surgery to relieve pressure building inside his skull. I don't have the facilities to do it myself." He turned to Deandrea. "We have to leave now. I'll come with you."

They helped Anne and Al into the copter. Within minutes, it was off.

*

Kyle peered over the railing. The smoldering remnants of speedboats slowly drifted farther and farther away with the current. Mike walked up to survey the carnage. Out fifty yards, several unexploded glider bombs remained bobbing in the waves. The shiny stainless-steel cones easily stood out from the surrounding charred debris. They were far from the yacht and drifting away, posing little realistic threat. But a random boat might come across one.

"Kyle," said Mike. "We shouldn't leave those things floating around. Mind taking them out before they have a chance to become a hazard?"

"Sure."

Mike left to go check on the others.

With the fires out, cleanup began. Everyone pitched in. The crew assessed the damage to the wiring harness and determined it was safe to restart the engines. The yacht roared back to life and headed home at thirty knots. A call came in. The Honduran Coast Guard was twenty miles away and asked for a status update. Henry thanked them but said help was no longer needed; the pirates were gone.

Two hours later, word came in from Deandrea that Al was in surgery. The prognosis was promising, but he'd need to remain hospitalized for several days. They removed the bullet from Anne's leg. She needed time to recover as well but would be fine. Deandrea was heading back, but Dr. Townsend would stay with them. When they were ready to leave, Peter would send his private jet down to pick them up.

*

As they progressed further north, a guarded calm descended across the yacht. But Mike couldn't completely relax; there was a nagging, unsettled mystery he needed to resolve. He wanted to revisit the issue of the missing gold. He and Peter went over it again and reasoned that the plane must have taken off with their gold. If so, it should still be in the air flying to Switzerland. Mike got up and went back to his room to get his satellite phone. He checked the current time in California. It wasn't too late. He called his old FBI boss in San Francisco.

"Special Agent Bill Andrews."

"Hi, it's Mike. I'm using a satellite phone, so the connection may not be the greatest."

"I can hear you fine. What's up?"

"We're on a boat making our way back from Nicaragua with a special guest. Sergio Cruz."

"You're pulling my leg!"

"No. We want to hand him over to agents once we get over the border."

"You captured Cruz? I don't believe it. How, with an army?"

"Yes, a small army. There were five of us, all former Special Ops. We flattened the PLVI compound and killed every blue shirt. All except one."

"How about the girl?"

"We saved Grace, she's with us. Unharmed."

"Okay, I know you, Mike, and you don't joke around. This is unbelievable news. You have Sergio Cruz, you saved Ms. Strauss, you destroyed their compound, and you killed every last PLVI blue shirt?"

"That's right. Now take a deep breath and help get this guy off our hands."

"My pleasure. Let me know when you'll be in port, and I'll arrange to have a team of agents waiting for you. Hell, I'm flying down to see this for myself. You realize there's a five-million-dollar bounty out for him?"

"I heard that. Nice chunk of change."

"When you get back, we need to have lunch, a long lunch. I want to hear the full story."

"Count on it. I'll call back with our exact arrival time in San Diego."

"Very good. Is that all?"

"No, actually, there's one more thing."

Mike explained their plan to deliver gold-filled bars to the PLVI for the ransom. But it had been stolen. It was worth twenty million dollars. They believed it was on its way to Switzerland. He described the unique markings on the bottom of the bars that could prove Peter's ownership and the name of the charter company. Bill said he would contact the Swiss embassy and put into motion a request for the Swiss police to meet the plane when it landed.

With those two issues out of the way, Mike could finally relax and unwind. He went to bed early and had his first full night's sleep in weeks.

*

The next day, Mike received a call. Swiss police identified and confiscated the gold. In a couple of weeks, Peter could arrange to have it sent back. They arrested three men. Two Russian military spy analysts and one high-ranking Nicaraguan Army officer. All three confessed after being presented with evidence. They'd planned to split the gold evenly and disappear. That news made the rest of the trip back even more satisfying but left a lingering mystery in their minds.

"How did Russians get involved with this?" wondered Peter.

"Remember the lecture in Monterey by Dr. Navarro? She mentioned a Russian spy station in Managua," said Mike.

"That's right, and they were monitoring PLVI activity. Apparently, they did more than that."

"I'll have to call Carlos. The CIA will find this all amusing, but he probably already knows everything by now," said Mike.

They were two days from San Diego. Grace slowly made her way around the ship and thanked everyone personally, including the NAIMERAs, for their part in the rescue. She debated whether or not to immediately return to Austin. After a long talk with Peter, she decided to return home. But she would also seek out the help of a therapist to work through any issues that might be haunting her from her ordeal.

Kim spent much of her time with the NAIMERAs. Mike and the other team members stopped by to check on them. Marty's wound was healing without any signs of infection. None of them raised any issues of concern from the combat.

For the rest of the trip, the former SEAL members turned back the clock, playing video games, exchanging stories, and drinking beer while renewing their friendships.

The yacht finally reached California, docking briefly at the port of San Diego, where Sergio Cruz was turned over, kicking and screaming, to the FBI. The team watched as four armed agents escorted him off the yacht.

"Thank god he's off the ship," said Grace. "Even tied up, he gives me the creeps."

CHAPTER 43

San Francisco, California

On the journey up toward San Francisco, Peter announced that he had one last request.

"I'd like you all to stay one more night. I've arranged a celebration dinner. I'll fly your family members in to join us."

They arrived mid-morning. Everyone stood on deck as they passed under the Golden Gate Bridge. They had made it home.

Peter reserved an entire restaurant high atop a San Francisco skyscraper in Union Square with panoramic views of the Bay Area. Deandrea's wife, Claire, came in from Hawaii. Sandy's son Marc flew up from Los Angeles. The dinner was exquisite—Waldorf salad, Kobe beef flown in from Japan, Nova Scotia lobster, Peking duck, followed by an assortment of desserts.

Peter stood up and held a glass of champagne. "It's not often I am at a loss for words. What we did is beyond amazing. I still can't believe it really happened. Thank you all for your part in rescuing Grace."

Grace interrupted. "Excuse me, but I need to say something, Daddy. After the accident, when I was kidnapped, I was frightened and confused. I didn't know what had happened to my fiancé, Alan. My heart was and still is broken. I was shuffled around and treated horribly. I was scared every time one of my abductors approached, certain they'd come to kill me. I almost lost hope. But you all never did. And like Daddy said, what you did was beyond amazing."

Grace held her champagne glass and raised it as she acknowledged everyone in the room. "I also want to say I just heard both Anne and Al are recovering well. They will be on their way home tomorrow."

The good news was followed by applause.

"Now, I'd like to thank the yacht crew, the team of ex-Special Ops: Mike, Sandy, Kyle, Deandrea, and Anne. Next, I want to say thank you to Kim, Daddy, and of course, the NAIMERAs. Thank you all for saving my life. There are others I will be forever indebted to—brave and selfless for their efforts. Without the combined contributions of everyone, I would not be alive. When I learned of the roles Maria Hernández and Nina Perez played, I asked Daddy to honor them."

Peter stood up. "Maria and her husband will receive the full reward I initially offered for information leading to Grace's safe return."

Grace smiled and lifted her glass. Everyone in the room did the same.

"We stand to collect a little reward bonus for Sergio's capture," said Peter. "Nina Perez will get part of that for her help."

Again, the entire room lifted their glasses and toasted.

One by one, Peter called Sandy, Deandrea, and Kyle up to thank them personally for their help and presented them each with an envelope. Inside was a certified check for one million dollars, with the stipulation it was meant as a retainer should there be another future mission. He followed with a handshake and salute.

Next, he called up the yacht crew members and presented them with an envelope containing a note of appreciation for their help, along with a generous bonus check.

Finally, he asked Mike and Kim to step forward. "Kim and I, as you may know, designed and created the NAIMERAs. Beyond that, she took over their development. They were spectacular. Thank you, Kim."

Everyone clapped.

"Mike. I don't even know where to begin. You made this all happen. How I got so lucky to hire the perfect person at the right time is beyond me. Kim and Mike, I can't imagine wanting to work at SGSI without you. I called a board of directors meeting later this week. I'd like you two to become part owners."

Kim and Mike looked at each other in a mild state of shock.

A loud round of applause erupted.

*

The next day, it was time for everyone to return home. Grace planned to spend a few days with her father before heading back to Austin. Mike accompanied Deandrea, Claire, Sandy, Marc, and Kyle to the airport.

"I can't tell you how grateful I am for your friendship," said Mike.

They all agreed, shared one last round of hugs, then went on their way.

*

The following morning was Mike's first real day on the job as the head of security. Sitting at his desk, trying to work through a stack of paperwork, he felt strangely bored. The past couple of months had been incredibly intense. Now nothing. Then came a light tap on his door.

Kim stuck her head in and smiled. "Are you experiencing the same feeling of melancholy I am?"

"You must be a mind reader," said Mike with a light chuckle.

"Okay, buddy, it's time to pay up. I'm here to take you up on your offer to replace my chai tea latte you spilled."

Walking slowly together, they shared a friendly glance. Kim moved closer and slipped her hand around his elbow.

—

ACKNOWLEDGEMENTS

I'd like to thank my friends and family for their kind words of encouragement. I especially want to thank my editors, Will Tyler, Elizabeth Ward, and Sara Kelly. Finally, many thanks to designer Mark Thomas for an awesome cover and interior.

ABOUT THE AUTHOR

Michael D. Ganzberger Michael spent thirty years working as a computer scientist at a U.S. national lab and five years active duty in the U.S. Navy. Born in Detroit, he's been a San Francisco bay area resident for the past 45 years.

To discover more about Michael and his books, please visit his website:

ganzberger.com

You can also comment with Michael on the following social media:

Instagram:

www.instagram.com/naimera.book

Twitter:

www.twitter.com/NaimeraB

Made in the USA
Middletown, DE
06 May 2021